Martin Boyd was born in 1893 of
Anglo-Australian parents. He was only a few
months old where the Boyd family made impressive
contributions to the artistic and intellectual life. At the outbreak
of the first world war he travelled to England and joined an
English regiment and later the Royal Flying Corps. In 1948, at
the height of his literary success, he returned to Australia to
make a permanent home near Berwick.

Most of his novels maintain an Anglo-Australian theme and
are based on his preoccupation with his own family. Martin
Boyd moved to Rome in 1957 and lived there till his death in
June 1972.

BY MARTIN BOYD

Martin Boyd

THE PICNIC

With an Introduction by
Brenda Niall

PENGUIN BOOKS

To Arthur Merric Boyd

Penguin Books Australia Ltd,
487 Maroondah Highway, P.O. Box 257
Ringwood, Victoria, 3134, Australia
Penguin Books Ltd,
Harmondsworth, Middlesex, England
Penguin Books,
40 West 23rd Street, New York, N.Y. 10010, U.S.A.
Penguin Books Canada Limited.
2801 John Street, Markham, Ontario, Canada
Penguin Books (N.Z.) Ltd,
182-190 Wairau Road, Auckland 10, New Zealand

First published by J M Dent & Sons Ltd, 1937
Published by Penguin Books Australia, 1985
Reprinted 1987

Copyright © Guy Boyd, 1937

Offset from the J. M. Dent hardback edition
Made and and printed in Hong Kong
by LP and Associates

All rights reserved. Except under the conditions described in the
Copyright Act 1968 and subsequent amendments, no part of this publication
may be reproduced, stored in a retrieval system, or transmitted in any
form or by any means, electronic, mechanical, photocopying, recording,
or otherwise, without the prior permission of the copyright owner.
Except in the United States of America, this book is sold subject to
the condition that it shall not, by way of trade or otherwise, be lent,
re-sold, hired out, or otherwise circulated without the publisher's
prior consent in any form of binding or cover other than that in which it
is published and without a similar condition including this condition
being imposed on the subsequent purchaser.

CIP

Boyd, Martin, 1893-1972.
The picnic.

ISBN 0 14 007955 6.

I. Title.

A823'.2

CONTENTS

ACKNOWLEDGEMENT

Roger Hone wrote 'Alec's' verses.
I thank him for permission to use them.

M. B.   1937

INTRODUCTION

The opening scenes of Martin Boyd's first major novel, *The Montforts* (1928), describe the arrival in Australia during the 1840s of an English gentleman-settler and his family. In *The Picnic* (1937), Boyd changes period and direction; this is the return home of the Australian-born descendants of a similar pioneering family, nearly a century later. Both novels explore cultural differences between England and Australia, using the newcomers' perspective to illuminate a sharply observed social world. In dealing with past as well as present, with the manners of English village life as well as those of the new society, Martin Boyd wrote with the authority of his own experience.

As a member of a distinguished Anglo-Australian family which maintained close ties with England for more than a hundred years after the first 'voyage out', he presented something of his younger self in the naive enthusiasm of *The Picnic's* central character Wilfred Westlake. Like Wilfred, Boyd had grown up with Arcadian dreams of English life, and as a young man tested them against reality. Wilfred's pleasure in matching landscape with literature is almost unqualified. For Boyd, who first saw England during World War I when he came from

Australia to join a British infantry regiment, delight was precarious; each 'home' leave from France was likely to be the last. He survived the trenches, and in 1917 transferred to the Royal Flying Corps, at a time when, as he said, pilots were killed 'almost before they had time to unpack their luggage'. In *The Picnic*, love affairs, tennis parties and village gossip make up a predominantly cheerful chronicle. Yet the picnic scene is dominated by political argument and ends in violence. Boyd's awareness that Europe was again moving towards war is the shadow on the grass in this 1930s novel.

Born in Lucerne, Switzerland, in 1893, Martin Boyd was the youngest son of Arthur Merric and Emma Minnie Boyd. Both parents were talented painters. Both came from families distinguished in Australian life from the early days of the colony. Emma Minnie Boyd, née à Beckett, was the granddaughter of Sir William à Beckett, the first Chief Justice of Victoria. Arthur Merric Boyd's father, Captain John Theodore Boyd, came to Victoria as military secretary to an early governor. Penleigh House in Wiltshire, the prototype of Plumbridge Hall in *The Picnic*, was the home of the à Becketts for generations; Martin Boyd's older brother Penleigh was born there in 1890. In Australia the Boyds and the à Becketts led the pleasantly ordered lives of the colonial gentry, for whom long visits 'home' to England were taken for granted. Martin Boyd's birth, however, coincided with a sharp decline in the family fortunes; the leisurely European tour of 1893, during which he was born, was for his parents the last such excursion. The collapse of the 1890s land boom in Australia brought them home from

Europe when Martin was six months old. The Boyds lived first at Sandringham on Port Phillip Bay, and later on a farm at Yarra Glen near Melbourne. It was a life of comfortable simplicity which suited the temperaments of Arthur Merric and Emma Minnie Boyd; and if the family was no longer rich it was by no means poor.

Martin Boyd was to look back on his childhood as an idyllic one. In his autobiography *Day of My Delight* he said of his father that 'although he was an artist he gave an impression of leisure and was responsible to no one for his time or effort'. Brought up to take financial independence for granted, Arthur Merric Boyd did not press his sons to find security in the professions although, in the early twentieth century, it might have been thought prudent to do so. Instead, he and his wife encouraged the creative talents of their children, and thereby fostered the Boyd family tradition in the arts which flourishes today. Of their three surviving sons (one died in childhood in a riding accident) all achieved distinction: Merric as a potter, Penleigh as a painter and Martin as a novelist. In the next generation, artistic talent within the family grew and diversified. Robin Boyd, Penleigh's son, became one of Australia's finest and most influential architects. Arthur Boyd, Merric's oldest son, has an international reputation as a painter. Merric's second son, Guy Boyd, is a distinguished and successful sculptor. David Boyd, the third son, has combined painting and pottery in another remarkable career. Martin Boyd's pleasure and pride in the family tradition in the arts may be seen not only in his autobiography, but in *The Picnic*, in which, through his *alter ego* Wilfred, he describes with insight as well as enthusiasm the lyric mood of a Penleigh Boyd landscape painting.

When he wrote *The Picnic*, Martin Boyd had been living in England for fifteen years. He returned to Australia in 1919, after his war service, but there he felt restless and reluctant to resume the training as an architect which the war had interrupted. He sailed again for England in 1921 and lived there until 1948 when he made another attempt to settle in Australia, which he still thought of as his real home. That failed, as had the homecoming of 1919; he had been away too long. In 1951 Boyd left for England for the third time, intending to stay only for a visit, but ill-health detained him. Finally, believing that it was too late to resume his Australian life, and disliking the English winters, he settled in Rome, where he remained until his death in 1972.

Martin Boyd is best known for his novels of Australian or Anglo-Australian life: *The Montforts* (1928), *Lucinda Brayford* (1946), and the 'Langton' tetralogy, *The Cardboard Crown* (1952), *A Difficult Young Man* (1955), *Outbreak of Love* (1957) and *When Blackbirds Sing* (1962). His 1930s work, reprinted after a long period of eclipse, may now be seen in perspective. *The Picnic* and other novels of that decade help to demonstrate the solidity of his literary achievement. Although he sometimes resisted being called a 'professional' writer ('amateur', signifying love of the art rather than of its profits, was a more congenial word) he took his work seriously. Each of the 1930s novels marks a stage in his growth as an artist and demonstrates something of his political, social, aesthetic and religious preoccupations. Each shows the gift for dialogue and the interest in the interplay of character which makes Boyd an entertainer in the best sense of the term.

The setting of *The Picnic* is a Sussex village modelled on the seaside resorts of East and West Wittering where Boyd spent much of his time during the 1920s and 1930s. His uncle, Charles Chomley, editor of the weekly journal, *The British-Australasian*, gave Boyd some casual journalism to do; he also helped his nephew survive on a very small income by lending him the Chomley summer cottage in East Wittering. Later, Boyd rented a cottage for himself in the same neighbourhood. It was a quiet place in which to write during the winter, and in summer he could go sailing as he had done as a boy on Port Phillip Bay. As a vantage point on English ways of living it was invaluable to the novelist. The characters in *The Picnic* are drawn from the collection of permanent residents and summer visitors whom Boyd came to know in West Wittering. He also watched Anglo-Australian encounters of the kind described in the novel. Miss Alice Creswick, the elderly Australian lady to whom he dedicated *The Montforts*, used to take a house in the neighbourhood and invite young Australian great-nieces to stay with her. Such comments as that of the Major in *The Picnic* ('I must say I regarded Australians as a purely wartime infliction') are recounted from Boyd's own experience of English insularity.

The Picnic had a satisfying critical and popular success in England. It must have pleased Boyd to read the reviews by the English poet Louis MacNeice and the Irish short-story writer Sean O'Faolain. Writing in the *Spectator*, MacNeice praised the comedy of *The Picnic* and the skill with which it avoided the two main hazards of writing about the English upper classes: 'obvious satire and submerged snobbery'. In *John O'London's Weekly*, O'Faolain said: 'There is wit, a lyric touch, good humour, even a sense of poetry, satire, a plot, undoubted entertainment, and the contrast of values is deliberate, interesting and amusing.' For these and other English reviewers, Martin Boyd was not 'an Australian novelist', but simply a novelist. The Australian reception of *The Picnic* was generally favourable, but reviewers were inclined to test the novel for Australian content. The influential Sydney *Bulletin's* reviewer was obviously in a quandary. How was he to sum up a good novel written by that literary undesirable, an Australian expatriate? His final paragraph is worth quoting as an example of an attitude towards expatriate writing which today seems odd and surprising:

The Picnic is well told, witty, kindly, illuminating, completely successful, a book to be grateful for – yet something is missing from it. Boyd has presented many facets of Australian character, but setting and circumstance prevent him portraying for the benefit of his English readers the most vital one. It is one that cannot be got from without. It is represented by Australians who are content to live in their own country and who accept their nationality naturally. For the interpretation of this we must turn to the indigenous school.

The verdict that the novel was 'completely successful', yet at the same time unsatisfactory because it did not portray the Australian at home, shows 1930s literary nationalism at its most confused. No doubt it irritated Martin Boyd, as did similar comments from other Australian reviewers about his status as an expatriate writer, but he might have been amused by the *Bulletin's* predicament. He would have been enraged to know that *The Picnic* was censored in Germany for its attack on Hitler's persecution of the Jews. The English-language Tauchnitz edition of the novel, published in Leipzig in 1937, shows clear evidence of tampering with the text: some of the political argument in the picnic scene was deleted. The deletions, though significant, are small. It is unlikely that Boyd ever knew of them, since he would have had no reason to check the Tauchnitz edition page by page against the original. If he had known of the censorship he would certainly have protested. At all times during his career he resisted editorial interference, even on minor matters. When he felt deeply, as he did about totalitarianism of Right and Left, he knew how to express his anger and disgust.

The Picnic has special interest among Boyd's 1930s novels in showing his preoccupations at a turning point in history. For him, political and moral questions were indivisible. The English reviewers who spoke of the novel's success as social comedy and the Australians who discussed its presentation of Australians did not do justice to the seriousness of its concerns. Today, nearly fifty years after the time of its writing, *The Picnic* may be seen as a whole.

Brenda Niall

CHAPTER I

'Is it twue that someone has taken Plumbwidge Hall?'

'Yes.   Some colonials, so Major Hinde says.'

'Oh! How disappointing!'

'Australians, I believe.'

'Oh, dear, that's dweadful. I had hoped some nice people would buy it.'

'No nice people have any money nowadays.'

'No; I'm almost wuined myself.'   Mrs. Malaby, with a hand on which there gleamed an emerald ring, toyed conspicuously with her string of pearls, lest any one should take her statement too seriously.

'Well, it may be better than having the place empty,' said Mrs. Hodsall. 'Vulgar people are often generous.'

'I'd wather have it empty,' said Rosie Malaby. 'If you'd had to twavel with Austwalians you'd agwee with me. I used to spend the whole voyage from Bombay in dodgin' them.'

'They may subscribe to local charities,' said Mrs. Hodsall with avidity.

'I'm afwaid I don't put money first,' said Rosie, loftily but untruthfully. 'I must make headway for Major Hinde and find out all about it. Do have some more shewwy.'

Rosie, a round neat little woman of forty-two, with rich, abundant, chestnut hair, and wearing a blue dress trimmed with scarlet patent leather, crossed the room to where Major Hinde stood beaming at Carola Hodsall and persistently patting her arm. Carola, stimulated by an unaccustomed glass of sherry, smiled with airy indifference. Rosie moved between her guests as though she were threading her way through a crowded reception, though actually there were only about a dozen people in the room.

Mrs. Hodsall, smiling with determined geniality, watched her fellow - guests, who were her husband's more important parishioners. She did not really approve of this form of entertainment. Before Rosie's arrival cocktail parties were unknown in Plumbridge. Every one was talking very loudly and seemed rather conscious of being at a cocktail party. She wished that Major Hinde would stop patting Carola, or at least that Carola had lost sufficient innocence to resent it.

Rosie occupied his attention, and Mrs. Hodsall beckoned to Carola.

'What have you had to drink?' she asked quietly.

'Only a glass of sherry, Mummy.'

'You mustn't have any more. There is some orange drink in a jug over there.'

'I wish Ursula would come,' sighed Carola.

'That is highly improbable,' said Mrs. Hodsall.

'Why?'

'I can't imagine that Lady Elizabeth would bring her here, or come herself.'

'Why not?' said Carola indignantly. 'I think Rosie is a darling.'

'Rosie?' exclaimed her mother.

'She told me to call her that.'

'It is most unsuitable. Daddy won't like it at all.'

'He heard me call her Rosie, and I saw him smile.'

This conversation took place with the subdued ferocity with which family arguments are conducted in public.

Meanwhile Rosie, having learned from Major Hinde, who heard it from the decorator who was re-papering his bedrooms, that two Australian ladies, a spinster and a widow with two boys, had taken Plumbridge Hall, and having expressed appropriate dismay, went on to discuss the chief topic of local interest, the domestic affairs of Lady Elizabeth Woodforde.

'Of course,' said Rosie, 'I weally can't blame him if he does leave her. They say she makes the most dweadful scenes. It's extwaordinawy that a woman of her birth can be so vulgar.'

'They're pretty rotten stock, you know,' said Major Hinde. 'The brother's no good. I believe he had to get out of the Blues.'

'I can't help laughing,' said Rosie. 'She made all these additions to Clovermead simply to attwact him and he pwobably won't come near the place. Still, I made something out of it. I should die of shame if I were she. What amuses me is that evewybody knows all about it. Ursula tells me evewything, poor child. Lady Elizabeth gives her a gwuelling time when

Mr. Woodforde goes on the loose, and she comes to me
for sympathy.'

'But does he go on the loose?' asked Major Hinde.
'He doesn't look that type to me.'

'Oh, you never can tell with men. Stockbwokers
always keep chowus girls. As a matter of fact it isn't
a chowus girl. It's a woman who wites for some
high-bwow paper. Ursula made me pwomise not to
tell any one, but it doesn't matter telling you.'

'Is there going to be a divorce?'

'The twouble is that Lady Elizabeth won't divorce
him, and he can't make up his mind whether it's worth
while to live in sin. He doesn't think it would be fair
to the high-bwow woman. Isn't it a scweam?'

Major Hinde grunted. He loved gossip but he hated
any sort of confusion or disorder, especially among the
upper classes.

'Are they coming here this evening?' he asked.

'I don't know,' said Rosie. 'Ursula said that she'd
twy and persuade Lady Elizabeth to come. But she
doesn't think there's any hope unless Mr. Woodforde
comes down for the week-end. For some weason Lady
Elizabeth thinks that if he comes down this week-end
he will stay with her, and that if he doesn't he will
have gone off with the high-bwow. If he does come,
she's sure to bwing him to show the neighbourhood
that she still has a husband. So my little party may be
quite an important occasion.'

Babs Oakes, a girl of thirty, carrying a pink gin,
joined them.

'Do tell me about the Australians,' she asked Major Hinde. 'Will they be quite impossible? I 've never met one.'

'I don't know much about them,' said Major Hinde. 'They may be quite decent—probably rather rough. By the way, I want you to come and see my new wallpapers. I think I 've chosen them rather well.'

'I 'd simply adore to,' said Babs.

'Are the Rounsefells coming?' asked Major Hinde.

'No. They 're in town,' Rosie explained.

'Thank God!' said Major Hinde.

Every one laughed.

Meanwhile Lady Elizabeth stood at the drawing-room window at Clovermead, about five minutes' walk from Rosie's house. Ursula, her daughter, had flopped into an armchair, and sat something like a discarded marionette, watching her. She admired the lanky grace of her mother's figure, her beautifully-made clothes, her animated, reckless face, of which the distinction was marred by the gash of too vivid lipstick. She admired the evidence of her mother's taste in the room, in the painted furniture, the silver mirrors, and the bleached pine panelling.

But at the moment she was most conscious of Liza's lipstick. She had chosen that colour because she thought Daddy was coming down, and whenever Daddy was likely to appear, Liza, in her anxiety to recapture his affections, committed an error of taste. Her fingers were fiddling with the curtain cord. Her eyes were drawn with her inner tension.

'Tom 's a fool,' said Liza. 'It didn't do any good my spending those filthy weeks on the Continent.'

'Oh, Lord! She 's going to cry,' thought Ursula in dejection. She had been with Liza for three hours, since a quarter to four, when it was possible that Adam would arrive. She had seen her mother progress from a faintly ludicrous excitement, through anxiety, to the destructive despair which was now beginning to grip her. She had been under a moral compulsion to reflect each of Liza's moods. She was beginning to feel like a wrung-out rag.

'Uncle Tom didn't absolutely promise that it would do any good your going away,' she said. 'He only said it might.'

'I should never have gone,' declared Liza. 'What is that thing, *coeli non animum* something? Your heart doesn't change with the skies.'

'Uncle Tom didn't expect that your heart would change, Mummy. No one expects that. But he thought that Daddy might miss you. It was just a psychological experiment.'

'So I am to be the subject of psychological experiment! No one knows what I suffer.'

'You tell us a lot,' said Ursula.

'You 're a cold-blooded little wretch,' said Liza, beginning to sniff at her handkerchief. 'I 've been a good wife to Adam and a good mother to you, and this is the treatment I receive.'

'Oh, dear!' groaned Ursula, and sat more than ever like a discarded marionette, with her feet straight out in front of her, and her arms hanging limp on each side of the chair.

Liza walked across to the mantelpiece and looked at the clock as if it could help her by going backwards.

'He might have had a breakdown,' she said.

'What's the good of pretending?' said Ursula, trying to squeeze a further drop of sympathy from her exhausted emotions. 'Daddy's car never breaks down. He used always to be down by five.'

'For six weeks I have been looking forward to this afternoon,' said Liza. 'I went on because Tom advised me to, from Paris to Vienna and down to Monte Carlo. When every fibre of my being was dragging me back here, I forced myself to go in another direction. You don't know what I suffered coming back up the P.L.M. Just over twenty years ago Adam and I came back that way from our honeymoon. Every time I looked out of the window I thought of it. Every remembered church and hillside stabbed me.'

Ursula lifted a limp hand and gave her mother's hand a little squeeze. Although Liza absurdly dramatized her grief, Ursula knew that at least two-thirds of what she said she felt, and that the other third was put on as much to numb her distress with a touch of unreality, as to force sympathy, to consume some part of Ursula's vitality as she ate up her own.

Liza went back to the window. Ursula's gesture had momentarily satisfied her. She went on talking, demanding, making scenes, because she never could

achieve an adequate response. She demanded so much
that people were afraid to give anything.

'I wasn't even met at Victoria,' she said. 'That has
never happened to me before.'

Ursula looked warily at her back, believing that
Liza was making up her mind whether to create a hell
of hysterics or to retire in silent tears to bed. She
hoped the latter. She felt herself on the verge of a
nervous breakdown. Actually Liza was in a reverie,
remembering her journey home. Her mind was often
more tranquil than her manner.

Twenty years ago Adam was a god, nordic, and
magnificent. He was six foot two, and the good food
which, like herself, he enjoyed (she was not sure that
this was not one of their first sympathies) had not yet
turned to so many extra pounds of flesh. His face was
sanguine, not scarlet. Anyhow, his colour and his bulk
had not changed her feeling for him. It was like *coeli
non animum* something—*mutantur*, that was the word.
The appearance changed but not the heart. At least
her heart had not changed. Why should his?

Why had it all gone sour and failed, the promise of
that journey home, up that same P.L.M., when they were
so young and full of delight? She was so distressed, she
refused so vigorously to acknowledge the rift, because
she was sure that it was caused not by something in
themselves, but by external circumstances. Her family
was rotten, she had to admit that—well, if not actually
rotten, greedy, shallow, and unscrupulous, and, of course,
as she was one of them she could not help being tainted

by their characteristics. But she had thought in those days that she was different from her sisters because she had disliked those traits in them and in herself, and had wanted to shed them. That was one reason why she had married Adam. She had idealized his bourgeois respectability. It was an odd thing to idealize, but she thought it would save her soul.

He would not realize that. She expected him to save her soul, while he apparently wanted to reverence her as the ideal of well-bred English womanhood. He wanted to be proud of her, not to save her. When from the nursery upwards one had been surrounded by astuteness and callous wit, it was impossible to eliminate these things immediately from one's attitude to life. She remembered the dismay she used to feel when Adam's face would become a solemn mask at her vulgarities. That was when he was first in love with her. Later he was angry or indifferent.

Then her brother and her sisters began to borrow money from him. Then he began to note likenesses between herself and her family, and in self-defence she would note his resemblance to his relatives. It was her family and his money which had come between them. He had made a very generous marriage settlement and thought reasonably enough that it should end there. If Adam had a fault, it was his belief in the sacredness of pounds, shillings, and pence. He was not mean, but money was sacred. In his relatives this trait was exaggerated. His sisters always told you how much their ugly, expensive furniture cost, and even the price of the food on the

B

table. Really she loathed that kind of vulgarity much more than her own, or the conscienceless extravagance of her sisters, and she began to detest the hint of it in Adam. But this did not make her love him less. She only wished he were different in that respect, and she used her dislike of his bourgeois traits as a weapon against his criticism of her aristocratic frivolity.

The situation was aggravated by the fact that it was Adam who was of the solid money-making class, and not the other way round. Aristocracy in its final stages is always feminine, so Liza's aristocracy, and consequently the rift between herself and Adam was intensified by her sex. Her family was in its full and final bloom in the early nineteenth century. Since then the petals had been steadily falling. Adam's family, wholesome, red-blooded, and materialistic was on the up-grade. He and Liza unfortunately had met half-way, grace and strength drawn together.

They began to have dreadful arguments; Liza would lie awake thinking out things to say to him. She would go away and write him long letters explaining the difference in their temperaments. When she was alone her mind raced all the time. Adam would not answer these letters. She did not believe really that they conveyed anything to him. He was amazingly clever apparently at drawing huge sums of money out of somebody's pockets down in the city of London, but absolutely incapable of understanding the simplest psychological issue. He read nothing but detective stories. In some ways he was like a sullen child.

She would agonize for hours over the letters she wrote him, or the arguments she would advance. 'When I come down to breakfast,' she would think in the night, 'I shall say so-and-so. I must remember that.' She would wake up and write some crushing argument on a little tablet by her bed, though often in the morning this appeared rather feeble.

Then after hours of mental gymnastics she would approach him with the result of her effort and he would most likely say amiably, if he was in a good mood: 'Don't be a fool, Liza,' and kiss her, and all that agony of reasoning which she had prepared at once became sheer waste. Or he might say: 'Don't bother me with all that nonsense. I 'm busy.' Then the tension would become too much for her and she would lash at him with her tongue—the aristocratic fish-wife, he called her.

She did find some satisfaction in that, because her tongue was often effective. But no wonder she was restless and thin as a lath. Who could keep up a combined sex and class war with one individual for fifteen years or so, and not feel the result?

Tom had advised her to go away, for at least six weeks. It was awkward, because the additions to Clovermead were just completed, but she went. She was about to make her last throw of the dice, and thought she might as well give it every chance of success.

Three or four years ago when Adam had his operation for gall-stones, she had wanted some quiet place for him to recuperate and she had taken a small house at Plumbridge, where Tom, his brother, was the local doctor,

and could both provide him with company and keep a
professional eye on him.

This house had been on a building estate created by
an Anglo-Indian woman named Malaby, who had bought
the most pleasant stretch of country in the neighbourhood and forced the purchasers of her sites to build
houses to her own design. They were mostly rather
fantastic erections which looked as if they had been
drawn in a child's copy-book. They were full of
quaintness, of beams and buttresses which supported
nothing, while often in other parts of the house the
walls were cracking for want of adequate support.

Adam had liked the place. The weather had been
good, his wound was healing well and the cottage
amused him. They had a short, sunny era of domestic
happiness, with Ursula and Alec, Tom's boy, back from
school for the summer holidays.

The house was so small that the servants had to sleep
in the village. It was like a pleasant form of camping.
It was the last time that she and Adam had been really
happy together. He liked her better when she was not
rushing restlessly to parties in London, or round the
country or the Continent on visits. But he did not
realize that he was so little at home that she had to
occupy herself somehow. She could not sit waiting
for him only to find that he arrived in a surly mood.
If she arrived in after him, excited and staccato from a
party or Wimbledon or Hurlingham or some function,
it was simply because she had to defend herself against
him, against her own love. She knew that he disliked

the smart kind of life she led, her made-up face, even her
gay and lovely clothes; but that was her 'life-style' as
Adler or somebody said. She could not change herself,
destroy herself, make herself an absolute door-mat for
him. And yet she had at intervals tried making herself
a door-mat, but it was a sort of passionate door-mat.
He did not like that either. So she became smart and
social and cold again, and their life was hell. She did
not dare be still and face her loneliness. She had to
camouflage it with feverish activity.

But at Plumbridge she had for a while achieved a
different life. Her 'life-style' for a month had changed,
and that was because she had Adam with her all the time,
and a ten minutes' mood of tiredness or reserve was not
important, because that was not the only ten minutes
during the day she would be alone with him. They
had had separate bedrooms for six years now.

If Adam could only have some gall-stones out every
year they might live happily together she thought,
except that now he would want Ella Hindley to nurse
him.

They had no country-house and Adam had suggested
that they should buy the cottage as a holiday place.
Liza was delighted. She had fallen in love with the
comic little house, because she had been happy there
with Adam. She changed its name from Chitral to
Clovermead, and it became a romantic symbol to her.

But after that brief, happy summer they soon returned
to their old relationship. She tried being a dutiful,
affectionate wife in London, but she could not help

irritating and then insulting Adam, to dispel the sense
of inferiority she had acquired by irritating him.

Adam took his business seriously. He had to, she
supposed, both because it was his nature and also to
make money, which, she had to admit, she spent freely.
But she had never until she married known a man who
went off to the City every morning, and took three
weeks' holiday a year. Or if she had known one she had
not *seen* him doing it. Adam irritated her often enough,
but that never seemed to make him feel inferior. Perhaps it was because he was so certain that everything
he did was right. When he irritated her she only wished
he was different in that respect, but when she irritated
him he wished that she was at the North Pole.

She simply could not be interested in his business.
When she tried to be he saw that she did not really
understand, and was contemptuous at what he called
her posing and lack of sincerity. He thought she was
insincere because she was lively. She was always
successful with people whom she met occasionally, and
could show interest in the most varied subjects. Adam
thought all that humbug, and she failed where most
she wanted to succeed, where she loved.

Adam had destroyed her confidence in herself. She
knew that she was dreadful when he was present. Even
her voice went wrong and became almost cockney.
She wanted to be with him alone but that bored him.
If she was with him in public that maddened him. And
it maddened her that he should have the impudence to
be ashamed of her.

'D'you think I don't know how to behave myself?' she demanded angrily. 'To have you standing by full of hostile criticism is enough to destroy any one's poise.'

That was when he told her she was like an aristocratic fish-wife.

'I'd rather be a live fish-wife, blue or red-blooded, than a ghastly money grubber.'

'You spend the money,' he said dryly, and there was no reply to that.

He told her that she was a perfect type of aristocracy.

This was no compliment as Adam hated the aristocracy, as much as any *tricoteuse* watching the guillotine. He said that the true aristocrat was the person who expected everything for nothing, as a natural right.

Then it seemed that Clovermead might be their place of reconciliation. They had no friends near, either hers or his, to accentuate their differences—only Tom who seemed to be fond of them both.

Liza was able to test Adam's attitude towards herself by his reactions to Clovermead. It was a barometer as well as a symbol.

For the first six months after his convalescence he retained his interest in the place and came down for frequent week-ends. Liza on purpose kept out of his way in London at that time, so that their week-end happiness should not have the anti-climax of a mid-week squabble. Perhaps she did this too well, and Adam, living contentedly in London with a rare glimpse of her, did not want to disturb his peace of mind with a week-end spent exclusively in her society. Or it may have been due to Ella Hindley, whom he first met at that time.

Adam came less and less frequently to Clovermead. She would ask him was he likely to be down for the following week-end, and she could not keep out of her voice the anxious nervousness which maddened him. When he refused she asked him why, and he said with a note of contempt for herself and for the cottage which she sentimentalized, that it was too cramped and uncomfortable, and that the architecture was a joke. Then to conceal that she was hurt and to repudiate her sentimentality she said: 'You suggested we should buy the damned house.' He hated her swearing, but when she was in a state of tension it was some release. Also it was a faint satisfaction to see him wince.

But when her flare of annoyance passed, and she was left deflated and anxious to conciliate Adam again, she went down to Clovermead and considered how the cottage could be enlarged and made more comfortable. A wing could be built out at an angle with large, light rooms, and the present building could be used as a dining-room and offices below, and servants' quarters above.

And now, after months of wrangling with Rosie Malaby, who in each brick of the new building had wanted to perpetuate her own atrocious taste, that had been done. But during the process of building Adam had receded farther and farther away from her, as if he knew that she was making a cage for him. Friends told her that he was seen at the theatre and lunching and dining in public with Ella Hindley, but she had no evidence yet that this association was more than platonic.

She had made the house charming. She had money and taste and she gave a desperate attention to each detail of comfort and decoration.

She wrote to Adam from Monte Carlo saying that she would be back on the Thursday afternoon, and suggesting that he should come down for the week-end and see the reconstructed house. It had been dreadfully difficult to write that letter. If she made it too cold he would be led to think that she did not care what he did, and sometimes, rarely and superficially, having reached a point of exasperation, she felt she did not care. If she made it too affectionate he might be irritated. She made four rough copies before she sent off what she thought was a brief, friendly note.

Years ago, she remembered bitterly, when she was returning from abroad Adam would come to meet her in Paris. Now, though she would have liked to spend a day there, she was careful to take a train which went straight through to Calais. And she was not even certain whether he would be at Victoria.

And he was not at Victoria, nor was a car sent to meet her. She had concentrated so on the thought of Adam that she had forgotten to let Ursula know her train. But he knew her train, and though she learned that he was on a visit in Yorkshire he could have wired for a car to meet her. He was returning to London the same night, last night that was. She did not wait to meet him but came straight on here to Clovermead. Her sense of ill-usage was so great that she knew that if she remained she would insult him. Nor was the London house a suitable or probable scene of reconciliation. It held the echo of too much discord.

She carried off Ursula, who came in from a party and was surprised to find her back, with her down to Clovermead.

During the night her sense of injury evaporated. She began the day with that hope which revived so persistently and perennially in her breast, and with so little justification. She spent the morning putting the last details to the house, and arranging masses of flowers. And now she stood beautifully dressed in this lovely setting, waiting with death in her heart.

'Mummy, we might as well go to Rosie's cocktail party,' said Ursula.

Liza gave a gasp. Her sense of being derelict and unvalued was overwhelming. How could Ursula make such a suggestion? The young were like that. They squeezed your hand one minute and showed callous indifference the next. They only thought of themselves.

'Can't you consider me at all?' she demanded.

'Mummy, I've been considering nothing but you the whole afternoon. I'm considering you now. If you stay here you'll get all fraught with self-pity and bring on a headache.'

'What does a headache matter?'

'Oh, I know, but why make everything more beastly than it is already?'

Liza gave a sharp glance at Ursula. She saw that she too was suffering from strain and on the verge of tears. She had a qualm of conscience, or else was guided by enlightened self-interest. If Ursula collapsed the focus of attention would be deflected from herself to her daughter.

It was true too that she could not bear to remain at home, mocked by her futile preparations. The party would distract her. She would feel heroic—laughing Punchinello with the broken heart.

As they reached Rosie's gate Tom drove up. Seeing Liza he got rather sheepishly out of his car. He was afraid his prescription had not worked. He could tell at a glance that Adam had not arrived. You could tell by Liza's clothes as well as by her face whether she was happy. When she was happy her taste was not quite so good. She was inclined to over-decorate herself.

'Hallo, Liza,' he said. 'Had a good time?'

'Don't be idiotic,' said Liza.

'Is Alec here?' asked Ursula to save her uncle from an attack by Liza.

'No; he has a job. He's going to be a road engineer and is working like blazes in a foundry. Beginning at the bottom, you know. It seems that if you want to end as a millionaire nowadays you have to begin as a newsboy. I should have turned him out to sell papers when he was ten.'

'That trip was absolutely useless,' said Liza. 'Adam hasn't come down.' The mentioning of Adam's name was too much for her. She put her handkerchief to the corners of her eyes.

'Oh, Mummy!' pleaded Ursula.

'Sorry, Liza,' said Tom uncomfortably.

'Do let's go in,' said Ursula.

'Ursula would drag me to this woman's house,' said Liza, putting away her handkerchief. 'I don't know why I should be expected to call on my builder, especially such a damned bad one.'

'Rosie's rather good fun,' said Tom.

'I'm not in the mood for fun.'

From the house came that high babel of voices which directs people to a cocktail party as a bell calls them to church.

It stopped abruptly as the maid opened the drawing-room door and announced Liza, Ursula, and Tom. Liza was glad that Tom was there. If she could not produce a husband, to arrive with a brother-in-law at least made it appear as if there was no family rift.

In the silence Ursula cried 'Darling,' and ran to Carola, who rose to meet her. Every one except Liza smiled at this spontaneous greeting.

Rosie said: 'Oh, Lady Elizabeth, I'm so delighted you could come. You must tell us all about your marvellous twip. Isn't Mr. Woodforde down? We were hoping to see him.'

'He's in Yorkshire on business,' said Liza. 'He may be down to-morrow.'

Rosie turned from Liza to Tom.

'How nice to see *you*,' she said, giving his hand a warm squeeze.

She was excited by their arrival. Her two pre-occupations were men and social advancement.

Rosie was the daughter of a Presbyterian minister in Belfast. After a restricted girlhood in that city, at the age of twenty she had married the manager of a bank in Bombay. She was half his age. He had died ten or more years ago when she had caught him up to three-fifths. Rosie returned to England far more of a pukka *mem-sahib* than the wife of any colonel. She spoke to her English servants as if they were natives, and still occasionally sprinkled her conversation with such words as *tiffin* and *wallah*.

She was one of those people who cannot touch property without making money out of it. Plumbridge was not too far from London. She bought a stretch of land by the river and built old-world houses. Her original idea was that they should be the houses of retired Indian army men and civil servants. The nearest she had come to this was with Major Hinde, who, however, had never been to India, and was not actually a major. But it was called the 'Poona Estate,' and all the houses had Indian names, except Clovermead, because Liza had kicked at living in a house called Chitral. But the houses had sold, which was the main thing.

Rosie being so obviously a woman of property expected to marry again. She was always well turned out, and she was pretty, if a little in the Rubens style, which extended beyond her chestnut curls to her figure. She was amusing and very good company, as she talked and laughed a great deal which made for vivacity, while men found her lisp endearing. But she was beginning to make up her mind that if she did not marry she might as well amuse herself.

She found Tom Woodforde rather amusing.

Tom was married but his wife had had a fall shortly after Alec was born, and she was a cripple whom one seldom saw. She was away a great deal with her sister in Cornwall, as the sea air agreed with her. Tom had to stay with his practice. For the rest of the year one was almost inclined to regard her existence as mythical.

'Besides,' Rosie confided to Babs Oakes. 'You can't expect a man to be faithful to a wife like that—not a fine strong man like Dr. Woodforde.'

She brought him a double whisky, and her excitement made her liveliness more catching than usual. Tom laughed at everything she said. There was that sense of amusement with each other which was like champagne to Rosie.

She knew that common politeness demanded that she should go and talk to Liza. This was the first time that Liza had been to her house, other than on business, and it was madness not to cement such a socially advantageous connection. But three pink gins and Tom's admiration had given her an illusion of power. She felt that she could afford to do as she pleased.

At length she tore herself away and crossed to Liza, who was amusing herself by contradicting Major Hinde.

'Isn't this awful news about the Hall?' said Rosie.

'What is awful?'

'It has been bought by Austwalians.'

'Does that matter?' asked Liza.

'It'll wuin the village. I know what Austwalians are like. I used to see them on the boat goin' to India. I'm sure *you* couldn't bear them.'

'I've met some. I rather liked them,' said Liza. 'They're unpretentious and they don't toady.'

'I must say I regarded Australians as a purely war-time infliction,' grumbled Major Hinde.

'Those dweadful voices!' cried Rosie. 'I have such a sensitive ear. I do think we are unfortunate here. One wouldn't expect to find the Wounsefells and Aus-twalians in one neighbourhood.'

Major Hinde went a little redder than usual.

'I must say the Rounsefells are too much for me,' he said. 'When educated people call themselves Commu-nists, I think they ought to be shot twice as quick as a working man. They ought to know better.'

'You can't blame people for being Communists,' said Liza. 'I sympathize with impatience.'

'Oh, Lady Elizabeth!' exclaimed Rosie, with in-sistent amiability, ignoring Liza's indulgence in *le plaisir aristocratique de déplaire*. 'This from you of all people.'

'If I were hungry I'd smash the bakers' windows,' said Liza. 'Only a fool wouldn't.'

Major Hinde, as has been mentioned, was not really a major. If he were he would have preferred Camberley to Plumbridge. He was one of those sober merchants who, after some mysterious connection with an army side-show, had emerged from the war years with military rank. He was an earnest little man, if extremely selfish about his personal comfort. The army might have its

faults, but it subscribed to principles of honour and fair
dealing which Major Hinde had found lacking in the
business world and the existence of which surprised
him. Having increased a reasonable private fortune
by the methods of the business world, he decided after
the War to settle down and live by the standards of an
officer and a gentleman. This ambition was chiefly
expressed in his rigidly conducted household, and in the
adoption of fantastically Die-hard politics.

He should have agreed well with Rosie, but whereas
he was, after all, moved by loyalty to an idea, Rosie's
chief concern was Rosie. Also he was always expecting
her to repair the cracks in his walls for nothing.

He was very upset that Liza should talk in this fashion.
It was painfully confusing to his mind. In the same
way he was furious when he read that peers were members
of the Labour Party. They were abandoning the ship
in which he had just secured a small but comfortable
berth.

He would have enjoyed in Liza's company a good
orgy of abuse of the working-classes. His sensitive,
self-indulgent little face showed that he was hurt. He
drifted over to where Ursula and Carola were seated in
the same chair, and began to tell them about his new
wall-paper.

Ursula interrupted him.

'Tell us about the Australians,' she said. 'Someone
says there are two boys. Will they be cowboys and ride
broncos? It'll be marvellous to have Plumbridge all
fraught with broncos.'

'I believe there are two young men about eighteen or nineteen.'

'One for me and one for Carola,' said Ursula. 'I shall be the cowboy's bride.'

'Cowboys are American, I'm afraid,' said Major Hinde. 'They have sheep in Australia.'

'What a blow! I hate mutton. But they will ride broncos, won't they? What are Australians really like?'

'An Australian colonel asked me to dinner during the War. When I arrived at his mess I found that he had forgotten about it and gone out. That is what they're like.'

'How lousy!' said Ursula indifferently.

'I have an uncle in Australia,' said Carola. 'He's the family skeleton.'

'Perhaps it's he who's bought the Hall,' said Ursula. 'What fun having your family skeleton there!'

'Oh, no! He's very poor and drunk,' said Carola. 'At least, he's disreputable in some way.'

'Perhaps he's rich and drunk now. People send their disreputable relatives to Australia and they always come back richer than the people who sent them. It's frightfully awkward.'

'And do Australians send their disreputable relatives to England?'

'I expect so. The steamers must always be full of disreputable people being sent backwards and forwards. That is why there are so many scandals on them.'

'If we marry the two cowboys, we'll go to Australia

C

and have scandals on the steamer.   That 'll be lovely,'
said Carola.

Ursula and Carola looked brightly into each other's
eyes and laughed exuberantly.   They were so pleased
with one another that everything they said seemed
wildly funny.

Major Hinde blinked at them.   He wanted to be
included in the lively conversation, but they seemed
unconscious of him.   His mind was obsessed by two
things at the moment—the gratifying failure of the
League of Nations to maintain peace, and the gratifying
success of his new wall-paper.   It was a lonely job
trying to find a listener to these two subjects.   It was as
bad as when he was a boy and there was no one to share
his interest in silkworms.

CHAPTER II

ET EGO IN ARCADIA

It was a month or so before Rosie's cocktail party that the Westlakes had entered the boat-train at Dover.

Christopher Westlake pushed past his brother into the seat by the window. Wilfred opened his mouth to protest, thought it useless, and with a gesture of disgusted resignation took the other place. But he was so used to Christopher taking the best of everything that it could not damp his spirits for long.

'Isn't this a marvellous train, Mum?' he said as they drew out of the Marine station. 'D'you think it's better than the Sydney express?'

Christopher was ashamed of himself for having grabbed the best seat. He stared sulkily out of the window.

Miss Westlake, sitting opposite the two boys and next to her sister-in-law, ordered tea.

'I love having meals on the train!' exclaimed Wilfred. 'It makes me feel cosmopolitan. Look, Mum, look at the primroses. Aren't those woods marvellous? They look as if they had just been washed with pale green.'

'That must be the tiny leaf round the elm boles,' said Mrs. Westlake with cultured reference.

'Gosh!' cried Wilfred, 'England makes me feel glorious already. Look at that farmhouse. It's absolutely tottering. It must be centuries old. I wish we could take it back to Melbourne.'

A very well-dressed woman with a tired worldly face gave a smile of not unfriendly amusement at the party of Australians. Christopher saw it and his face went crimson.

'Shut up,' he said savagely, and jabbed Wilfred with his elbow.

'I won't shut up,' said Wilfred hotly. 'And keep your elbow out of my kidneys. What's the good of coming to Europe if you're going to behave all the time like a mentally deficient bull?'

Christopher's blue eyes, which at times could be starry and strangely innocent, now went small and glinted dangerously.

'Wilfred!' begged Mrs. Westlake.

'What have *I* done?' he demanded, his voice rising.

Christopher's face was now darker than his curly hair. He stood up, again pushed his way roughly past Wilfred, upsetting some of the tea which Miss Westlake had just poured out, and walked down the pullman. He was suffering agonies of shyness but he could not stay beside Wilfred without using violence. He went farther down the train and sat in another carriage.

'Look what you've done!' said Mrs. Westlake.

'I didn't do it,' said Wilfred, mopping at the spilt tea. He could have saved the tea, but he let it spill for the satisfaction of seeing Christopher exposed as a complete boor.

'You don't make allowances for Christopher.'

'He's older than I am. I shouldn't have to make allowance for him. He ought to make them for me. He's not a lunatic, is he? Or perhaps he is.'

'He doesn't like being noticed in public,' said Miss Westlake. 'Neither do I,' she added dryly.

They succumbed to the self-conscious silence that follows a squabble.

This was a red-letter day of Mrs. Westlake's life, and she was determined to enjoy it, in spite of the complications of motherhood, which usually obliged her to put her sons' welfare and pleasure first. Since she was five years old and was given story-books with an English setting, she had longed to go to England. She was now fifty-one and this was her first visit. Before she was five she had longed to go to Heaven. European palaces and ruins and picture galleries were the focus of her later aspiration, and just as inaccessible—in fact, more so, as it needed wealth and freedom to go to Europe, whereas Heaven might be reached through such inexpensive means as a snake-bite or a motor accident.

But she lived in hope. When she had educated her sons, and Wilfred had left the university and would be, she hoped, earning his own living, she would spend some of her money on herself and journey to the promised land. It was hard to have to wait so long, as although the fixity of her desire remained as strong as ever, the eye for beauty grew less keen, and the edge of her appetite for culture less sharp. Also her legs would be less inclined to bear her over the acres of the Louvre, or along the galleries of the Uffizi, or up the belfry at Bruges, while the ecstasy which she had imagined obtainable on Alpine summits was ruled out for ever.

Mrs. Westlake, like convicts who have a portion of

their sentence remitted for good conduct, was rewarded
for her loyalty of purpose by having the date of its fulfilment advanced by four years. This was owing to the
death of Mr. Samuel Uniacke, a very rich squatter, who
was equally single-minded in his devotion to Mrs.
Westlake's sister-in-law, Beatrice, who at this moment
sat beside her in the boat-train. Miss Westlake, years
ago, had refused to marry Mr. Uniacke on account of his
greater age. Far from taking this as a slight he had left
her all his money, except a thousand pounds, which went
to the Old Colonist's Home.

Miss Westlake had been devoted to her brother, a
commonplace, rather brutal man, and though she could
never forgive any woman who had the effrontery to
marry him, she had to be good to Matty simply because
she was Norman's widow and the mother of his sons,
who among living people came first in her regard. She
had a distinct preference for Christopher, who most
resembled her dead brother.

To most people this would not have been a recommendation. Mr. Westlake, during their four years of
married life, gave his wife a dreadful time. He had
never been violent, nor drunk, nor ungenerous, nor, as
far as she knew, unfaithful. In fact, the latter possibility
would not have occurred to her. He would merely,
when she had arranged an especially nice meal for him,
suggest that something else would have been preferable.
When once she hinted that he should show some appreciation of her effort he said: 'Don't you worry. I'll tell
you soon enough when anything's wrong.' He bought

carpets and furniture without consulting her, and ridiculed her aesthetic objections. After his death she taught her sons that their father was perfect in every way, an example and an ideal, but by degrees she refurnished the house.

Miss Westlake, suddenly finding herself a rich woman, decided to spend a proportion of her money on her nephews, and Matty, being their mother, naturally reaped some of the benefit. So instead of travelling to Europe at a remote and uncertain date, as a 'tourist' passenger, carefully considering each sixpence spent on lemon squash lest it should be needed for admission to some treasure-house of art, she surprisingly found herself a first-class passenger on the *Orion*, with not only unlimited lemon squash at eleven, but even with an occasional bottle of champagne for dinner.

This remission of sentence was not entirely pleasing to Mrs. Westlake, who had a conscientious difficulty in enjoying what she had not earned. Pleasure should be the reward of effort. At tea in a well-conducted household one ate bread and butter before cake. She had planned her life in this order, but now, before the end of the bread-and-butter stage, she was suddenly loaded with rich plum cake. It upset her cultural digestion.

When she embarked at Port Melbourne it was to have been a personal triumph. Unaided on her small income she would have educated her sons well and have taken a trip to Europe, two prerogatives of the rich. She was now robbed of this, and beneath her outward appreciation was a sense of frustration and resentment. The

Orient line first-class passengers were more rich than
cultured, and had nearly all been to Europe before.
They were more interested in Bond Street than the
Bargello, and she could not share with them those
thrills of anticipation which she might have enjoyed
with some schoolmistress on a one-class boat.

The Westlakes landed at Naples and travelled over-
land. Mrs. Westlake had a second disappointment. She
valued culture, not because a work of art gave her a
glimpse of understanding or a thrill of beauty, but
because she had a good memory, a sense of propriety,
and liked what was established and authoritative. She
had always confused art with uplift. What was the use
of art if it was not to refine manners and improve morals,
and make the cultured individual more socially desirable
than the non-cultured? She knew, of course, the great
artists had in a spirit of reverence painted naked women,
and she took it on trust that it was respectable and even
necessary to admire these works, but she was quite
unprepared for the voluptuous riot of the Italian Renaissance. This pagan fecundity and perversion, these
shameless Ledas and complacent Ganymedes which,
without warning, confronted one in sudden corners of
galleries or gardens, provoked a most uncomfortable
internal conflict between her twin faiths in art and uplift.

She only escaped renaissance improprieties in Italy
to be embarrassed by the sanitary arrangements of the
French. She was thankful to arrive at last in England,
her real Mecca, where she hoped she would not so often
have to pretend not to notice things. Though England,

she found, was less satisfactory in this respect than
Australia, where public modesty is never offended.

To-day, after so much half-recognized disappointment,
Matty Westlake was determined to enjoy herself. She
would have liked this journey from Dover to London
to be gay and a little sentimental, with some recollection
of the characters of Dickens. The boys had spoilt that
with their quarrel, but she was still determined to extract
full measure from her first glimpse of England. There
on the railway bank were some primroses. Already she
had seen the brushwood and primroses that had drawn
homeward Browning's April longings. That was one
thrill she could note in her diary.

'What are those round buildings, Beatrice, with white
cowls on the top of them?' she asked.

'Those are hop oast-houses,' said Beatrice.

'Ah, yes. The hop-fields of Kent,' said Matty
appreciatively.

Beatrice had often been in England. Before Sam
Uniacke's legacy she had had a quite comfortable income,
and she had travelled to Europe at least every five years.
This was another suppressed grievance of Matty's.
Beatrice, who was not cultured, was free of all those
places for which her own hindered spirit yearned. She
walked with ignorant eyes and unraptured senses through
those cathedrals and galleries which Mrs. Westlake
believed would produce in herself an ecstatic response.
Beatrice even at times professed a contempt for
culture.

Beatrice at this moment was feeling a contempt not

for culture, but for Matty's affectation of it. Miss
Westlake, as far as her means had allowed, was a woman
of the world. She now hoped to be one completely.
She liked good food, pleasant music, and fine architecture,
so she travelled about where she could find them. She
liked beautiful scenery for itself and even for its association, but she did not want to have Matty continually
at her elbow with Catullus at Sirmio, Byron at Chillon,
Tennyson at Milan, and Burke at the Petit Trianon.
And now they couldn't even take the boat-train to
Victoria without Matty dragging up Dickens and Browning. Matty had a genius for destroying the atmosphere
of comfortable worldliness which Miss Westlake liked
about her. An earnest provincial refinement clothed her
like her neat but always slightly unsuitable clothes.
She should have travelled from Paris in tweeds, not in
her best black dress which would become a head mistress
on Speech Day.

When Miss Westlake pointed this out Matty said:
'Oh, but it is an occasion—my first landing in England. I must wear something a little festive.'

Matty was always sacrificing real suitability to her own
sentimentalities. It was tiresome to have the social
gratification which she should feel at the connection with
Matty's family so largely negatived by Matty's personal
lack of *nous*.

Beatrice's father had emigrated to Australia at the age
of twenty, and had become a successful auctioneer and
estate agent. Of her grandfather she knew no more
than that he lived in Twickenham and that his name was

Christopher. It should have been an advantage for Norman to marry Matty.

Because Matty was a Plumbridge.

The Plumbridges had arrived in Melbourne before the gold rush, and after the last convicts had been sent to Tasmania, that is, in the vintage years of Victorian gentility. In Sussex there had been Plumbridges before the Conquest. Matty's grandfather had been a judge in Victoria. Her more remote ancestors included an eighteenth-century bishop, a seventeenth-century cavalier colonel, a sixteenth-century poet, and a thirteenth-century crusader. Even so, Beatrice, who though not snobbish would have enjoyed a solid social background, failed to derive much advantage from the connection. The Plumbridges, instead of taking up the Westlakes, were inclined to drop Matty.

Of her two nephews Beatrice preferred Christopher. Wilfred was so obviously a Plumbridge. He appeared to combine the logic of the judge with the gaiety of the cavalier and the romantic ardour of the poet. If the god Hermes had taken advantage of a curate's wife, the result might have been something like Wilfred. His mercurial vivacity was restrained by an obvious gentle-manliness. The top of his head was very high. He moved quickly, but with a slightly awkward diffidence, especially if he passed a group of other boys in the street. At school he had been laughed at, but not unkindly, owing to his natural benevolence and naïve enthusiasms. He was always extremely attentive to Beatrice, and a little too grateful.

Christopher, on the other hand, though often surly and sometimes outrageous (as now when apparently he was travelling all the way to London in the lavatory; it did not occur to Beatrice that he might be sitting in another carriage), was a sop to her pride. He favoured his grandfather. He too was good-looking, not with Wilfred's pointed, mercurial good looks, but with a superb, sunny resplendence. His blue eyes shone, glinted, or glowered, according to his mood, in a round, sanguine face. His hair was hyacinthine gold.

No wonder he hated notice, as he had not long left the monastic seclusion of school, and people were always staring at him. She attributed his annoyance to the sensible modesty of the Westlakes, and did not know that he had sufficient Plumbridge in him to enjoy publicity and admiration, and was only vexed with himself for not being able to carry it off without self-consciousness. Matty and Wilfred both lived more or less in fear of him. Ultimately in any family matter his sheer physical will-power dominated their finer discriminations. That this was a triumph of matter over mind did not worry Miss Westlake. It was also a triumph of Westlake over Plumbridge.

Also Beatrice occasionally took a perverse and mischievous pleasure in being unjust, though often she felt she was serving a larger justice. For example, just now Wilfred had merely suffered the brief physical pain of an elbow in his side, which would not do him any harm, while Christopher had borne the agony of exposure to the notice of strangers, of an unrelieved pressure of passion, of a further exclusion from human contact. Beatrice had merely hinted at a restoration of the balance.

As the train drew into Victoria Christopher reappeared in the pullman. Each nursing a private grievance the four Westlakes breathed the air of London. But soon Wilfred's grievance evaporated in excitement at being told that the gardens of Buckingham Palace were over the wall on the right of the street, and Miss Westlake felt that, after all, there was some satisfaction in having one's generosity appreciated, while even Christopher commented on the skill of the taxi-driver.

.   .   .   .   .   .

A motor tour of the west of England in the spring is the *plat du jour* of the Australian tourist. Beatrice had done it before, but she could not deny Matty the fulfilment of one of her chief ambitions.

In Australia roses bloom all the year round. In the coldest month the wattle flames along the banks of the Yarra, and in mid-winter the streets of Melbourne are fragrant with violets and with the sweet-scented boronia. Matty and her sons had never seen this bursting of the brown earth and bare trees into leaf and blossom. When they set out the daffodils were in bloom and willow catkins hung in the hedgerows. When they returned it was through a land transformed with a magical rapidity, such as she had never imagined, into an enchantment of hawthorn and bluebells, of dazzling green woods and golden fields of buttercups.

At last Matty felt that she had arrived at the promised

land.   The riotous fecundity of nature in its vegetable
forms did not offend her.   Beatrice endured her rhap-
sodies more equably as they were accompanied by less
literary allusion.

On the way back they called at Plumbridge to see the
tombs of Matty's ancestors.   Beatrice was inclined to
be sceptical about these ancestors as twice she had
accompanied Australian friends to the original homes of
their families, which during two generations in the
antipodes had grown to legendary palaces, only to find
them small and rather insanitary farmhouses.

Also, although Matty's relatives were grand about
their English origins, Matty herself modestly disparaged
the legend.   Her grandfather Sir Wilfred, the judge, had
inherited Plumbridge Hall from a cousin, but after a
few years had sold the place and returned to Australia,
as the climate was better for his lumbago.

'I believe there is a tomb or something in the village
church,' said Matty.   Wilfred was crazy to go and see
it.   He was ravished by everything English.   But
Christopher said:

'England is just like the Fitzroy Gardens going on
for ever.'

The rows of elms by Plumbridge church evoked this
comment.

The church smelt of stone and stale incense.   The
evening sun, slanting through the west window, made
dabs of brighter colour on the painted rood screen, over
which bled a modern crucifix.   On the right a blue
madonna accepted placidly a vase of wilting tulips.

There seemed to be an excessive richness and clutter of candles round the high altar. It looked as though the vicar, having passed through the enthusiasm of the Oxford Movement, had sunk into a casual continental Catholicism.

Matty was shocked. Catholicism was to her like Communism or Fascism or being a Jew—something not quite respectable. One expected it abroad, where they exhibited statues of Leda and Ganymede and where the public lavatories were so public, but not in a place where the members of one's own family were buried.

'Where is the tomb?' asked Beatrice.

They strolled round the church, Christopher following with an affectation of lack of interest. There was always something about the interior of churches which repelled him. They made him think of dead bodies. He had after their first continental orgy gone on strike with regard to church interiors. But he had followed in here to see this family tomb of which there was so much talk. He was irritated by Wilfred's exaggerated eagerness, and was also afraid that the tomb might not be as grand as they expected, and that they would all be made to look fools before Aunt Beatrice. In fact, this seemed highly probable, as they had been round the church and had as yet found nothing bearing their name.

'It must be here,' said Matty. 'It can't have been moved.'

Beatrice smiled sardonically, but she too was a little disappointed.

They were standing by a stone screen in the north aisle.

'What's in here?' said Wilfred, and dived through a low archway. 'I say, here it is!' he called excitedly. 'There are tons of them.'

This was literally true. In the middle of the chapel where they found themselves lay the crusader, Walter de Plumbridge, with his legs crossed and no nose. On the wall was a grandiose classical monument to the bishop. In a corner was a bust of the Elizabethan poet, and there was even a brass tablet to the memory of Sir Wilfred Plumbridge, 'Senior Puisne Judge of the High Court of Victoria, Australia.' In a coloured window the Plumbridge arms appeared repeatedly with various quarterings and impalements, and the floor was covered with the slabs of lesser members of the family.

Matty could not suppress a smirk. Wilfred was enraptured. Christopher could hardly endure the lack of inner co-ordination brought about by this sudden vicarious distinction.

'This place makes me feel frightfully grand,' said Wilfred, grinning.

This frank acknowledgment of his own confused emotions seemed to Christopher so indecent that he growled:

'When people boast of their ancestors it means that the best part of them's underground,' and walked out of the church.

Wilfred could not help laughing with pleasure at being associated with so much defunct aristocracy. He read aloud bits of inscriptions, saying: 'Look here, Mum, listen to this: "She was pious without enthusiasm." She must have been frightfully cautious!'

Mr. Hodsall, who happened to be in the vestry, heard their voices. Actuated partly by curiosity and partly by resentment, he came out to defend, as it were, his church from the tourists. He left it open for purposes of devotion, but apart from a sentimental schoolgirl who brought tulips to the Virgin, it was seldom entered during the week by any one but cheerful trippers. It angered him to hear their bright voices shattering the mystical atmosphere which it was his object to create. If he found them there he would at once attempt to restrain them by the example of his own modulated tones.

His appearance in the archway of the screen was so silent and sudden, that Matty gave a start.

'You are admiring our crusader,' he said. 'He is Sir Walter de Plumbridge. The family lived at the Hall here until quite recently.'

Wilfred nudged Matty, wanting her to announce their identity, but she felt that to do so would be to make too exorbitant a social claim, and that she would be unable to keep either a cringing humility or a smirking boastfulness out of her manner.

Mr. Hodsall showed them a few points of architectural interest and shepherded them quietly to the door.

'Who lives at the Hall now?' asked Wilfred.

'It is empty.'

'Could we see it?' He looked from Matty to Beatrice to see if they were agreeable to this.

'I suppose you could. It's for sale. You may need

D

an agent's order, but the caretaker at the lodge might
let you in.'

'Is it a big house?' asked Wilfred a little anxiously.

'Yes. That is why it is still empty. It has a fine
staircase and a good deal of Grinling Gibbons carving,
and a ghost, of course.'

'Whose is the ghost?'

'It is supposed to be that of a Lady Jemima Plumbridge. She formed a liaison with a handsome footman
who was shot by her husband. It was in the seventeenth
century,' he added, by way of cloaking this scandal with
the decent dust of time.

'Was he hanged?' asked Wilfred.

Mr. Hodsall smiled.

'The gentry were seldom hanged in those days,' he
said, 'except, of course, for political offences.'

Wilfred looked at him with bright-eyed interest. He
nudged Matty again for her to tell him they were Plumbridges but she only frowned.

Beatrice asked how far it was to the Hall. Mr.
Hodsall directed them, and excused himself from accom-
panying them as he had to say evensong.

'He's a jolly nice man,' said Wilfred. 'I thought
English people were frightfully stand-offish.'

'English people who are sure of their own position
are among the most friendly in the world,' said Beatrice.
'Only second-rate English people have tried to patronize
me as an Australian.'

'I'm not sure about that,' said Matty. 'We were
asked to be nice to some English cousins who came out

to Melbourne in the summer before the War. It was all we could do to get them to be civil to us.'

Miss Westlake shrugged her shoulders.

'That was a most extraordinary story for him to repeat,' said Matty.

'Why didn't you tell him you were a Plumbridge?'

'There was no occasion to—especially after he had told us that.'

'I'd rather be disreputable than dull,' said Wilfred.

Sometimes he felt an absolute thrill of delight at being alive. One of these thrills was overtaking him at the moment. He grinned ecstatically as he half danced to where Christopher was scowling by the car. Sometimes there seemed to be little bursts of light in his brain, when he saw clearly something which previously he had dimly felt to be there. It was almost like recognizing a lover. Arriving in Florence gave him that sensation, and he had it again now.

He liked that church, looking rich, antique, and half pagan in the evening light. It made you think that people believed in the supernatural. In Australia there was nothing to suggest the supernatural, which rather impoverished life. Also it was very stimulating to see one's own name (Wilfred's second name was Plumbridge) on a tomb of the thirteenth century.

'We're going to see the family seat—seat of my trousers,' he sang exuberantly.

When he was in these moods everybody loved him —even Christopher.

The last owner of Plumbridge Hall had been a Sir

Isaac Epstein. He had bought the place from Sir Wilfred and had died, aged ninety and childless, a year ago. He had improved the plumbing, and had added a huge castellated billiard-room at one end of the façade and a huge domed conservatory at the other end to balance it. He had also built a castellated gatehouse at the entrance to the park. These additions gratified rather than repelled the Westlakes, especially as on a stone panel over the gateway was inscribed: 'This gateway to the ancient home of the Plumbridges of Plumbridge was erected by Sir Isaac Epstein. A.D. 1895.'

The caretaker seemed suspicious of their request to see the house, but when Beatrice told him that the vicar had sent them, he hobbled off with an air of dutiful boredom to fetch them the keys.

They crossed a stream by a stone bridge, rounded a clump of chestnuts, and came in view of the house. Its long straight rows of windows glittered in the late sun, and the seventeenth - century brickwork was rose - red. Below a terrace a wide lawn stretched to the stream. Cedar trees beyond the lawn gave an atmosphere of dignity and peace.

There was a faint gasp from the occupants of the car.

'Sink me!' exclaimed Wilfred, who had seen the film of *The Scarlet Pimpernel*. 'It's a palace.'

They pulled up by the front door. Christopher shut off the engine and they felt that intense silence which pervades an empty house.

Wilfred grinned broadly.

'I say, Mum, did your relatives really live here?' he

said. 'You must feel frightfully grand.   I'm beginning
to feel rather ducal myself.'

'I had no idea it was such an imposing place,' said
Matty.

'You could put twenty-five Deepdenes into it.'
Deepdene was the name of their villa in Kew.

Beatrice looked at the house with approval.   At any
rate, the Plumbridge's background was equal to their
pretensions.

'Come on.   Give me the key,' cried Wilfred, and
jumped out of the car.

He burst shouting into the empty hall, pleased with the
sound of his voice echoing along the stately, dusty rooms.

Christopher seemed a little dazed.   He sat for a while
in the car and then went off by himself.

Wilfred was in a state of aesthetic intoxication.   He
went ahead of Matty and Beatrice, exclaiming and
pointing out beauties of carving and panelling.

'Why on earth doesn't Cousin Walter live here?' he
asked.   'Can't he afford to?   He must be cracked.'

He stood with Matty in the big drawing-room.

'Can't you imagine the people living here?' he said.
'I can just see them in knee breeches and wigs dancing
in this room.'

The Restoration denial of puritanism, the evidence of
pride of life, the voluptuous swags of fruit and flowers,
the columned mantelpieces, the carved and coloured
arms of Plumbridge, produced another burst of light in
his brain.   In some odd way which he could not understand this architecture seemed to endorse his philosophy

of life. His love for England and English things nearly brought the tears to his eyes—for this rich placid room, for the candle-laden chestnuts in the park, for the blue-bells and the scented may blossom beyond, for the grey church among its green elms.

'Wouldn't it be absolute heaven to live here?' he cried.

'It would not be very suitable to our way of life,' said Matty.

'Why not?' His demand was sharp.

When Wilfred spoke to her like that a kind of blight descended on his mother. Their bond of sympathy was so great that he could not bear any disagreement with her. Until he was about fifteen he had always seen more or less eye to eye with her, but recently, especially on this trip, he had found his appreciations and emotions verging widely from hers. This made him angry as his pleasures were not so great unless she shared them. In his early years he had echoed Matty. He expected this agreement to continue and expected her mind and understanding to stretch with his own. It vexed him when she failed in turn to be his echo.

'We should feel out of place here,' she said, hurt and sulky.

'I shouldn't. I should feel absolutely at home,' he retorted.

Matty gave him a look that was almost malevolent. Her own relatives were arrogant, lavish, worldly, snobbish, and often snubbing. Against them she had built up her refined, sentimental, domestic life, had made it secure with strong maternal ties to her sons, particularly to Wilfred. But Wilfred showed increasing signs of hankering after the flesh-pots of the enemy camp. This house seemed to reek of her relatives' personality. It was arrogant and lavish, a suitable forcing-house for Plumbridges. For Wilfred to admire it was the act of a traitor. She turned silently and looked out of the window.

Wilfred went through a further stately doorway into a little circular domed ante-room. In delight he forgot his annoyance with Matty.

'Mum,' he called. 'Come and look. Here's an absolute jewel of a room.'

Matty made an effort to conceal her resentment and followed him.

'Isn't it perfect?' he said. 'It would just do for a sitting-room for you.'

She was about to say that she would hate to live in such a formal room, but became aware that Wilfred had fixed an expectant and intimidating eye on her.

'It is prettier than the others,' she said weakly.

Christopher walked away from the house across the wide lawn until he came to the stream which bounded it. For a while he poked about among the reeds and stones trying to see if there was any fish in the stream. He noticed a door in the long brick wall on the west side of the lawn and went over to explore. The door was stiff but not locked. As he pushed it open it scratched on the stones behind it, and crushed the young grass which had sprung up in those last few days of rapid growth.

Through the door was a neglected orchard. The trees were heavy with apple blossom, a deeper pink in the late sunlight. The grass was long, untrodden, and of the cool, but brilliant green of early May. In the grass were flowers—daisies, stitchwort, and blue speedwell. Against the wall the clumps of fern-like cow parsley were on the point of bloom. In this sheltered place nothing was broken or disturbed. The caretaker had removed dead wood, but nothing was clipped or pruned. Each leaf and petal, whether of weed or flower, achieved its own perfection.

Christopher stood still, faintly wondering at the place and at the silence. Wilfred's voice no longer echoed from the house, and there was only a minute buzz of insects. Until now he had affected contempt for the English countryside, which was so universally tidy, like one large garden. There were none of the dead trees, of the parched spaces and the dangers that one met in the Australian bush. As he stood there, watching the trees and the flower-starred grass, he forgot his contempt. The perfect unblemished growth of this place on the verge of its summer strength seemed to be in some way the mirror of his own growth. This garden and his own body were in the same splendour of late spring. He was always conscious that there was no spot of weakness or decay in his body. His discontent was partly arrogant that he had met no match for his physical magnificence, and partly humble because of the dumb stretches of his mind.

As he stood still, breathing quietly and deeply, he

became aware that he was experiencing something. The place seemed not so much a mirror of himself as himself to be part of the place. The same rhythm was in them both. In his body was a strange blending of peace and of power and of desire. It was like a slow, heavy intoxication.

Beatrice also had wandered off by herself. She gave a brief glance at the reception rooms of which the merits were obvious. After that she explored the upper floors and the kitchen regions. She noted the number of bathrooms and the position of the pantries. She crossed a paved yard at the back of the house and peered through the cobweb-coated windows of the laundry.

When at last she came out to the front of the house she found Matty sitting alone in the car.

'Oh, there you are,' said Matty. 'I wondered what had happened to you. It's very late. We ought to go. Christopher has disappeared. Wasn't he with you?'

'No,' said Beatrice. 'How d'you like the house?'

'I'm very interested to see it, of course, but I thought it would be older. It's a very plain front.'

'It's Queen Anne, or possibly earlier.'

'In Melbourne Queen Anne style houses have bow-windows and turrets.'

Beatrice grunted.

'Well, I suppose we'd better go if we want any dinner. Christopher! Wilfred!' she called.

Wilfred, his eyes bright with excitement and longing, appeared in the classic frame of the doorway.

'Oh, I wish we could live here,' he cried.

'Christopher!' called Matty. 'Go and look for him, Wilfred.'

Beatrice strolled across the terrace and down on to the lawn. She noticed the door in the wall and went over to it, not so much in search of Christopher as to see what was on the other side.

She saw Christopher standing with his back to her. His body was dark against the setting sun, but his hair was a golden halo. His stillness startled her.

'Christopher!' she said sharply.

He turned slowly and passed his hand across his eyes. 'What!' he said.

'We're going. Why didn't you answer?' She looked at him curiously. 'Do you feel faint?' she asked.

He said 'No,' and followed her back to the car.

At the gatehouse they stopped to return the keys to the caretaker.

Beatrice handed Christopher five shillings. 'Give him this,' she said.

'Thank you, sir. You're a gentleman,' said the man, agreeably surprised.

'I'm not a gentleman. I'm an Australian,' growled Christopher.

.   .   .   .   .

They drove to Southwick, the nearest large town, where they put up at the Crown Hotel.

At breakfast the next morning Beatrice told the others that she did not want to go sightseeing, and that they could do the cathedral, the famous alms-houses, and the castle by themselves. She would meet them at luncheon.

They came in to that meal hot and hungry from their sightseeing. They had climbed up one of the cathedral towers, and seen the instruments of torture in the castle. They sat down happily in the hotel dining-room. Heavy beams ran across the ceilings and the wide Georgian windows opened on to the cheerful noise of the street.

'By Jove, I'm ready for some beer,' said Wilfred. 'Good English beer in this good English pub. Isn't this place frightfully English, Aunt Beatrice? It couldn't be anywhere else, could it? The best hotels in Australia haven't this atmosphere, have they? I'd rather be here any day than at Menzies.'

The waiter stood smiling at their table.

'Beer,' said Wilfred. 'Pints of beer.'

'No. Don't have beer,' said Beatrice. She took the wine-list from the waiter and ordered a large bottle of champagne.

'Beatrice! Champagne at luncheon,' expostulated Matty.

'It's an occasion,' said Beatrice.

'Yes, rather,' said Wilfred. 'Every day's an occasion now. I wish I could live in England for ever.'

'You may,' said Beatrice quietly. 'I have bought Plumbridge Hall.'

Wilfred's jaw dropped.

'Oh, sink me!' he gasped. 'Honestly! Oh, Aunt

Beatrice, my stomach's too empty for this sort of thing.'
He collapsed into weak, gurgling laughter.

On the other hand, Matty's face fell with dismay.

'You haven't really,' she said accusingly.

'I have. Why not?'

Matty could not explain why not. Her reasons were
so bound up with her inhibitions that it would have
been an indecent agony to expose them, even if she had
been able to express them in words. She was a negative
snob, without whose existence positive snobbery would
be impossible as there would be no one to be impressed.
The enjoyments of wealth and position seemed so tremendous to her that she shrank from them as she would
shrink from a too passionate love affair.

Consciously she felt that Beatrice was driving a
wedge between herself and her boys.

'You can't have bought it yet. You must be able to
back out,' she said.

'I have no intention of backing out,' Beatrice said
calmly. 'I went out there again with the agent this
morning.'

'What on earth should she want to back out for?'
flared Wilfred, confirming Matty's fears.

'It will cost thousands a year to keep up that house.'

'I have thousands a year,' said Beatrice dryly.

Her father and her brother had been natural business
men, adventurous, acquisitive, fond of good living, and
not too sensitive. Their fondness for good living had
prevented them from amassing large fortunes, as
although they would never miss an advantageous

opportunity, neither would they forgo immediate comfort.

Beatrice was running true to type. Plumbridge House was an advantageous opportunity. She was clear-sighted about this. Whatever people might say about that sort of thing being exploded, she realized that it would be more than helpful for two Australian boys at the university to have an English county background. If she bought Plumbridge Hall she acquired this added spiritual asset with it, which she would not get with any other house she might buy in England. This did not prevent her from beating down Sir Isaac Epstein's executors £4,000 on the deal.

If she did not keep up a large establishment she did not see how she was going to spend her income. The inspiration had come suddenly upon her as she stood in the kitchen at Plumbridge yesterday evening, and was confirmed when she found Christopher in the orchard.

She saw that the place had in some way deeply affected him. She intended ultimately to settle it on Christopher, to give him that security of background which she felt he urgently needed. She was glad to see now from his smile of secret satisfaction that she had been right.

Matty, whose sensitive reluctance was shared by no one, sipped wretchedly at the champagne which the waiter had poured into her glass.

CHAPTER III

POLITE PASSAGES

LIZA had been on the verge of tears all through luncheon. When the servants left the room she collapsed. She had been rung up by one of her sisters who had seen Adam and Ella Hindley together at Bognor Regis on Sunday.

'But they might just have driven down for the *day*,' Ursula repeated, until she was almost crying with nervous strain herself.

At last, Liza, having wrung the last ounce of sympathy from Ursula, went up to her room to rest. Ursula went round to be comforted and cheered by Rosie. Uncle Tom was there and Rosie seemed to be completely changed. Usually she made so much fuss over Ursula.

To-day she said the same friendly things, but they seemed to have been dipped in acid instead of in honey.

Uncle Tom was as nice to her as usual, but Rosie's manner was so impatient that at last Ursula left, uncomforted. She wandered alone about the fields and lanes. She felt depressed about Liza and hurt about Rosie. Surely Rosie and Uncle Tom were not behaving like Daddy and Ella Hindley. It made the world too evil. It seemed dreadful to her that people over forty should have either passions or romantic aspirations. Their bodies had become such odd shapes by then.

'I do hate adults and adulteresses,' she said.

It was very strange. When you were a child you thought that only young people behaved badly. When you got a bit older you saw that it was the grown-ups who behaved really badly. The offences of children were trivial.

She sat on a stile and sang: 'Would I might be hanged.' She had a high, sweet voice. There was nowhere to go, nothing to do. She picked a daisy and pulled off its petals, saying:

'He loves me. He loves me not.'

Pip, her dog, sat by the stile with his tongue out, watching her.

At last she set out for home, and turned into the right-of-way which ran behind Plumbridge Hall. As she passed, Christopher, carrying a heavy stick, emerged from behind the laundry.

They stared at each other, he with a mixture of interest and arrogance, she with a sudden violent admiration which it took her a moment to conceal. He noted her startled eyes and his arrogance increased.

'What are you doing here?' he demanded.

'I'm going home.'

'You can't go this way. We live here now.'

'This is a right-of-way,' she said. 'It's been one for hundreds of years.'

'It's going to be shut now.'

'You can't shut a right-of-way. It's against the law.'

He flushed angrily and she felt a little afraid. Pip trotted over from sniffing round a corn-stack across the lane. He gave an uncertain bark at Christopher, and after a desultory wag of his tail slunk behind Ursula.

'Is that your dog?' said Christopher.

'Yes.'

'I'm going ratting,' he said. 'You can bring him if you like. He'll be useful. I'll be getting a dog soon, only we haven't been here long. You'd better get a stick.'

'I hate rats,' said Ursula.

'So do I. All the more fun killing 'em.'

'I didn't mean it like that. I mean I'm afraid they'd run up my clothes and bite my face.'

'You're all right with a good stick.'

He went along the lane to where some broken hurdles were lying against the back of the stables. Ursula, surprised at herself, followed him. Christopher's personality excited her. She had never seen any one so resplendent, so bursting with life. The mixture of innocence and anger in his eyes was exciting. And so was his way of speaking to her as if he had always known her.

Christopher pulled an upright from the hurdles, tested its soundness by banging it on the ground, and handed it to her.

'Have you ever killed a snake?' he asked.

'I've hardly ever seen one.'

'You could kill a snake with that. What's your dog's name?'

'Pip.'

'What a name! Come on, Pip.'

The dog came up to him with a tentative advance at friendliness. They went over to the corn-stacks.

'Go on, Pip! Fetch 'em out! Fetch 'em out!' Christopher encouraged, and thrust into the stack with his stick. A rat ran out of the side of the stack. Christopher gave a yell and leapt after it. He laughed and bashed at it with his stick. Soon it gave a convulsive quiver and lay still. He picked it up by the tail and said: 'That's a good one,' and then flung it aside. This performance was repeated with variations for about an hour. Ursula bashed half-heartedly at a rat if it came near her, but she did not kill one.

'You want to put more go into it,' said Christopher crossly. 'They won't hurt you.'

'I haven't much go,' said Ursula. 'I'm all humanitarian.'

When he was chasing the rats he laughed and leapt and danced. He tried to jump on them with his heavy shoes. His eyes were small and glinting and his white teeth gleamed as he laughed. Ursula thought he was like some African savage, only white. She was a little repelled and yet fascinated, and thought that anyhow this sort of amusement was common to most young men.

After a while Christopher stopped for breath. He flung himself on the ground and pulled the dog's ears. Their friendship had been endorsed in the blood of their enemies, the rats. Ursula leant against the corn-stack where it was sliced like a huge loaf of bread.

'Are you Australian?' she asked.

E

'You know that already, do you?' he said with self-conscious sullenness.

'I knew that Australians were coming to live at the Hall.'

'We've a right to live here. We've bought it.'

'Of course you have. I didn't say you hadn't,' said Ursula cheerfully. 'It's not a disgrace to be an Australian, is it?'

'Some people think it is.'

'I don't,' she said.

'That's good of you.'

She didn't know whether this was meant as sarcasm and she did not reply.

'Will you come in and have tea with us?' said Christopher.

'That would be very *outré*.'

He did not know what she meant and was sulky at his own ignorance. After a silence he brought himself to ask her:

'What does that mean?'

'I don't know really,' said Ursula. 'It's a word Mrs. Hodsall uses. It means something no nice girl does.'

'Who is Mrs. Hodsall?'

'She's the vicar's wife.'

'What's she like?'

'She's like a sergeant-major who has taken holy orders but is still slightly fraught with sadism.'

'What's sadism?'

'It's something *outré*.'

'Like coming in to tea?' He grinned at her. 'Will you come in to tea?'

'I don't know you. I don't even know your name.'

'It 's Buggins,' said Christopher, 'Oliver Buggins.'

'Mine is Woodforde,' said Ursula politely. 'Ursula Woodforde.'

Christopher was annoyed that she had not flinched.

'Do you like my name?' he asked, smiling rather evilly.

'I think Oliver is a very nice name,' she said. 'But I thought your name was Westlake. My mother's maid told me that the postmistress told her that it was Westlake.'

'So they talk about us in the post office?'

'Naturally people are interested in new arrivals. Don't they gossip in Australia? I adore a good gossip, all about who 's been living with who — I mean with whom.'

Christopher went scarlet.

'Good heavens!' he exclaimed.

'Pardon me!' said Ursula. 'I 'm not as *outré* as I sound, but I 've been brought up among very loose-tongued relatives.'

Christopher stood up and went round the corn-stacks collecting the rats he had killed. There were nine of them. He laid them in a row on the ground. The largest one he brought over to Ursula. He sat beside her and examined its dead body in detail, pointing out to her the delicate structure of its ears and claws and teeth. She edged away. She did not like to see him pawing over this dead creature as if it were a flower or a curious stone. He seemed to be aware of her shrinking and forced the rat more insistently on her notice. At last she said: 'I must go home. I'll be late for tea.'

'I suppose we're not good enough for you to have tea with us,' he said.

'Don't be idiotic.'

He smiled secretly and walked beside her along the lane. At the end of the laundry he halted.

'Will you come again to-morrow afternoon?' he asked her.

'I don't like ratting much.'

'We'll do something else if you like,' he said.

'I may have to go to London to-morrow.'

'Shan't I see you again?' he asked a little wistfully.

'Oh, yes. We're here a lot.'

'When shall I see you?'

'I expect my mother will call on your mother and I shall come with her. Then you can ask me to tea.'

'I may not be here next week.'

'Where will you be?'

'At a coach at a village beyond Southwick. We're going to Cambridge in the autumn.'

'Who are "we"?'

'My brother and I.'

'What's your brother like?'

'He's all right,' said Christopher. 'We'll be here at week-ends,' he added.

'I see. Well, good-bye, Mr. Buggins.'

'Don't be silly.' He smiled in a superior fashion.

'What d'you mean?'

'My name isn't Buggins. I just wanted to see what you'd say. It's Westlake—Christopher Westlake.'

'Oh, you're too much for me,' said Ursula crossly. She turned down the lane. He looked after her. His eyes were wide and innocent and hurt like those of a wild animal caught in a trap. She felt him looking after her and turned. She saw his hurt look and smiled. She was amazed and her heart gave a kind of twinge when she saw the extraordinary sweetness of his expression as he smiled back.

. . . . . .

Ursula would probably have had difficulty in persuading Liza to call at the Hall, if Liza had not taken a dislike to Rosie. As Rosie had spoken disparagingly of Australians Liza had called at once, before Beatrice had thoroughly settled in.

Beatrice was prompt and direct in action. Her mother came of pioneer stock. Her maternal grandfather had set out into the bush with his goods and chattels in a couple of wagons. He did not wait for a properly equipped house to be ready for his occupation. Beatrice having completed the purchase of Plumbridge Hall, spent three days in London furniture shops, buying the barest necessities of beds, china, linen, and tables, and moved in the following week. Curtains and the luxuries of furnishing she intended to buy at her leisure. They dined in a room without carpets and went to bed

in rooms without curtains, but the weather was warm
and the windows were not overlooked.   The servants
she engaged were a little suspicious of this makeshift
establishment, but were otherwise contented, having
never been so well fed in their lives.

A slightly scandalized butler, who felt that he was in
danger of losing caste in such a household, admitted
Liza and Ursula to a drawing-room which contained
only two sofas covered in lining, and a vast Louis-
Quatorze writing-table, glowing with ormolu and
tortoiseshell.

If Beatrice had been the bejewelled and nasal vulgarian
that is the average playwright's idea of a rich Australian
Liza might have been rude or grand or even confidential
about her domestic difficulties.   But among well-bred
people she behaved perfectly.   She always reflected her
surroundings and behaved as people expected her to,
which was at the root of her trouble with Adam.   He
always expected her to do something to irritate him.

When she saw Beatrice's composed and pleasant
manner and heard her speak with no trace of accent,
she said:

'I 'm afraid I have called too soon.   I must apologize.'

She was really ashamed of herself, because she had
only come out of curiosity.

She took an instant liking to Beatrice.   Beatrice had
that agreeable antiseptic quality which is seen in sensible
middle-aged women.   Liza found it soothing to her
inflamed nerves.

Beatrice too was pleased by the appearance of Liza.

She liked the best of everything. When she had not a great deal of money she had travelled about the world, gratifying the lust of the eyes, cultivating her taste, and, when possible, people of breeding and intelligence. If once she had made a friend, of whatever position, she would never desert her, but she preferred her friends to have good clothes, inquiring minds, and a knowledge of the world. She saw that Liza's clothes were exquisite, that her face had been beautiful, and that her manner had distinction. She was frankly pleased.

Liza introduced Ursula, and after a little desultory conversation, Beatrice asked her if she would like to see the house.

They were in the hall when Wilfred's voice in the gallery said: 'Hell!' and six new tennis balls came bouncing down the stairs, followed by Wilfred in white flannels.

He stopped abruptly on the bend of the stairs, and stood with his hand clasped over his mouth as if to shut in any further expletives.

'I say—I'm sorry,' he said. 'I dropped the tennis balls.'

'This is my nephew Wilfred,' said Beatrice.

Ursula looked up at him with her bright, rather bird-like eyes. Wilfred ran down the last flight of stairs and shook hands with Liza and then diffidently with Ursula. He began to pick up the balls.

'I didn't know any one was here,' he said.

'Don't worry,' said Ursula. 'Mummy often swears.'

Liza laughed uncomfortably.

'This is the dining-room,' said Beatrice, opening a door.

'Are you going to see over the house?' asked Wilfred, his eyes lighting with interest.

'Yes,' said Ursula.

'Aren't you going to play tennis?' asked Beatrice.

'There's no hurry.'

'My nephew has ideas on decoration,' Beatrice explained to Liza.

Liza gave an appraising glance at Wilfred.

'You must come and look at my house,' she said. 'I've just added to it.'

'That would be marvellous,' said Wilfred. 'I'm going to be an architect.'

Christopher who had arranged to play tennis with Wilfred came from his room out into the gallery. When he heard Ursula's voice he started and went to the balustrade where he stood looking down on the group below.

He saw Liza and Beatrice go through into the dining-room. Wilfred and Ursula lingered a few moments talking brightly together and then followed them. He could hear Wilfred talking and laughing, and Ursula's clear voice, echoing in the huge uncarpeted dining-room.

His face went red. He stood there gripping the dark oak of the balustrade. His jealousy was painful and violent. He had not mentioned his meeting with Ursula to any of the family, not so much from secretiveness as because his feelings were so involved that he could not have spoken naturally.

He had never had any easy contact with another human being. He came nearest to it with Beatrice, but there the friendship was implied rather than expressed. He loved Wilfred with an intensity which, if his brother was aware of it, he was apt to regard more as a nuisance than a blessing. When Wilfred was cold and airy, Christopher was inclined to bully him to create a contact. Wilfred's logical mind and dislike of pain were repelled by a love so oddly revealed.

With Ursula he had made his first easy contact. Not knowing her or who she was had given him confidence —also the fact that she did not know him nor his background—his reputation for ill-temper and 'difficulty.' Their meeting had been fresh and free.

He loved those free and airy creatures like Ursula and Wilfred, just as he loved birds and swiftly-moving animals. Himself he felt bound to the earth. His movements were slow. In his mind ideas unformed into words moved swiftly, but his speech was slow. All the time he felt like someone imprisoned. He shot birds and killed animals because, at least, it gave him power over the things which had the freedom he was denied. He bullied Wilfred for the same reason, because he felt that Wilfred, if he would, could lead him to share his freedom.

With Ursula he had actually and immediately shared the freedom. He had felt almost no impulse to bully her, except for that brief moment when he had mystified her by inventing that stupid name (he went a deeper red remembering it) and when he had forced the dead rat on her reluctant notice. She had the same airiness, the quickness and lightness of Wilfred, the quality he loved, but without the wish to escape him.

The night after he met her his sleep had seemed to be informed with a new peace and tenderness. He had not actually dreamed, but there had been a feeling that he had been bathed in some blessed light.

And now he thought that Wilfred was stealing the source of this miracle. Wilfred who had so much contact and freedom was denying him his first glimpse of it. He did not see how any one could resist Wilfred. Wilfred expected to be liked, which was half the battle. He went forward confidently and engagingly, unconscious of the possibility of rebuff.

He was in some ways so like Ursula that Christopher did not see how they could possibly fail to attract each other. Air would mingle with air and blow away on laughing breezes, leaving him dumbly rooted in the earth. He heard them now, their voices a cheerful babble, growing fainter as they passed through the dining-room into the rooms beyond.

Beyond the dining-room was a lobby in which was another staircase. Christopher wrung his hand in an undecided movement, and then dashed along a passage and down this staircase. Like Wilfred, he halted, confused, at the lower turning.

He had the furious look of youth, but he was also anxious and his eyes were not small and glinting but wide and starry. Liza looked up at him with amused admiration, as he stood white and gold in his flannels against the brown panelling.

'Hallo,' said Ursula. 'Here 's the sunburst.'

'Aren't you going to play tennis?' Christopher demanded rudely of Wilfred.

'Sink me!' said Wilfred. 'There 's all day to play tennis.'

'What a marvellous house!' Ursula exclaimed. 'Lovely young men come popping down all the staircases. Are there any more stairs?'

Liza said 'Ursula!' reprovingly, but she laughed with the others. Christopher looked bewildered.

It was a new experience to have even his black moods treated with a light friendliness. He saw the open admiration of Liza and Ursula, the affectionate glance from Beatrice. The fever of jealousy and the dread of exclusion drained from him, and as always when this happened he felt almost physically weak.

He came uncertainly down the remaining stairs and was introduced to Liza and Ursula.

Ursula said: 'I 've already met him among the haystacks.'

Beatrice looked surprised—Christopher with a kind of grateful humility followed the tour of inspection of the house.

. . . . . .

There were soon other callers at the Hall, though the County did not begin to leave cards till the autumn. Liza, although more than County, was not indigenous

to Sussex, so for immediate social purposes she was
ineffective. All those who had been at Rosie's cocktail
party came in quick succession—Rosie herself, the
vicar and Mrs. Hodsall, Major Hinde, and Babs
Oakes.

Rosie showed her surprise, explicitly to her friends,
implicitly to Beatrice and Matty, that they were not more
uncouth, though she did say: 'I can't bear those dweadful
voices. I have such a sensitive ear.' Actually Rosie
could not tell C sharp from B flat, and none of the Westlake's voices were unpleasant. The boys were inclined
to drawl and to slur the last word of a sentence, while
Matty in over-refinement was apt to call a house a
'haoose,' but they had no twang.

When any one called at the Hall all the Westlakes
trooped into the drawing-room to see the visitor. This
custom might have had its origin in the pleasure and
curiosity with which a traveller was received on remote
Australian stations.

Rosie said to Major Hinde: 'I was overwhelmed when
four Austwalians came into the woom. But what a
glowious cweature the elder boy is.'

She had not concealed her opinion from Christopher
himself. She had eloquent eyes. Also she said: 'I
have heard about you from Ursula.'

It was evident that what she had heard was to the
good.

Christopher felt that somehow his feeling for Ursula
was endorsed. That made him grateful to Rosie, but
he felt more than gratitude. His unconscious male

aggressiveness had awakened in her an instant feminine response, which was blended with a touch of maternal yearning.

There had never been much sympathy between Matty and Christopher. She had not sufficient perception to understand his moods, and the affection she showed him was largely artificial and dutiful. Rosie's glance soothed at once his boyish need of caresses, though it was only a caress of the eyes, and his male vanity. Even her attitude to Australia and the faint malice of her references to her friends could not impair his loyal attachment.

They sat round listening to her bright destruction of local character. Wherever she went Rosie held the floor. 'Poor Lady Liza,' she said, 'I'm so tewwibly sowwy for her. She never knows whether she has a husband or not. Weally it's better to be a definite widow, I think.' She laughed a lot as she spoke, which gave people the impression that she had a keen sense of humour. 'I never know whether to ask if Mr. Woodforde is down. It makes it so difficult. I do think people ought to make up their minds, and then they should put in *The Times*, under the engagements: "A divorce has been awwanged and will shortly take place between Mr. Adam Woodforde and Lady Elizabeth Woodforde, daughter of the late Earl of Ashby."

'Of course,' she went on. 'Ursula is the one I'm sowwy for. Her mother gives her such a dweadful time. Whenever Adam plays up Lady Liza takes it out of Ursula, and then Ursula comes and tells me all about it, poor child. She has a gwuellin' time. It amazes me that a woman of Lady Liza's birth can behave like that. They say she's just like a fish-wife. She's an amazin' chawacter. She's a Jekyll and Hyde. To see her in public you wouldn't believe she could go on as she does in pwivate.'

'I'm afraid I find it hard to believe,' said Beatrice coolly.

Rosie felt a little vulgar, and in revenge turned the conversation to Australian-English comparisons.

'How do you like our countwy?' she asked Wilfred.

'I absolutely adore it,' said Wilfred.

'But I expect you are homesick sometimes for your own home?'

'Not yet. I've been homesick for England all my life.'

'That is nice and flattewin' for us. But how could you be homesick for a countwy you had never seen?'

'You can have an inherited nostalgia,' said Wilfred, who had read this phrase somewhere.

'Oh! That sounds vewy gwand. You are goin' to stay long?' she asked Beatrice.

'I have bought the house,' said Beatrice laconically.

'So you feel quite at home here?'

'If we don't feel at home here,' said Wilfred with a touch of heat, 'I don't know where we would feel at home. Mother's family lived here from the time of Edward the Confessor.'

'But I thought they lived in Austwalia,' said Rosie, affecting mystification.

'Australians were originally English, weren't they?'

'I suppose they were,' said Rosie, as if this were open to question. 'So your people lived in Plumbwidge,' she said to Matty. 'Do you know which cottage they lived in?'

'They lived in this house,' said Beatrice.

'Mother was a Plumbridge,' said Wilfred, grinning.

Rosie gave a slight gasp.

'Oh, I had no idea. Are you sure of the relationship?'

'My grandfather,' said Matty mildly, 'was Sir Wilfred Plumbridge. There is a monument to him in the church.'

'How extraordinary!' said Rosie, in consternation pronouncing an 'r.' 'I'm so glad. I mean it's splendid to think of a county family gettin' a place back again. It's nearly always the other way wound nowadays.'

She was disconcerted by the necessity of readjusting her attitude. She had a great respect for the county families and an inexhaustible sympathy for the aristocracy. Their privations were a constant grief to her. Her cheeks flamed with indignation at swollen death-duties, and she would exclaim 'How intolewable!' when a peer for financial reasons was obliged to relinquish the mastership of hounds. With Major Hinde she revelled in indignation at the splendours and miseries of dukes. This was very disinterested of her, as her own income was remote from ducal, and the aristocracy, on the rare occasions when she met them, were unfailingly rude to her.

Matty, feeling that perhaps she had been pretentious

in claiming relationship to her own grandfather, miti-
gated the boast by saying:

'Of course, I am not used to English country life,
nor to a big house like this. I hope I shan't find it
overpowering. It was my sister-in-law's idea to buy
it. I did not really want to.'

Wilfred's clear brows puckered. When Matty said
this sort of thing he felt an inner disintegration, as the
fibres which bound him to his mother were strained by
the need of repudiating her attitude. She had no pride
in life, and could enjoy nothing unless it had the excuse
of uplift. Even in this place which should be her
natural home she must affect the humility of the Lord
of Burleigh's wife, who had died of a surfeit of
grandeur.

'Cousin Walter's house in Torrak is just as big as this,'
he blurted out in loud, absurd anger, and flushed at
making a fool of himself.

'We very seldom went there,' said Matty.

Rosie looked surprised.

A diversion was caused by the men bringing in the tea.

'Won't you stay and have tea with us?' said Beatrice
politely.

'I oughtn't to stay so long on a first call,' said Rosie.
'But perhaps things are more informal in Austwalia,'
she added in an attempt to regain the ascendancy.

'In the country, when travellers have come a long way,
one is pleased to see them. That may make us less
formal,' said Beatrice. Nothing vexed her more than
for people to be suspicious of disinterested friendliness.

She did not press the invitation and rose to say good-bye. To accentuate her informality she went with Rosie out to the front door and stood there for a minute or two talking to her. Matty, eager to remedy any bad impression she might have made, followed them.

Christopher flung himself on the sofa. Wilfred stood looking thoughtfully out of the window. A thin jet of steam rose from the silver kettle. Its faint hissing was the only sound to disturb the silence of the afternoon. Through the open windows came the smell of cut grass and the scent of roses and violas from the bed below. For Wilfred the house still had the spell of an enchanted palace to which he had miraculously gained admission. The sense of the past was a heavy drug under which he almost swooned with pleasure.

At the moment his peace of mind was disturbed by the brush with Rosie.

He turned slowly and began to heat the teapot.

'Wait for Mother and Aunt Beatrice,' said Christopher, who had had a heavy luncheon.

'Why?' said Wilfred.

'Because I say so.'

'Don't be a fool, I'm thirsty.'

He put the tea in the pot and poured on the boiling water. Christopher had an impulse to restrain him by physical force. He was angered by Wilfred's possessive interest in the house. He knew already that Aunt Beatrice was going to leave it to himself, and yet Wilfred was making a kind of spiritual claim on the place which

F

Christopher felt was an infringement of his rights. He let Wilfred go on but he glared at him sullenly.

Wilfred was thinking of Rosie. She was an irritant in his mind which he tried to remove by critical analysis.

'I don't think Mrs. Malaby's as nice as the other people round here,' he said. 'She's one of those hard, bumptious women who try to boss you—like that Mrs. Bastow on the *Orion*. I hate women who think because they're women they can say anything they like. If a man said the same things he'd get a black eye.'

'You wouldn't give it to him,' said Christopher insolently.

'I'd give it to any one who was as impudent as that hard-faced bitch,' said Wilfred hotly.

'Shut up!'

'I won't shut up. I've got as much right to my opinion as you have, haven't I?'

'Shut up!'

'You're mad. If she's a hard-faced bitch I'll say so, and you can't stop me. I'm not going to take my opinions from you. You've got about as much judgment as a bull.'

The blood rushed to Christopher's face and his eyes went pink. Rosie had looked at him with love, which had blinded him to any of her failings. To hear Wilfred criticize her produced a surge of anger, which he knew must appear unreasonable, and this increased his rage. He was always being placed in these positions, where the reason for his anger was inarticulate, while Wilfred managed to secure for himself all the appearance of reason, good temper, and justice.

He seized Wilfred's arm and shouted: 'Shut up, will you! Shut up!'

Now that Christopher had lost his temper, Wilfred, as he always did in these circumstances, became much calmer. He had to retain the weapons of reason, the only ones that he could use successfully against Christopher's force.

'You filthy little skunk!' Christopher shouted.

'You're crazy,' said Wilfred calmly.

'You're afraid. You're trembling with fear!' shouted Christopher. He gave Wilfred a push, and his chair went over.

'You can smash me into a mince-pie if you like,' said Wilfred, 'but I'm not afraid of you. I'll just have to be a mince-pie, that's all. But you're a fool if you do. And if you injure me badly I'll jolly well have you up for assault, even if you are my brother. Then you'll look a fool.'

'You'll look the fool,' growled Christopher.

'I can carry off looking a fool. You can't.'

The butler, hearing the chair fall, poked a scared head into the room.

'It's all right, Lucas,' said Wilfred in a rather high voice. 'We're just having a slight discussion. I'll ring if I want you.'

The man withdrew.

'You can't ring here. This is going to be my house,' said Christopher.

'This is idiotic. You 're like a child of ten,' said Wilfred.

'Have you ever been flung through a window?' roared Christopher.

'Fling away, but you 'll spoil Aunt Beatrice's new rose-beds,' said Wilfred.

Christopher let go Wilfred's arm and gave him a stinging blow on the side of the head. Wilfred's sang-froid departed.

'You bloody swine!' he cried. He picked up a silver butter-dish, the nearest thing to his hand, and flung it at Christopher. The rolls of butter stuck on his hair like burrs, and the dish made an angry bruise on his forehead.

As in surprise and pain he put his hand to his head the door opened and Beatrice, followed by Matty, came in.

'Can't you use your fists like a man?' she demanded of Wilfred.

'What use are my fists against him?' cried Wilfred. 'If you give me a sword and a red rag I might have a bull fight with him. He 's very brave to knock me about, I suppose, but I 'm a coward to defend myself. He 's absolutely crazy. He loses his temper because I have my tea when I 'm thirsty.'

'Pick up the butter-dish,' said Beatrice.

Wilfred reluctantly picked it up. Christopher was pulling the rolls of butter out of his hair, and putting them on to an old Worcester plate.

Beatrice looked at him with an annoyance which was

directed against the others. 'You'd better go and wash,' she said. 'Matty, ring for some more butter.'

She followed Christopher out of the room.

'You ought to consider Aunt Beatrice,' said Matty to Wilfred.

'She dotes on Christopher. She may as well have the consequences of her doting,' said Wilfred.

'What starts these squabbles?' asked Matty. 'They are dreadfully upsetting.'

'I don't know,' mumbled Wilfred, helping himself to cake. 'They just happen.' He would not meet Matty's eyes.

He took his tea and went to the window.

'Why did you say that,' he complained, breaking the silence with difficulty, 'about our not being used to big houses?'

'I only mentioned what was true.'

'It isn't true—not in the way she'll take it. People think that Australians live in bark huts, anyhow.'

'I hate pretentiousness,' said Matty, cross but uneasy.

'I can't see there's anything pretentious in enjoying what you've got.'

'It's absurd for us to be housed like this. Look at this room. It's like the inside of a palace.'

'Good Lord!' cried Wilfred, exasperated. 'Why shouldn't we live in a palace if we want to, and if we've got the palace to live in? All our ancestors lived here.'

'Your father was an auctioneer,' said Matty.

'Well, what of it? Are we to go round branded all our lives because of that? I suppose we should ring bells like Indian lepers and call out: "Don't come near me, I'm the son of an auctioneer." You'd take the gilt off any gingerbread.'

His voice was high. He gave his mother one furious glance and went out, slamming the heavy oak door.

Matty, trembling with distress and anger, leant against the resplendent table. Her anger was directed against Beatrice more than Wilfred. Matty as much as any orchid had been bred to a particular atmosphere in which alone she could flourish. Her tastes, her prejudices, her affectations, were those of the refined circle of an outer suburb of Melbourne in the first decade of this century. They could only thrive in the unfortunately or fortunately rare ethos of their origin. Those who live in the suburbs of London are reputed to have a narrow but refined outlook. Those who live in the suburbs of a colonial capital have gone through a further dilution of refinement, and as the dominions are always about twenty years behind the mother country in intellectual fashion, it followed that Matty could only be truly at home in a provincial household of the 1880's. Only in such a house could her artistic enthusiasms, her intense modesty, and her deference to the hall-marked, provoke no sense of discomfort. Europe to her girlhood's circle was a rich mine from which one might occasionally bring back some jewel to adorn the elegant limits of life in Kew (Vic.), but one would not dream of going to live in the mine. It forced her life from play-acting to reality. In Kew she had, perhaps unconsciously, played at cultured gentility. Mrs. Nelson, a neighbour who had returned from Europe, told her that her dining-room was like that of an English country house, and they sometimes made playful allusions to her manorial dining-room. The fine photographs of classical buildings, the Parthenon, the Temple of Vesta, which hung in her hall again made her house a mirror of culture. She and Wilfred had together enjoyed so much these refined arrangements. Wilfred had catechized Mrs. Nelson about English houses, and had used her information to add clever embellishments to Deepdene. Their shared interest in the house had been one of the chief bonds between herself and her second son. Now Beatrice had not only robbed her of the adventure of making her own carefully-planned expedition to the European mine, but forced her to live in its glittering depths, where she could hardly breathe, or to change the metaphor to one which Matty would not have dreamed of using, she was like a woman who, from enjoying the graces of an unfelt flirtation, is suddenly snatched into bed with her lover.

Wilfred's snobbery was the natural soaring greed of youth, her own the avoidance of embarrassing contacts, and by continual play-acting she had avoided the most embarrassing contact of all—that with life. Wilfred was thirsting for life more abundantly. Beatrice had exposed the difference between them. She had endangered Matty's only real and valued contact which she had been able to maintain within the convention of her playacting, that with Wilfred. She had forced her from the pretty stage of provincial gentility where she shone, into the solid position of gentry where she did not know her lines. She could not cut away from Beatrice and return to her own life as Wilfred would never forgive her. The only thing she could do was to decide that she would continue with Beatrice, but, in turn, she would never forgive *her*.

At the moment, after this open rift with Wilfred, she felt she could not bear to speak to her sister-in-law, and she left the drawing-room. As she passed through the hall with its fine staircase, its lofty, painted ceiling, its heavy gilded chandelier, she hated the house for its dignity and its lack of daintiness.

CHAPTER IV

SONGLESS, BRIGHT BIRDS

'I THINK the younger one is rather graceful,' said Sylvia Rounsefell, watching Wilfred through a pink-rimmed single eye-glass, 'but there's something irritating about him. The brother's a magnificent blond beast. Give me another cigarette, Aelred.'

Her husband fixed a cigarette in her long pink holder and deferentially lighted it for her. He then sat back with a strange brightly-coloured dignity and watched the tennis party to which he and Sylvia were not actually invited. His forehead was high and hairless, his beard red, his tie of spotted white linen, his trousers of blue linen. He wore no socks, but his shoes were of white canvas and red leather.

The Rounsefells were the envy, the contempt, the pride, and the joke of Plumbridge. They lived mostly in Mecklenburgh Square, but last autumn they had acquired a farmhouse beyond the village, where at Christmas time, with some even more exotic-looking friends, they had held a decorative parody of medieval revels. Before that they had lived at Syracuse.

Aelred Rounsefell was a publisher. At least, he printed books which if they had not been so exquisitely produced would have been listed in French catalogues as 'curious and amusing.' But with the spread of Fascism it seemed that soon the Mediterranean would be no longer safe for pornography, and the Rounsefells returned to Bloomsbury. They were as tireless as the Athenians in their search for some new thing. They were so advanced in culture that to them Plumbridge was a delicious or disgusting anachronism, according to their mood.

After luncheon that day, Sylvia, having just arrived from London, was in the mood for anachronisms.

'Let's go and see Malaby,' she said. She called all her women friends by their surnames.

Aelred always acquiesced in her whims.

Rosie's maid told them that she was playing tennis at the Hall.

'Who's there?' asked Sylvia eagerly. 'Has someone bought it?'

'Yes, madam. An Australian lady.'

'What's her name? How old is she?'

'Just middle-aged, I should say.'

'Does she live there alone?'

'No, madam, Mrs. Westlake and two young gentlemen live with her.'

'Two young gentlemen! Are they rich?' Sylvia laughed at her own ill-mannered curiosity.

'They have eight servants and a chauffeur.'

'How many cars?' asked Sylvia gaily.

'Two, madam.'

'Only two cars! Let's go and call on them,' she said to Aelred, turning away indifferently from the maid.

'Rich Australians,' said Aelred doubtfully. 'They'll
have as much sensibility as the Bayswater Road.'

'I want to see the eight servants and the two young
gentlemen. Come on. It will be amusing. We can
leave if we don't like it.'

Though capable of extravagant generosity they could
also show that complete selfishness which makes people
ignore the line between assurance and aggressiveness.

Lucas, the butler, like a crow in charge of two birds of
Paradise, led them down the lawn and announced them
to Beatrice. As they approached, the group by the
tennis pavilion exchanged glances of rueful amusement.

'Good heavens!' Rosie exclaimed to Tom Woodforde.
'Here's Bloomsbuwy! What incwedible guys!'

Sylvia, when she had carelessly apologized to Beatrice
for calling in the middle of a party, turned and regarded
the other guests with the drowsy insolence of a *grande
amoureuse*. She left Aelred to compensate with exaggerated courtesy for her own cavalier manner to
Beatrice. Aelred had a soothing deference which made
every woman conscious of her sex, and every boy
vaguely surprised that he was not a girl.

Sylvia was no fool. She saw at once that her eclectic
culture would have no effect on Beatrice, however much
she might talk of people called Aldous and Vanessa.
She used her affectations to give herself background and
status. She controlled them as a sybarite might control
his appetites to make them yield him the maximum of
satisfaction. From childhood she had determined to
be someone. Her origins were uninteresting and she

had no great wealth to give her social prominence, so she decided to exploit her taste and her flair for the latest movement in art or literature. She had the sense to limit her orbit and to shine brightly within those limits. Matty in her refined suburb had tried in the same way to give her life distinction, but her light, reflected only from the distant dying sun of Victorianism, was unable to shine far, while Sylvia's, continually replenished from the hot new rays of surrealism, or whatever cultural comet she might be worshipping at the moment, was able to impress and cause to wilt even people as little touched by cultural movements as the semi-county society of Plumbridge.

Meanwhile Beatrice accepted Aelred's subtle flatteries with a slightly sardonic pleasure.

Sylvia felt a sudden distaste for the locals, and when Beatrice was called to the house to interview a builder about some alterations, she drew Aelred apart to sit by her and watch the tennis and the people.

She puffed at her cigarette and replaced the pink-rimmed monocle in her eye.

'I do think Malaby's obscene,' she said. 'D'you think she has seduced the doctor yet?'

'No, not from the way she's going on,' said Aelred judicially. 'She's still too eager. She makes excuses to touch him.'

'What d'you think these people would be like if they didn't believe in chastity?'

'They'd be fatter.'

'Malaby is'nt a sylph.'

'Yes, but she doesn't believe in chastity.'

'It must be awful to have to practise what you don't believe. I should die,' said Sylvia. 'D'you think Malaby really wants to seduce the doctor, or just to play with the idea of doing it. She has such marvellous outbursts of gentility. D'you think she values her chastity or her reputation most?'

'She doesn't value her chastity at all. But she's determined to get something valuable for it if she gives it up. All provincial women are like that. It's a form of commercial dishonesty, like selling your rubbish to the dustman.'

'I wish you wouldn't make analogies, Aelred.'

'Why not?'

'It's like a clergyman. D'you think the doctor would enjoy more Miss Oakes's virginity or Malaby's ripe experience? Why don't you seduce Miss Oakes, Aelred? I think you ought to. It would be kind.'

'I'm not a charitable institution.'

'She would probably be rather brittle in bed. I believe the blond beast is in love with Ursula Woodforde. He hates playing with Oakes against her. He really is attractive. He won't pick up any balls for Oakes, but when Ursula's serving against him he sends balls down to her. I love that sort of vicious rudeness. It's a drop of vital blood among all these people who've been kept on ice.'

'Malaby hasn't been kept on ice.'

'She mistook the oven for the refrigerator.'

'Shall I seduce Malaby?'

'Don't be silly, Aelred. Do look at Oakes. She's almost in tears. Every time the blond beast leaves her to pick up her own balls, it's a reminder of her frustrated girlhood, and that no man has ever seen her with her clothes off. And she has a pursed-up look too. She's shocked because the blond beast isn't behaving himself. These people don't know how to lose their virginity and keep their sense of propriety. That is the whole problem of provincial life—to do the two things together.'

'D'you think Malaby will solve it?'

'Malaby has no sense of propriety. She has no sense of anything. She's a muddle of echoes. But Oakes has some significance. She's eternal, like those weedy purple columbines. I rather like her. I wish she'd burst openly into tears. If she began by losing her sense of propriety she might end by losing her virginity. Give me another cigarette, Aelred.'

The ping of the tennis balls, Wilfred's and Ursula's frank, clear cries of delight or annoyance as they won or lost a point, Rosie's caressing murmurs to the doctor, punctuated by her exclamation of 'Bwavo!' as Christopher won a point, a thrush in a lime tree, and the tinkle of silver and china as Lucas, followed by a footman, brought the tea down the lawn, produced a pleasant afternoon noise.

'I'm glad we came here,' said Sylvia. 'I always like watching people do things. It's odd that people without any taste can produce a scene like this which has a sort of character and unity. Oh, look at Carola! That swish forward of her hair when she stooped to pick up

that ball was absolutely enchanting. It catches me here.'
Sylvia put a pink-nailed hand under her left breast.
'Look at her now, throwing her hair back. She's
absolutely fair and flowering. It's a shame that she's
stuck here with all this inhibited gentility. I wish the
blond beast would fix his passion on her instead of
on Ursula. He's lovely. It's marvellous to watch
him. He's like a congested boar when he looks at his
brother or Oakes, and when he looks at Ursula his eyes
are like crucified stars. He's much too good for her.'

'I like Ursula,' said Aelred.

'Oh, no, Aelred! She's dreadful. All upper gang-
lion. I can't bear her sharp mind and all that bird-like
twittering. Oakes has quite a good chin, but she holds
it as if someone had given it a push.'

'Sexually starved people always hold their chins in,'
said Aelred.

Sylvia stroked her chin thoughtfully and laughed.

Ursula at the moment was not at all bird-like. She
had spent the morning discussing with Liza whether
Liza should swallow her pride and go to London in the
the hope of seeing Adam. She knew that her mother
was determined to go, but first she wanted to chew
thoroughly every reason for and against, partly because
it gave some release to her obsession with Adam, and
partly so that she could blame someone besides herself
if the expedition was not a success. She wanted Ursula to
go too but Ursula refused, not only because she could not
face Liza's tantrums if Adam was not there, but because
she wanted to come to the tennis party and see Christopher.

Liza tackled her with this.

'I believe you 're attracted by that boy,' she said.

Ursula's silence admitted it.

'It 's ludicrous,' said Liza. 'He 's not even an under-graduate yet.   And he looks as if he had a temper.'

'He left school eighteen months ago. He was at Melbourne University for a year before he came to England.'

'Where was he at school? You can't marry an Australian.'

'You married someone from Surbiton. That 's much worse.'

'A lot of good it 's done me,' said Liza, with the levity with which she would suddenly punctuate her grief.

But Liza's careless remark had crystallized Ursula's attitude to Christopher. She realized that she did want to marry him, and she did not know if he wanted to marry her, and because he was not yet twenty she knew that everybody would think even an engagement absurdly impossible.

They had only met about half a dozen times since that afternoon when he had hunted the rats, but one Sunday they had been alone together for hours, playing singles and picking raspberries in the orchard. They had hardly touched the verge of sophisticated love. Their feelings had been expressed indirectly by glances, gestures, and even by mild chaff.

And it was true that Christopher was difficult. Though she would not call him bad-tempered.   He was behaving in an extraordinary fashion to Babs Oakes. It made

Ursula more depressed. She had wanted to tell Rosie all about Liza, but when she arrived Rosie was engrossed with Uncle Tom, and talking to him in that bold, girlish fashion that it made one uncomfortable to watch. So she could not confide in Rosie, nor could she confide in Carola because her cousin Alec was talking to Carola, and Alec had confessed to Ursula with lyrical hyperbole what he thought of Carola, so she could not bear to interrupt them, and Christopher had not arrived on the court until after two sets had been played.

She longed to be alone with him.

'Game and—thanks a lot,' said Wilfred.

Babs, almost in tears, made for Rosie and Tom.

'I think Australians are horrid,' she said.

It upset her dreadfully when her experience clashed with the tenets of her childhood. Her mother had told her that a gentleman always did this, a lady never did that. A gentleman never kissed a girl until he was engaged to her. A gentleman would endure with respectful patience a prolonged period of arch teasing, and perform difficult and even dangerous tasks at a lady's whim. This was so when Babs's mother was a girl, and Babs was not going to cheapen herself by behaving in any other fashion than as a wayward queen of beauty. Time and again she had seen her mother's precepts exploded, but she clung bravely to her faith.

'No decent man likes made-up women,' she affirmed, and with a shining nose she would send some unfortunate male a hundred yards to find her handkerchief, or in a distressingly coy moment to pick her a rose,

G

and then she would be aggrieved that they were not charmed. This afternoon Christopher had bluntly refused to fetch her handbag from the house, and now had left her to pick up her own tennis balls.

'It's those dweadful voices I can't stand,' Rosie said to her. 'The boys' voices are not bad, but that monotonous flat sound the mother gives forth makes me want to scweam.'

'Would your screaming be more musical?' asked Tom.

'Oh, doctor!' said Rosie, laughing crossly.

'I can't stand the boys,' said Babs. 'Christopher's not fit for decent society. He has no manner at all.'

'You can't expect a young Gweek like that to have manners,' said Rosie. 'He'll get all he wants without them.'

'What'll he get?' Tom inquired lazily.

Rosie laughed loudly.

'I can't tell you before a *jeune fille*,' she said, looking at Babs.

'I can't understand how Miss Westlake could ask the Rounsefells,' said Babs.

'Perhaps she didn't ask them,' said Rosie, inadvertently accurate. 'Aren't Alec and Cawola sweet together? I adore love's young dweam.'

Tom grinned placidly. He was not deceived by Rosie's sensibilities and enthusiasms.

Wilfred, released from his game, went over to where the Rounsefells sat apart in supercilious culture.

'How d'you do?' he said, shaking hands. Sylvia stretched out her hand, back upwards, rather as if she

were in the habit of having it kissed. Aelred stood up
and bowed with the deference he showed to all grace
and beauty.

'I'm awfully sorry my aunt was called away. I
expect she'll be back soon.'

His assurance and manner of the perfect host amused
Sylvia.

For a moment he stared at her, bright-eyed. Her
hat had a broad transparent brim which softened most
becomingly the lines of her face. Thick golden curls
clustered round her neck, and from her ears hung
heavy gold earrings of Flemish filigree, which matched
her necklace. Her dress was hand-painted silk of rusty
pink on beige. Her pink enamelled toe-nails peeped
prettily from her sandals and she wore lace gloves. She
was more of a *poule luxueuse* than Wilfred had ever met at
close quarters, but of a *luxe* distinguished and superb.
He had read somewhere of a 'queen superbly swaying.'
She was like that. He smiled with pleasure at a conception so completely realized.

'I hope you don't mind our intruding on your tennis
party,' said Aelred.

'Oh, no. I'm awfully glad you came. I love crowds
of people.'

'Are we a crowd?' asked Sylvia, pretending to be
piqued.

'No. Of course not. I mean I like an air of gaiety,'
Wilfred explained, a little confused at his gaff.

'How lovely!' exclaimed Sylvia. 'An air of gaiety.
It suggests the 'nineties.'

'It is delightful to meet someone in Plumbridge who likes an air of gaiety,' said Aelred.

'Don't you like Plumbridge?' asked Wilfred uncertainly.

'I like the landscape,' said Sylvia, 'but not the figures.'

'I love it all,' said Wilfred. 'It's my home.'

'Isn't Australia your home?'

Again this irritating suggestion that he ought to be packed off by the next boat—that if once one's father or grandfather had embarked for Australia, one no longer had any right to live in England or to call it one's home. Wilfred frowned.

'In a sense it is,' he said, 'but you see my people have lived here since the time of Edward the Confessor, so I think I have the right to call this my home.'

His voice trembled a little, partly with exasperation at again having to give this explanation and partly with elation at its conclusive effectiveness.

'What! Lived in Plumbridge for a thousand years!' Sylvia laughed. 'No wonder they needed to go to Australia for a change!'

Wilfred smiled, but with slight irritation.

'They lived in this house,' he said. 'Mother was a Plumbridge.'

'You're one of the real county families then.'

'Yes,' said Wilfred, blushing slightly at having this acknowledged by an English person.

Aelred looked away, bored. Having an illegitimate grandfather he had a complex about gentle birth and could not bear any reference to the artificial distinctions of genealogy, especially as the Rounsefells for the last three months had called themselves Communists.

'Aelred, did you hear?' demanded Sylvia. 'This young man is one of the indigenous aristocracy.' She seemed amused by the fact.

'Is there any indigenous art in Australia?' asked Aelred.

'There are Streeton and Hans Heysen,' said Wilfred.

'What are they?' Aelred showed polite interest. Wilfred was amazed.

'They are our most famous artists,' he explained.

'In what style do they paint?'

'Oh, fairly modern,' said Wilfred uncertainly.

'Post-impressionist,' suggested Aelred.

'Not exactly.'

'Do they express the Australian ethos?'

'Ethos?'

'Have they the vibration of the Australian earth in their painting? Is it the vital expression of a new culture?'

'Oh, yes; I think it is.'

'Where could one see specimens of their work?'

'We have some here—in the dining-room. Would you like to see them?'

'Yes. Do let us see the work of the most famous Australian artists,' cried Sylvia.

'We'd better go after tea. I'll show you the whole house if you like.'

'I love seeing houses.' Sylvia was beginning to enjoy herself. 'Is that golden creature your brother? Do bring him over.'

'I'll try,' said Wilfred, smiling apologetically in advance for any recalcitrance Christopher might show.

'Is he very difficult then?'

'He is sometimes. He becomes savage without any cause.'

'I adore that,' said Sylvia. When Wilfred left them to fetch Christopher she began to laugh. 'This is like a dream, Aelred,' she said. 'An Australian county family and famous artists one has never heard of, and a blond beast who may become savage at any moment, and a young man straight out of the 'nineties.'

'Christopher was standing close to Ursula. Enchantment enclosed them. His skin felt as if he were stroked with dove's wings. She could not look at him as her love would be exposed in her eyes. He stood beside her and helped her to strawberries and cream. He put the sugar on the strawberries for her and their hands touched. He helped her to food as if it were an act of worship.

'Mrs. Rounsefell wants me to introduce you to her,' said Wilfred.

'What for?' growled Christopher, with the dazed indignation of one awakened from a lovely dream.

'I can't imagine,' said Wilfred lightly.

Ursula looked defensively at Wilfred.

'Are you coming?' he asked.

'No,' said Christopher.

'You must. It's horribly rude not to.'

'I'm busy.'

'You're not. She can see that you're not. She's looking at you.'

Christopher looked round and saw Sylvia watching him expectantly. He put down his plate of strawberries with a gesture of obvious annoyance and went over to her.

'He's in a rage at having to leave Ursula,' said Sylvia to Aelred. 'What fun!'

Wilfred said: 'This is my brother Christopher,' and stood by to smooth out any unpleasantness.

Sylvia looked at him appreciatively. She often said that young men were uninteresting lovers. They thought too much of themselves and their own satisfactions, but she allowed it would be tolerable for such a specimen as Christopher to think of himself. There was something classic and Greek about his brow and hair, and something of refined negroid about his nose. An embrace from him, she felt, would have tremendous significance. It would combine an innocent but extreme African sensuality with a strange spiritual return to classic sunlight. She told Aelred this later when she dressed him down for snatching this agreeable morsel from under her nose.

Aelred always pounced on the young and charming —if a girl, to remark on the texture of her hair or the angelic intricacies of her ears; if a boy, to extract the sweetness of his intellectual aspirations.

'You have just been in Italy?' he said to Christopher.

'About three months ago.'

'Tell me. Did you feel any sense of home-coming there?'

Christopher looked at Aelred as if he were about to expose him to some public humiliation. He did not reply.

'You are the classic type,' Aelred went on. 'I wondered if you had any inner consciousness of that when you found yourself in the Italian ethos. You did not instinctively respond to it? When I first went to Italy as a boy of eighteen, I had an amazing sense of spiritual liberation. You didn't feel that?'

'I don't know,' said Christopher, who was not going to own up either to any aesthetic deficiency or to any experience which might lead him into deeper quagmires.

'The shape of the head and body are the central motif in any racial culture,' said Aelred didactically. 'You can't imagine a Chinese landscape peopled with any other type of face than the Chinese. Even the Chinese dogs are in harmony with it. Certain people are definitely disharmonious with certain landscapes. I should think you would feel most at home in the Eastern Mediterranean. You're sure you don't remember any sensations of being peculiarly at one with the southern Italian landscape.'

'We didn't go farther south than Naples,' said Christopher, bewildered and surly, but Aelred was never dismayed.

'What type am I?' asked Wilfred, partly from curiosity and partly to draw attention to himself before Christopher burst out into some atrocious rudeness.

'The English type,' said Aelred a little contemptuously. He had taken a dislike to Wilfred. He was a reminder of his own misguided youth when he had been enthusiastic about all the wrong things: the poetry of Swinburne, the prose of Wilde, the paintings of Rossetti and Burne-Jones, the Wardour Street of the aesthetic world, from which Sylvia had led him, up the Charing Cross Road with its advertisements of contraceptives, into the pure air of Bloomsbury.

Wilfred, however, was pleased.

'Is there an Australian type?' asked Aelred, 'or hasn't it developed yet, as the American type has developed?'

'Australian men are supposed to be tanned and lanky,' said Wilfred, 'but those are only stockriders really. They drink so much tea.'

'It has a deeper cause than that,' said Aelred. 'Does that type suit the Australian landscape best? I imagine it would rather. That probably is the Australian vibration—the lanky trees, the lanky men.'

Christopher with the barest gesture of apology went back to Ursula, who was listening dazedly to Major Hinde's account of his new wall-paper. Christopher abruptly led her away. Major Hinde looked after them with an expression of greedy pathos. All the time he was hurrying away from loneliness, and all the time it was catching him up. He was so interested in his house, his garden, and his food, because houses and food were connected in his mind with domestic happiness. His instincts were those of the nesting bird, but he was so preoccupied with the nest itself that he felt it would spoil his arrangement of it to share it with any one. He tried to escape his loneliness and satisfy his

homing instincts by telling people about it. His face
was red, selfish, and brutal, but his eyes were those of
a lost child, until he had fixed a listener, when they became like the ancient mariner's. If he were interrupted
in the middle of a recitation about his experiences with
a certain kind of lawn sand, or where he bought his
meat, he would wait with polite impatience until the
interrupter paused, and then he would pounce on the
conversation, beginning to the word where he left off,
and continuing until the last weed had withered on his
lawn, or until he had made his final crushing retort to
a rebellious butcher.

In telling Ursula about his difficulty in choosing the
spare room wall-paper he felt that he was sharing his
nest with that delightful young creature, and when
Christopher led her away he had a dumb smitten expression, as if someone had wrecked his home.

He waylaid Wilfred who was carrying two cups of
tea to the Rounsefells.

'I hear that you are a young man of taste,' he said
firmly.

'Oh, I don't know,' said Wilfred, blushing with
charming diffidence.

'I should like you to come and see some decorations
I am doing to my house.'

'I should love to,' said Wilfred, 'I'm awfully interested
in houses.'

Major Hinde purred.

'That is excellent,' he said. 'You must dine
with me.' He began to catalogue his wine bins, but

Wilfred excused himself to take the tea to the Rounsefells.

. . . . .

'Where are we going?' asked Ursula.

'Wait and see,' said Christopher. He pushed open the rusty door into the orchard, where now the grass was mown and vegetable gardens were being laid out along the northern wall. As it was Saturday afternoon there were no gardeners about.

Christopher looked at Ursula with a rather sunny air of triumph. He led her to the far end of the orchard where an old apple tree made some chequered shade. Then he lay beside her on the dry grass.

They lay about a foot apart facing each other. They played with bits of speedwell or clover, or anything of minute interest which they could find in the grass. They spoke very little but sometimes their fingers touched.

Ursula had always been easily loquacious about love. Its effect on Liza had not made it appear very desirable, and the nearest she had come to it was in her happy companionship with Carola. But now Christopher had produced in her a dazed and dumb condition.

She was playing with a pink clover flower, which he took from her, and then held her hand. She looked up and the blue light in his eyes was almost more than she could bear. The touch of his hand was like fire which ran through her. She tried to ease this intensity of feeling by some of her usual prattle, but the words would not come.

. . . . .

Matty was lying on a magnificent four-poster bed, hung with old rose damask. All the furniture of her room was grandiose, chosen by Beatrice with the faintly malicious intention of forcing her into assurance of manner.

The curtains were drawn against the afternoon sun. Matty had one of her headaches.

Beatrice, who had never had a day's illness in her life, came in without knocking.

'You'll have to come down,' she said. 'I have to see the builder about the alterations to the larders. The most extraordinary people have called. The woman has no stockings and tomato-coloured toe-nails. They're called Rounsefell.'

Matty forgot her headache.

'The Rounsefells!' she exclaimed. 'I'm most anxious to meet them. I believe they know T. S. Eliot.'

'Who's he?' said Beatrice, and went off to attend to the builder.

Matty hurried to the dressing-table. She did her hair rather severely and put on a dress of speckly brown silk which she had bought at Liberty's. Then wearing her glasses, which normally she used only for reading, and carrying a volume of *The Forsyte Saga* and a copy of the *New Statesman* she went down the lawn to her first meeting with the English intelligentsia.

'Do look at this, Aelred,' said Sylvia as she approached. 'Did you ever see such refinement?'

'Is it Tennyson's princess obliged to take a position as governess?' suggested Aelred.

'No. It's the boys' mother. The younger one is just like her. But how did she produce the blond beast. She must have been in Belgium in 1914 or else they mixed the babies in the nursing home.'

Matty came across to them.

'You are Mrs. Rounsefell,' she said, in much the tone in which someone might say, 'This is Westminster Abbey.'

Sylvia acknowledge the fact and introduced Aelred, who said: 'We have been admiring your boys.'

For some reason Matty felt this remark to be slightly improper.

'Oh,' she said, and looked round at Wilfred.

Wilfred, who had been nervously watching the meeting between his mother and the Rounsefells, extricated himself from the grip of Major Hinde's glittering eye, which had again ensnared him, and came up to find how successful it had been and to smooth out any provincialisms of which Matty might be guilty. He had a generous boy's hot unreasoning loyalty to his mother. He had the sensitiveness of a critical mind to her idiosyncrasies. He endured the wretchedness of the conflict between these two things, but did not know yet what caused it. A great deal of Wilfred's time was spent in patching up his pride, not in himself but in his mother.

'Where is Christopher?' Matty asked.

'He's gone off somewhere.'

'He ought to be handing round the tea.'

'He went with Ursula,' said Sylvia, smiling.

'Go and fetch him,' said Matty to Wilfred

'Oh, no.   It would be a shame!' cried Sylvia, genuinely shocked at the idea that handing tea to Rosie and Mrs. Hodsall should take precedence of the delights of love.

'They're all right,' said Wilfred.

'What are you reading?' asked Aelred with courteous interest.

'*The Forsyte Saga*,' said Matty.   'I'm afraid, for the first time.'

Wilfred watched anxiously for the Rounsefell reaction, now that they were approaching cultural grounds.

'Is it good?' asked Sylvia carelessly.

'But *you* must know it,' said Matty as if she were telling a professor of Egyptology that he must know about the pyramids.

'Why?' asked Sylvia.   'I hate reading about bourgeois life.'

Their mutual animosity flickered a moment on the surface.   Matty suffered one of her habitual puzzled disappointments, when reality did not fit in with her preconceived ideas. Rosie, whom she despised, had referred contemptuously to Sylvia as a high-brow, therefore Sylvia should have proved a kindred spirit with herself.   But this Nell Gwynnish creature with the pink toe-nails was as remote from her conception of an intellectual Englishwoman as a barman from a bishop.

Aelred, however, could enjoy himself with almost any woman.

Those who were not seductive were, consciously or unconsciously, amusing.   He enjoyed Matty's wriggling

walk, the peculiar reverence with which she said 'intellectual,' her general air of being a period piece. He
proceeded to ravish her mind. With subtle deference
he elicited her literary and artistic tastes. They were all
that he expected, a bowdlerized edition of his own tastes
at eighteen. What had annoyed him in Wilfred pleased
him in the mother.

Matty found her first sympathetic listener since Melbourne. Aelred knew every picture and building in
Italy, France, and England which had captivated her
attention. She opened to him her treasure-house of
appreciation, and he went in and picked over the jewels.
He was able to praise, to criticize, and explain all that
had charmed or puzzled her. She confessed with the
same note of penitence in which she had admitted her
delay in reading Galsworthy, that she did not care for
Botticelli's 'Venus rising from the Sea.'

'The most satisfying works of art,' explained Aelred,
'are composed of erotic fragments. They are most
noticeable in that picture. Technical skill and even
beauty of colour and form are subsidiary to the main
purpose of a painting. That purpose is to reveal a
condition of nature. The most illuminating condition
we know is that of erotic awakening, therefore the work
of art which has the most significance is that in which
this theme is implicit.'

This was contrary to Matty's most cherished beliefs,
but Aelred put it forward in such a well-bred manner
that she could only agree, delighted at last to feel the
impact with an educated mind.

Aelred continued probing her mind and playing with her inhibitions, touching here and there on a tender nerve, delighting in her shock and her acquiescence, and cloaking his subversiveness in such elegant language that Matty, though thrilled, was unaware how far she had been seduced from the standards of Kew, Victoria.

'The most distasteful of all aesthetic attitudes,' he said, 'is that of the man who puts the fig-leaves on the statues. One should either view beauty whole or not at all. Many people who want to appear cultivated refuse to allow the artist his own intention. They deny, for example, Shakespeare's obvious meaning in his sonnets. They ignore the erotic fragment in the statue or the painting, without which the artist could not have felt the urge to paint it. The truly constructive critic must enter wholly into the spirit of the artist, otherwise he makes a travesty of aesthetic appreciation. If you don't like his spirit leave him alone, but don't emasculate the giants to fit in with late Victorian propriety.'

'You don't mean that we should enter into every mood of every great poet,' said Matty, deferential but doubting. 'Shakespeare often reflects the grossness of his age. We can admire his greatness surely while still regretting those aberrations. We have advanced some way since them.'

Aelred smiled.

'Have you been into the church here?' he asked.

'Yes.'

'Did you notice the Elizabethan tomb with the cherubs on the corners?'

Here there was a double intention in his question. He ignored the fact that the tomb was of one of Matty's ancestors by way of keeping her in her place.

'I have seen it, of course.'

'Epstein was down here and he spent an hour looking at those cherubs. They are living children with blood and bone and the germ of human passions. There are some modern cherubs in the lady chapel. If they ever lived they are dying of pernicious anaemia, physical and spiritual. They show exactly how far we have advanced since the Elizabethan age.'

This final thrust gave Matty the extreme pleasure of having her own opinions over-ruled by an authoritative male.

'I don't know that I entirely agree with you,' she said. 'But I have enjoyed this talk enormously, and hope we may continue it later. Here is my sister-in-law. I'm afraid she will be annoyed because I haven't kept the tennis going.'

Sylvia meanwhile had drifted over to Rosie and the doctor. By a few eclectic references she made Rosie feel a fool, so that to save her face she left them. Babs Oakes could never bear the proximity of Sylvia. It made her squirm as if she were asked to sit by a tarantula.

Sylvia then was free to pursue a very diverting discussion of caesarian operations and cists on the womb. Wilfred drifted awkwardly between his mother and Aelred, and Sylvia and the doctor. Aelred deliberately ignored him, and when he went back to Sylvia he heard

H

her describing, apparently with amused relish, the removal of an internal growth from her sister-in-law.

'It was as big as one of those huge Jaffa oranges they sell at Marks and Spencers,' she said.

Wilfred stood bewildered, looking at the lovely scene which he had so desired. He had wanted his life to be like a Wilde play—witty and set in stately homes and beautiful gardens. He seemed likely to realize his ambition but he felt suddenly afraid. If circumstances came half-way to meet him his imagination could supply the rest. For so long his imagination had had to give more than fifty per cent to reality, when on holidays in Tasmania he had pretended that a ruined stone church surrounded by elms was in England, or that Port Phillip Bay was the Mediterranean. But now reality had overpowered imagination, which no longer could fix his ambition.

Here were the lawns, the terrace, the stately home, the tranquil cedar trees, and here was the gay and witty crowd; but it was quite different from what he had imagined it would be. There was an alien force behind it; it was stronger than himself.

This mood hardly lasted more than thirty seconds, but for that time fear held him in its grip.

Mr. Hodsall saw him standing with a troubled face and spoke to him.

'You're dreaming,' he said.

Wilfred shook himself and smiled.

'Sometimes my mind goes racing on like an engine that isn't pulling anything,' he said.

'Is that what was happening then?'

'Not exactly, sir.'

Wilfred had hardly met Mr. Hodsall since their first visit to Plumbridge when they had inspected the church. He responded now to his friendly interest and remembered how much he had liked him then. He had had so much to occupy himself in the meantime that he had forgotten that he had liked him—a boy's will being the wind's will.

'What were you thinking of then?'

'I don't know. I suddenly seemed to see everything from a different angle.'

'That is interesting.'

'I don't like it very much. I like to see things in a straightforward light, but sometimes in spite of myself the light comes on them from an extraordinary angle, and I see everything as a caricature.'

'Do you find it difficult to control your imagination?'

'Yes; sometimes I do. If I can't sleep I begin to imagine something, for example, what would have happened if I had made a different reply to a question someone has asked me. Then I build up a whole long conversation from that. And I worry about Christopher, too. I imagine awful stories in which he murders someone and is hanged.'

'Oh! That's not good,' said Mr. Hodsall.

'I know, sir,' said Wilfred. 'I hate doing it, but sometimes at night all the things that are wrong with one's life loom up in enormous proportions.'

'Is there much wrong with your life? It appears to be exceptionally full of promise.'

'I don't belong anywhere,' said Wilfred. 'That is what I was thinking just now. I want to belong here, but people don't seem to want me to. Mrs. Malaby, every time I meet her, mentions that I'm Australian, and then says: "Oh, but I mustn't point that out, must I? Colonials are touchy." Being an Australian apparently is like having a wart on the end of your nose. But if she had a wart on the end of her nose I wouldn't point it out every time I saw her and then say: "I'm sorry, I forgot you're touchy about facial disfigurement."'

Mr. Hodsall laughed.

'I should let those things sink to their proper proportion,' he said. 'You won't have to suffer that kind of thing from well-bred people.'

'But if I have to meet the other sort,' complained Wilfred.

'There's only one remedy for the difficulties and humiliations of human intercourse,' said Mr. Hodsall.

'What is that, sir?'

Mr. Hodsall hesitated a moment.

'Love,' he said in a shy, sensitive voice.

Wilfred did not reply. He did not know exactly what Mr. Hodsall meant. As he was a clergyman he probably was speaking in a religious sense, but there was the awkward possibility that he might mean something else.

Wilfred, preoccupied, watched Carola and Alec. Carola suddenly turned away from Alec and ran over to join Rosie, who was sitting alone after her rout by Sylvia. Alec stared disconsolately at his tennis racquet, and flipped its strings with his finger. He looked up and caught Wilfred's eye and smiled.

'Excuse me, sir,' said Wilfred politely, and went across to Alec.

Mr. Hodsall followed him with a rueful eye.

'In season and out of season,' he murmured. 'It's impossible without impertinence.'

He started as Major Hinde's voice behind him boomed:

'Ah, vicar! I want your advice about my dahlias.'

.   .   .   .   .

Carola, with what is called coltish grace, put her arm round Rosie's waist.

'Alec's silly,' she said.

'What's he done?' asked Rosie.

'He told me I was like an angel with an earthly body and a sense of humour.'

'And what did you say?'

'I said I hadn't enough sense of humour to think that was funny.'

'And what did he say to that?'

'He said it wasn't meant to be funny—that I—oh, I can't repeat it.'

'You can wepeat it safely to me.'

'Anyhow, I told him that I liked being friends with him, but that I didn't want to be sentimental.'

Rosie laughed.

'Poor Alec!' she said.

'Where's Ursula?' said Carola.

'She went into the orchard with Chwistopher.'

'Let's go and find them.'

'They mightn't like that.'

'Why? They're not a case, are they?'

'Vewy much so,' said Rosie, laughing.

'How beastly! Oh, what a bore! Do you like Christopher, Rosie?'

'He's wather magnificent, isn't he?'

'It doesn't hurt your eyes to look at him, but I think he's like a dog which you're not sure won't bite you. He laughed in my face.'

'What does he laugh at?'

'I don't know. He never laughs with you, but suddenly, to himself when no one else is laughing. If he deceives Ursula I'll be livid.'

'Deceives her?' Rosie shrieked with delight.

'Well, that is one of the things men do to girls, isn't it?' said Carola crossly. 'I thought they were always deceiving them.'

    •   •   •   •   •

Meanwhile Beatrice, having disposed of the builder, came back to the tennis courts. It was as if a head master came into an undisciplined classroom where the boys were throwing darts, fighting, drawing, or making assignations, according to individual temperament.

Beatrice would not have been happy in the Elysian fields. Idle grace and philosophical discussion were little to her taste. As she came down the wide lawn from

the house the scene that met her eyes was somewhat
Elysian. The white and green-stained balls lay about
on the deserted courts. Aelred and Matty were earnestly
discussing the relationship of the Beautiful to the True.
Wilfred and Alec, standing apart, were sniggering with
exclusive amusement, while Sylvia, a shade of Aspasia
or Helen, was enjoying with the doctor the vicarious
intimacy of the operating theatre. The other guests
had either disappeared or else reclined in chairs, satisfied, seeing it was so hot, to be idle for a space.

When Beatrice was well fed and contented she was
quite pleased to see people in pairs, but it is only natural
that those who have been denied the pleasures of love,
in their weaker and more irritable moments should be
vexed by the sight of others' success. Beatrice was
thirsty and fussed by an inarticulate and obstinate
builder. To her view, though everybody was pleasing
himself, the party had gone to pieces. What was the
use of paying a great deal to have the tennis courts put
in order for this season if they were not played on?
When she gave a tennis party she expected the ping of
balls and the calling of scores to be incessant from
three o'clock till cocktail time. Tea should be taken in
relays.

But some subversive atmosphere, some exotic zephyr,
had been wafted in with the Rounsefells. At once
people had ceased to act and had begun to talk, a state
of affairs which Beatrice detested. In the middle of
the group, near the deserted tea-table, which nobody
had bothered to move into the shade, so that the

strawberries were hot and the cream sour, reclined
Sylvia, looking too like Queen Venus and talking of the
insides of other people's bodies, while displaying so
much of the outside of her own.

'Why haven't you kept the tennis going?' Beatrice
demanded of Matty, as if she had let a kettle off the boil:
'Where is Christopher? Wilfred, go and find Christopher and arrange another set.'

Everybody at once stood up with an air of apology
except Sylvia, who affected bewilderment at this sudden
activity.

Beatrice said: 'Major Hinde, will you play with Miss
Oakes against Mr. Hodsall and Dr. Woodforde?' She
stood by to see her orders executed.

In about three minutes Wilfred came back with the
truants.

'Have we been vewy naughty?' asked Rosie, with
an arch smile.

'You four make a set,' said Beatrice, ignoring the
smile. 'Wilfred, you had better play with Mrs. Malaby
against the other two.'

'I've promised to show Mrs. Rounsefell our pictures,'
said Wilfred.

There was an awkward silence. Sylvia smiled,
enjoying Beatrice's struggle with inclination and
manners.

'Very well,' said Beatrice, 'but hurry.'

Wilfred led Aelred and Sylvia up to the house. He was
angry and humiliated at his aunt's brusqueness. How
could one create an Oscar Wilde scene of witty urbanity

if Aunt Beatrice turned even a game into a moral obligation?

'I hate games,' he said, 'unless they're played for pleasure.'

'How can you live in this atmosphere?' asked Sylvia.

'What d' you mean?' he said defensively.

'People who live like this'—she waved a lace glove towards the house—'live for nothing but games.'

'This house was built mostly in the eighteenth century,' said Wilfred. 'They didn't live for games then.'

'In the eighteenth century,' said Aelred, 'games were taken more lightly, and hunting and shooting still retained something of their original necessity. Modern life has taken the pleasure from one and the virtue from the other. Country house life no longer has any aesthetic significance.'

Wilfred thought this rude, but his resentment was killed by surprise when Sylvia said: 'It's a nice survival though, like a man's nipples.'

He sniggered, and then felt puerile when the Rounsefells showed no amusement, nor any sign that they thought this simile out of the way.

'Here they are,' he said, opening the dining-room door. 'That is by Streeton'—he indicated a canvas over the sideboard—'and here is the Hans Heysen. That's Christopher by McInnes. It was painted just before we left.'

Sylvia put up her pink eye-glass and examined the brilliant sky and deep purple river of the Streeton, the stringy gums and sunlit dusty air of the Heysen, and the startling beauty of Christopher, illuminated against a brown curtain.

Wilfred stood by, awaiting praise of this virtuosity.

The Rounsefells went from one picture to the other and said nothing.

Sylvia turned to the table which was laid for dinner. It was done with blue Bristol glass, large pale clematis, and love-in-the-mist.

'That's rather pretty, Aelred,' she said.

Aelred gave it a glance.

'It always surprises me to find that this *confort bourgeoise* still exists,' he said.

Wilfred winced.

'Does your butler do the flowers?' asked Sylvia.

'No; I did them,' said Wilfred. 'What do you think of the pictures?' he asked.

'They don't convey anything to me,' she said indifferently. 'Except the portrait. That's excellent of its kind.'

'But they're clear enough,' he said a little exasperated.

'Oh, yes, they're photographically clear, but any one might have painted them.'

'They don't express any distinctive culture,' said Aelred. 'They are just Australian scenes in the English traditional style. I thought there might be an Australian style.'

'Those are in the Australian style,' said Wilfred.

Aelred did not reply.

'Why don't you make your aunt have this panelling painted?' asked Sylvia.

'Paint oak panelling!' exclaimed Wilfred.

'Why not?' said Aelred.   'It was often painted in the eighteenth century.'

They were back in the hall.

'You could do this hall in mauve and pick out the mouldings and the balustrades in pink.   It would make the house more gay and fair.   You could make the plums on the coat-of-arms pink.   Pink plums are much nicer than blue ones, don't you think so, Aelred?'

Aelred's reply was in the nature of an erotic fragment.

'There's another Australian picture in here,' said Wilfred anxiously.   He opened the drawing-room door, feeling that he had to wring some word of approval for his national art from the Rounsefells.

Wilfred had moved the grandiose boule table to the far end of the room.   A long Persian carpet in russet and old gold led up to it.   Above, against the mellow panels, hung a painting of a deep glade where wattle trees hung gracefully above a brown river.   The tarnished gold and tortoiseshell of the table, the autumnal carpet, and the brown walls, made an admirable setting for the yellow blossom in the picture.

'Wait a minute,' said Wilfred.   He drew thick brocade curtains and switched on a light concealed in a cylinder beneath the picture, which made it alive in the darkened room.

'It's by Penleigh Boyd,' he said.

Sylvia smiled.

'Did you arrange this, too?' she said.

'I like that, Aelred,' she went on.   'It's much the

best. It has poetry and sensibility. It's rather Watteauish, the work of a soul in exile.'

Aelred was examining the Grinling Gibbons carving on the mantelpiece. Without asking Wilfred's leave, he drew the curtains back again, so that he could see better.

'The artist should be at home in the world,' he said, 'not in exile. Nostalgia destroys a work of art.'

'We're going to have a grey and yellow chintz in here,' said Wilfred, 'in a Georgian design.'

'Why don't you have a modern design?' asked Sylvia, suddenly interested and pitying Wilfred's traditional ideas.

'Is your dress modern?' he asked. 'It goes well in here. Is it a repeating pattern?'

'Oh, Aelred, how marvellous,' cried Sylvia, 'to meet someone in Plumbridge who asks about repeating patterns.'

Aelred who had been angered by the Australian pictures, which he had not expected to be half so good, was slightly appeased by this sign of intelligence in Wilfred.

'Come back and dine with us,' said Sylvia.

'Yes, do,' said Aelred, turning on once more his caressing manner.

'I'd love to,' said Wilfred, 'but I don't know if I can get away.'

'Can't you leave your butlers and your love-in-the-mist?' chaffed Sylvia.

'It's not that——'

'Come on. Come with us now.'

'I must change, and I must go and tell Aunt Beatrice.'

'Why? Don't be stuffy,' said Sylvia. 'I like people who do things spontaneously. I long to meet someone who, if I said to him: "Will you come to Baghdad with me? I'm leaving in half an hour," would say "Yes, I'd love to," and not want to tidy up first.'

Wilfred smiled uneasily. He was dismayed that the Rounsefells were not themselves going back to the tennis court to say good-bye to Beatrice.

'I'd love to come another night,' he said.

'We're going back to London to-morrow,' said Sylvia.

Again the sensations he had experienced down by the tennis courts returned to Wilfred. He felt somehow oppressed and afraid. Sylvia's expectant eye was on him.

'All right,' he said ungraciously. In a confused and hurried fashion he left a message with a servant, saying he would be out to dinner, and, feeling that he had betrayed something much deeper than mere politeness, he went with the Rounsefells to Walnut Tree Farm.

.   .   .   .   .

Ursula was the last to leave the tennis party. Christopher stood near as she said good-bye to Beatrice.

'Lady Elizabeth's in London,' he said suggestively.

'Are you alone?' asked Beatrice kindly. 'You'd better stay and dine with us. The boys will drive you home.'

The twinkling candle flames, the love-in-the-mist, the large pale stars of the clematis, and the Bristol glass seemed to Ursula a suitable decoration for the tables of heaven. Above the flowers was Christopher's face, angelic in repose, if perhaps something like the angel of a bull, placid and powerful. His eyes were an echo of the floral decoration. For most of the meal they were fixed on hers, but now and then one or the other would lower his glance as the happy fusion became too obvious or an almost intolerable joy.

Beatrice's vexation of the afternoon had now worked up beyond speaking point to a state of suppressed anger. She would not have dreamed of asking Ursula to stay on to dinner if she had known that Wilfred would not be there. It was throwing Christopher at her head.

As neither Christopher nor Ursula played bridge Beatrice organized a game called 'rummy,' of which the only object could be to keep Christopher and Ursula under her eye, as no one wanted to play, and Christopher made the game pointless by manipulating the cards so that Ursula should always win.

When it was time for Ursula to leave Christopher said that he would drive her home. Beatrice felt that she could not reasonably object, but told him not to be long.

It was two hours before he returned from the five minutes' drive to Clovermead. Beatrice, who had been waiting up, met him in the hall. His face was rosy, his hair ruffled, his eyes wild and wondering, as if he had seen a god.

.   .   .   .   .

Major Hinde offered Babs a lift home. He felt rather rash and a bit of a dog, as he was terrified of the unchaperoned society of a female, unless she were adolescent or safely married. He was anxious to protect not so much himself as his home from their acquisitive hands.

Babs discontentedly accepted his offer. Although her face bore the marks of the thirties her mind lingered in the teens. She felt ill used that she had not the society of someone younger. Christopher, who drew her like a magnet, had treated her like a despised aunt.

'How do you like our Australian friends?' asked Major Hinde, turning his exquisitely kept Vauxhall saloon carefully into the main road.

'I think they're awful. Christopher's ruder than any one I've ever known.'

'He'll get licked into shape. He ought to go into the army—I told his mother so. The other boy is a nice lad. I must say I was agreeably surprised, though I *have* met some very decent Australians. We can't say much when we remember the Rounsefells are English, eh? If they *are* English. D'you know what I'd do with people like that? I'd take the lot and dump them on a South Sea island.'

'I expect she'd like that,' said Babs.

The major snorted.

'You must come in and see my dahlias,' he said. 'They're remarkable.'

'I ought to get home,' said Babs uncertainly. Major Hinde was a bore, but he was a man after all. If one could not be led into the orchard by an ardent youth one might as well be shown an old man's dahlias. She followed him round the garden and listened to the history of nearly every flower in the herbaceous border. Every now and then she made fretful, fading efforts to take some part in the conversation, but it was like a scooter trying to check a steam roller.

'Now you must come and see my wall-paper,' he said.

'I really must go,' said Babs. 'I'll be late for dinner.'

'It won't take a minute.' He led her in at a side door and up into a newly-papered room, overlooking the rose-garden. The paper was of small pink roses.

'What d'you think of that?' he said complacently. 'I shall call this the rose room.'

Babs sat down on the bed. She did not know what made her do this. Christopher had produced a kind of madness in her, and the steady purr of Major Hinde's voice had aggravated it to a state of hypnosis. She had never been alone in a bedroom with a man before, not even a man of Major Hinde's age. How old was he? Sixty? The incident was an adventure to her. It was against all her mother's advice and teaching. She was being immodest and making herself cheap. 'Put a high value on yourself and others will estimate you highly,' her mother had said. Well, it hadn't worked. Babs at last was the victim of honest doubt. The brazen Rosie and the wanton Mrs. Rounsefell flouted all her mother's maxims, and men clustered round them. True they did not make themselves cheap. They had no need to. But they did make themselves noticeable. If Christopher had not been rude to her perhaps Babs would have gone on valuing herself highly, but now she felt provoked, slighted, curious, excited, ready to see what men really did.

Giving expression to this wild mood she sat on the bed.

'I didn't know whether to bring the paper above the picture-rail, or to end it there,' said Major Hinde. 'But I finally decided to carry it up to the cornice. It makes the room seem higher.'

Babs leant back on her elbows to look up at the cornice. She felt that her attitude was wildly immodest.

'Do you sleep here?' she asked. Her eyes were unfocused and strange.

'No,' said Major Hinde. 'Don't crush the bedspread.'

He was astonished and indignant that Babs immediately burst into tears. He told everybody in the village of the incident.

'I'd no idea she was so touchy,' he said. 'I didn't speak to her at all harshly. I merely asked her not to crush the bedspread!'

.   .   .   .   .

The rays of Venus seemed to be powerful if slightly perverse on this Saturday evening.

Rosie had invited Dr. Woodforde in for a sherry and, as his wife was away staying with her sister in Cornwall, had persuaded him to stay and dine with her.

'I may be called out to a patient,' he demurred.

'Wing up and tell your maid that you're here, and to wing up if any one wants you,' she said.

I

'H'm!' he said, but did it.

At eleven o'clock he stood up and murmured something about going.

Before dinner she had offered him a bath. As he stood in her pink and perfumed bathroom, drying himself with a towel embroidered with the initials 'R. M.,' he felt already that a degree of domestic intimacy with her had been created.

The *dîner à deux*, waiting on themselves as the maid was out, the subsequent liqueurs and the shaded lights of Rosie's little morning-room, which she called her 'nook,' increased this to such an extent that now they began an argument of which perhaps only Tom realized the full implication. He became candid and amused.

Rosie only half enjoyed the candour, and she tried to be amused. In these matters she preferred the idiom of romance to that of rationalism. A doctor had his disadvantages.

'Weally you are extwaordinawy,' she said. 'I 've never talked to any one like this in my life before. I wonder I 'm not dying of shame.'

Tom smiled. He was like a large red-faced boy, good-naturedly teasing his sister. Sylvia had rather taken the gilt off the gingerbread that was Rosie. Sylvia, he imagined, had no illusions about love. She would not use Rosie's clichés about 'giving oneself' and 'dying of shame,' and yet he was sure she would conduct a love affair with charm and even give it a more than sensual significance. However, as he had no intention of beginning one, at any rate in Plumbridge, the comparison only served to weaken any effect of Rosie's persuasiveness.

'You can't have many offers like this,' she pouted.

'It's not an offer. It's a request,' said Tom.

'Weally!' Rosie laughed with deliberate good-nature. 'I wonder I don't turn you out of the house.'

'I thought you wanted me to stay in it.' As long as the argument remained amiable, he rather enjoyed it.

'You're dweadful. I offer you evewything and you don't even show any gwatitude.'

'Thank you very much,' he said obligingly. 'But you're asking me for a good deal too. If I lose my reputation I'm ruined. Besides, you know it's not biologically true that a woman gives herself. It's the man who finds love exhausting. Look at all the fat wives and thin husbands.'

Rosie gave a shriek of laughter.

'You are a scweam,' she said. 'Have another *chota peg*.'

'Do you know the effect of whisky on the liver?'

'How *can* you be so pwosaic?'

She squirted a little soda into the glass and handed it to him.

'Is there any one else?' she asked, ignoring the existence of his wife.

He lost his pleasure in the discussion. He drank the whisky and stood up.

'Don't go,' she pleaded, and seized one of his hands. 'I shall be so cwoss if you do.'

'You won't be cross because I'm going.'

'Why shan't I?'

'You 'll be cross because it 's uncomfortable to change an opinion. You believe that all men are selfish brutes, only living to seize every sensual opportunity. When they don't, you think either that it is a deliberate insult, or that your ideas are wrong, which is even more humiliating. See, Rosie?'

'Oh, you 're howwible. Go, then. I don't care what you do. It seemed such a wonderful opportunity.' She sat up on the sofa. She crushed her tiny handkerchief in her hands and tears filled her eyes.

He looked at her shrewdly, puffing out his cheeks with rueful amusement.

'Well, thank you for the dinner,' he said a little awkwardly.

'Damn the dinner,' she almost wept.

'Aren't you going to see me to the door?'

'You know where it is.' She sat blinking at the decanter and the empty glasses. He shrugged his shoulders and took up his blazer and scarf from a chair. She had made him sit in his tennis shirt because it was so hot. At the door he turned.

'Well, good night,' he said a little shamefacedly.

Suddenly she rose and followed him out into the hall. She put her arms round his neck and joined her mouth to his in a prolonged and what is known as an experienced kiss.

'There,' she said. 'You didn't deserve that.'

He chuckled and slapped her on the rump, much as one might dismiss a pony into a field.

.   .   .   .   .   .

In spite of the glamorous night and the general air of temptation, the only successful seduction that evening, at least among the upper classes, was of Wilfred, and this took place solely in the realms of the mind.

Wilfred, though hardly of the type to appeal to an empire builder, was a nice boy. He had been so since the age of thirteen when his cold and mischievous nature had changed into one of generous warmth and response to all that he felt was admirable. Since then, though his more robust relatives were inclined to think him an effeminate liar, he had not once offended against his own code of conduct. Sometimes indignation made him rude, or injustice made him passionate to the point of murder, but rudeness to the insolent and murder of the detestable were not actually against his code, which was that of the public school. Having acquired this code from afar, and having like his mother a natural enthusiasm for the highest he saw, he took it much more seriously than the average English public schoolboy, as he soon discovered from Alec.

As he walked back with the Rounsefells he felt that his honour was horribly besmirched. People often could not help being common through ignorance, but deliberately to behave in an underbred fashion seemed to him almost a violation of natural order. Nor was he looking forward with pleasure to his explanation to Beatrice.

However, a few of Aelred's cocktails soon dispelled his uneasiness, and he was jerked out of his preoccupations by the return from a sketching exhibition of two of the Rounsefells' friends. The man had a huge nose, a black beard, and a check shirt. The woman had a round, placid Madonna-ish face. Her hair was cut in a fringe, and she wore a plain, tight, navy-blue dress which revealed every curve and wrinkle of her plump body. She only spoke about twice during the evening and when she did she used words which usually are only written by rude boys on back walls.

A resentful-looking country girl came in to lay the table, but Aelred went out to cook the dinner. With surprising facility he produced a white soup with spring onions floating in it, an omelette, a roast chicken, and a salad which contained garlic and bananas. The table-cloth was of rough cotton in blue and orange stripes, and they drank Italian wine out of flasks. It all seemed to Wilfred enjoyably continental and Bohemian, if occasionally a little startling.

The Rounsefells seemed amusedly aware that he was startled, and increased the effect. They talked about schools and sex, and spoke as if Communism were the only possible political solution. They laughed over the liaisons of their friends, and as far as Wilfred could gather, not only marriage but sexual differentiation was a thing of the past.

The bearded man's name was Francis and the lightly-clad woman's Freya. They had different surnames, but apparently they were sharing the same bedroom. Yet though their conversation was so frank, it did not seem improper. Sylvia made Wilfred think of things that were beyond impropriety, like that statue of Leda in Italy.

They dawdled drinking round the disordered table

until half-past nine, when the resentful-looking country girl poked her head round the door and, in a voice made furious to cover her nervousness, asked if she might either clear away or go home.

'Oh, yes; let her clear,' said Sylvia.

Aelred, forgetting his Communism, muttered that the girl did not know her place.

Wilfred, in polite oblivion of this domestic contretemps, turned to examine a picture on the wall. It was of a woman in Victorian pantalettes lying under a monkey-puzzle. It was deliberately out-of-drawing and painted mostly in spots.

'What is this?' he asked.

'Magic from the subconscious,' said Sylvia lightly.

'I'm quite prepared,' said Wilfred earnestly, 'to believe that it is good if you can tell me why. What actually is the merit of it?'

'The calligraphy is rather pleasing, don't you think?' said Aelred.

'But if this is so much better than Streeton,' said Wilfred, 'will you show me some of this man's work when he was back at Streeton's stage?'

Aelred, with a kind of lofty sulkiness, turned to make the coffee. Freya looked at Wilfred as if he was a different species of animal.

'You see,' said Wilfred, eager and apologetic, 'I'm quite ready to believe that these modern paintings are good, but no one can explain to me what is good in them. Take Van Gogh's chair. What is really good in that? Couldn't I draw one as well?'

'It is just a chair, pure chair. It has the very essence of a chair. If you were asked to convey "chair" in painting, do you think you could do it as well?' asked Francis.

'I'm tired of Van Gogh,' said Sylvia. 'Provincial people who want to be modern always buy prints of *Roses Lauriers.*'

Aelred took Francis and Freya off to his room to show them a huge book of photographs of oddities in nature which he had just published. These illustrated how the erotic fragment motif were found throughout nature, in the shapes of buds and branches, leaves and stones.

Wilfred was left with Sylvia, who explained to him that there were no obvious aesthetic standards. The really cultivated depended entirely on their individual sensibility.

'But tell me about yourself,' she said; 'about Australia and everything. Bring over the wine and cigarettes first.'

Gradually he exposed everything of himself to Sylvia. She was so serious, so free, so friendly, so interested. She asked him about his emotional life at school. What vices had he indulged?

'Go on. Tell me,' she said. 'There's no reason why you shouldn't.'

His career to date was disappointingly innocent, but he had never revealed to any one what he told to Sylvia. She labelled it all. His admiration for the head master, his warm-hearted friendship with Higgins Minor, were given the correct Freudian diagnosis.

'You see,' she said, 'at a co-educational school that couldn't have happened.'

'No.' Wilfred agreed doubtfully, though he could not quite see why his mild hero-worship and his companionable love for Higgins were mental diseases.

The talk became a little less intense and personal. Wilfred's career was followed to his present abode at Plumbridge Hall.

There was a moment of silence. The mention of Plumbridge Hall disturbed Wilfred, bringing him abruptly back to the present. His gentlemanly instincts began to repudiate this conversation with Sylvia. He wanted to return to the surface.

'You must come and dine with us,' he said in a slightly stilted manner.

Sylvia detected his change of mood.

'With the love-in-the-mist and the butler?' she said. 'You only ask me because you have an inferiority complex.'

Wilfred gasped. He had been too relaxed, too confiding, too admiring, to be suddenly angry.

Diffidently he stood up.

'I'd better be going,' he said. 'You see, I didn't tell Aunt Beatrice I'd be out.'

'Bother Aunt Beatrice,' said Sylvia, unaware or else not caring that she had offended him. 'Stay and tell me some more.'

Aelred came in, and, ignoring Wilfred, said crossly to Sylvia:

'Where's that vellum bound *Golden Ass*?'

'I don't know,' said Sylvia indifferently.

'Well, good-bye,' said Wilfred. Sylvia ignored him, so he turned to Aelred and said: 'Good-bye, sir.'

Sylvia burst out laughing.

'Aelred will poison you if you call him "sir,"' she said. 'Call him Aelred, every one does.'

'Oh, are you going?' said Aelred, suddenly courteous again. 'We'll walk with you. We may hear the nightingale. Francis! Freya!' he called. 'We're going to hear the nightingale.'

'So are we—in bed,' called back Francis.

Sylvia laughed.

'What enthusiasm!' she sighed.

Aelred laughed and Wilfred began to laugh out of politeness, and then realized that he felt completely exhausted. It was unlike any tiredness he had known before. It was as if he had undergone an operation, as if his spiritual inside had been taken out, pawed over, and put back again, which was exactly what had happened. Sylvia's gibe had been just as if the surgeon, having the warm palpitating entrails before him, for fun had poured on them a little vitriol. That had stung, but it was the previous exposure, the judicial assessing of his secret loves and hopes, his moral struggles and yieldings, which had provoked this incredible weariness. No mere physical seduction could have left him so drained.

After a good deal of delay while Aelred looked for Sylvia's cigarettes, they set out.

As they passed Rosie's house at the end of the village, they were the witnesses of a remarkable sight. It so

happened that at that moment she was saying good
night to Tom Woodforde. The light streaming through
the front door made a flaming halo of her hair, while
Tom was silhouetted against it in an outline of rugged
manliness.

Sylvia and Aelred stood and stared. Aelred chuckled,
but Sylvia said, with a touch of venom: 'They look just
like an advertisement for Lifebuoy Soap.'

She was as annoyed as if she had learnt that Rosie had
a collection of paintings by Laurencin or Modigliani.

Wilfred was horrified. It was astonishing and re-
pulsive to him that people over twenty-five should kiss
each other for pleasure.

At the park gates, feeling more tired than ever, he
again attempted to say good night.

'Don't go in yet,' said Sylvia, 'come and hear the
nightingale. They sing in the wood at the end of this
lane.'

He was afraid to give Aunt Beatrice again as an excuse.
Sylvia would think he was a schoolboy. He could not
say that he was exhausted. He had the good manners
which take into account the implication of every
remark.

'Let him go,' said Aelred indifferently.

'No; he ought to hear the nightingale,' said Sylvia.
'There are no nightingales in Australia. It's a land
where bright blossoms are scentless, and songless, bright
birds. I read that somewhere only the other day, in
the *Empire News*, I think it was.'

'It isn't really,' said Wilfred. 'The magpie is absolutely

lovely when you hear it on spring mornings. They
were going to call it the Melba bird.'

Sylvia laughed.

'Were they?' she said. 'Well, now you must come and
hear an English nightingale on a moonlit night. Come
along.' She took his hand and drew him up the lane.
Feeling no response to her friendly pressure, after a
few yards she let his hand go again.

Wilfred felt awkward at having his hand held, and
snubbed when it was let go.

He wanted to hear the nightingale, but he did not
want to go with the Rounsefells. Like Matty, he expected everything hall-marked to yield him a thrilling
sensation. Few of these things had failed him. Capri,
Fiesole, Chartres, Fontainebleau, and the ruins of Glaston-
bury had all produced their moments of wondering
rapture. He responded naturally to the authentic.

He had looked forward to hearing the nightingale
as much as to seeing the chanting choirs of Milan. For
such moments he preferred to be alone, or if possible
with some beloved friend, as awe-struck as himself.
He wanted to go too, when he was strong and alert,
and could give the fullness of his being to the heavenly
sound—to let his heart ache and the drowsy numbness
pain his sense; to experience with Keats that rich
nostalgia for all ancient beauty, for dryads, for dance and
Provençal song, for the courts of emperors, for Dionysus
and his leopards, for the magic casements of fairy-land,
and to feel in his own heart the sadness of the homesick Ruth. All this memory and beauty was to be

released on the night air, mixed with the soft incense hanging on the boughs. He had a feeling that the Rounsefells, if they knew what he expected, would think he was bourgeois or something.

They stood about in the lane for what seemed to Wilfred to be hours. At last a few liquid notes were dropped casually into the night.

'Sh!' said Aelred, holding up his long-fingered hand.

Wilfred walked a little way on, going as far as he could from the Rounsefells without appearing rude. He turned towards the wood, but he could still see them out of the corner of his eye. They reminded him of a Victorian picture he had once seen of a man and a woman standing by a hedge. It must have been a sampler or a valentine. The man had a wide hat and a beard like Aelred's, and the woman's mittens were not unlike Sylvia's lace gloves. They were in a lane just like this, and there were moonlight and leaves behind them. He thought that Aelred and Sylvia must have come here with the intention of looking like a Victorian picture.

He shut his eyes and tried to wring from his exhausted brain and deflowered spirit visions of ancient heroes, of lovers in Greece and the golden islands of the south listening to the same fluid melody which now came from the hedge beside him.

'That's rather pretty,' said Sylvia. She sang three notes, the chief motif of the nightingale.

'You've frightened it away,' said Aelred.

'It doesn't matter. We 've heard enough. Come on, Wilfred. How d 'you like it?'

'It 's not quite what I expected.'

'Did you think it would be like the magpie?'

'No; it didn't convey quite as much as I expected.'

'Beauty should not convey anything,' said Aelred. 'It should merely please by its colour and design. The arrangement of those notes is perfect.'

Wilfred was about to say: 'But if the arrangement doesn't convey anything, how can it be perfect?' but he thought better of it.

Soon he escaped inside the gateway whose battlements had proved so ineffectual against the Rounsefell invasion.

.   .   .   .   .

Beatrice need not have been so concerned at Christopher's illuminated face and late return. At least, it was not due to the cause she suspected. He had driven Ursula straight home.

At Clovermead the lights were on in the drawing-room and the hall.

Christopher stopped the car and Ursula leant against him, but more for comfort than for love.

'Mummy 's back,' she said in despair.

'Shall I come in?' he asked. 'It might make things easier for you.'

'If Mummy doesn't want things to be easy,' said Ursula, 'the whole Brigade of Guards wouldn't ease the situation.'

She opened the car door and turned towards him. Their hands touched tenderly. They made a sound which was more like the murmur of pigeons than a coherent good night.

Driving back Christopher wished that he had kissed her, but their love at present was more in a state of ecstasy than of action. He drove slowly, not to disturb his mood.

As he approached Rosie's house his headlights caught what appeared to be a bright red ball above her gate, which he saw to be Rosie's curly head. She was leaning over her gate, breathing the cool night air. There was something kind and lonely in her attitude. He stopped the car.

'Who is that?' she asked, trying to peer behind the glare. For one mad moment she thought that Tom might have returned.

'It's me,' said Christopher with a kind of expectant friendliness.

'How nice of you to stop. I was just beginnin' to feel that life was a hollow sham.'

'Why? It's a lovely night.' His voice was husky with emotion.

'Yes. But it's not lovely alone. I couldn't stay indoors by myself. Do come in and have a dwink.'

'I've just been taking Ursula home,' he said, as they came into the 'lounge-hall.' Rosie made him sit there as she did not want him to see the whisky tray with two glasses in the 'nook.'

She brought a fresh tray and clean glasses.

'Will you have a John Collins or a Blue Nile?' she asked. 'It's a night for a long dwink, don't you agwee?'

Christopher blindly said a John Collins and trusted her not to debauch or poison him. He felt that his horizons were widening.

'Ursula's a darlin',' said Rosie. 'I'm awfully fond of her. You're lucky.'

'Why?' He was alert but not exactly suspicious.

'Need you ask?' She raised her eyebrows.

Sylvia was often apt to refer to second-rate people and second-rate minds. Once when asked what she meant she said: 'I don't mean stupid people. I rather like stupid people. I mean clever people who are satisfied with the obvious flavours. Malaby has a second-rate mind,' she added.

Christopher was at the age which enjoys obvious flavours, at which they are still fresh. Therefore, although their conversation, which dealt with the mysteries of love, was revealing and even intoxicating to Christopher, and though it provided vicarious sympathetic satisfactions to Rosie, it was rather too banal to be described at any length.

It lasted for an hour and a half. When it ended he was not sure whether he was in love with Ursula or with Rosie. He only knew that he was in love.

Apparently the Uranian Venus who governs strange attractions must have been powerful in Plumbridge that night, otherwise it is difficult to explain why both the Westlake boys should have been subjected simultaneously to emotional titillation by different middle-aged women.

At least, it could be said for Rosie that her second-rate
stimulus was not destructive. She sent Christopher
home in love with the world and with life, whereas
Sylvia's advanced analysis left Wilfred completely
ravished.

Rosie, as she bade Christopher good night, gave him
a kiss which, if less prolonged than that which Tom
Woodforde had presumably enjoyed, was only quasi-
maternal.

As she stood for the second time that night, silhouetted
in her hall doorway, for the second time the Rounsefells,
on their way home from the nightingale, passed and
saw her.

This time Sylvia was furious. Occasionally when she
was tired or jealous the spirit of puritan ancestors would
awaken in her.

'Good God! She's caught the blond beast,' she
exclaimed. 'Does she spend the night kissing men on
the doorstep?'

They walked on thoughtfully. After a while Sylvia
gave her husband's arm an affectionate squeeze. In
spite of their talk the Rounsefells' devotion was mutual,
bourgeois, moral, and exclusive, and at the moment
they felt, after their fashion, lofty-minded from the
song of the nightingale.

.   .   .   .   .

Beatrice, having dismissed the servants long ago,
curtly sent Christopher up to bed and bolted the front
door herself. Then slowly she mounted the lovely

K

staircase. Nymphs, cupids, and coats-of-arms floated above her on the ceiling.

'What an unfortunate ending!' she said aloud, thinking of her first tennis party. She switched out the brilliant chandelier, so that the moonlight was visible in criss-cross squares on the floor of the gallery.

It was then that Beatrice saw the ghost. At least, it seemed that a white, misty figure came along the gallery from the direction of the servant's wing, and dissolved into thin air outside Matty's room. But before Beatrice had switched the light off she had glanced up at the chandelier, and her eyes were dazzled.

'I suppose it's that Lady Jemima,' she said. 'I must be tired.'

CHAPTER V

AFTER the tennis party the Hall became the centre of social life of the neighbourhood, that is, of the immediate neighbourhood. Apart from Liza, who in this district was slightly *déclassée*, the higher aristocracy had not called, much to Wilfred's surprise and disappointment. The higher aristocracy consisted chiefly of the duke at Plumwood, and of the Waddingtons. Mrs. Waddington was the daughter-in-law of that famous Edwardian beauty Mrs. Almeric Waddington whose photograph used to be sold in shops in Bond Street. People stated untruthfully, but not unnaturally, that King Edward VII had presented Mrs. Waddington with Belamor, the magnificent estate half-way between Plumbridge and Southwick, where her son now lived.

When Wilfred suggested that they might call, Beatrice said:

'English county society is nearly as snobbish and cliquy as that of Melbourne.'

But for the present she was contented to give her tennis parties and provided her excellent meals for smaller fry, who consumed them with avidity, but did not hesitate to remind her frequently of her Australian origin, in order to discount any effect of patronage.

147

At luncheon on the day after the tennis party Beatrice mentioned that she had seen the ghost.

'Crackers!' exclaimed Wilfred. Having recently heard this expression used by a very dressy young man at his coach's he had adopted it in place of 'Sink me.'

'What was it like?' asked Christopher suspiciously.

'It was a lady in white,' said Beatrice, smiling with tolerance of her own credulity.

'There are no such things,' said Matty, who was invariably 'right-thinking.'

The footmen, fiddling with vegetable dishes at the side-table, winked at each other. The butler, who felt it slightly *infra dig.* to serve in this Australian household, especially under the ill-assured Matty even though she was a Plumbridge, looked more sour than usual at her denial of the fine country-house tradition of supernatural visitation.

The servants at the Hall had something of the attitude of agnostic acolytes. Even some of Beatrice's Australian habits distressed Lucas, particularly that of always escorting her guests to their cars, and worse still of going out on to the drive, like Sister Anne in *Bluebeard*, to see if they were coming. Christopher particularly was a trial to him. One of the footmen was called Timothy. This youth was a platinum blond, if not an albino. Christopher when in a good mood called him Timothy White, when dissatisfied he shouted at him as if he were a dog which certainly Lucas found more in the tradition of country gentlefolk.

After Matty's dismissal of the subject, above stairs no

further thought was given to the ghost, but Timothy White had the second housemaid on the verge of hysteria by supper time.

· · · · · ·

Every week-end the boys came home in the long scarlet sports-coupé which Beatrice had given them, this type of car being their own choice, though their envious fellow-students called it: 'The Jew-boy's gin palace.' Nearly always Beatrice arranged a tennis or dinner party for them. She said: 'Some day we must have a picnic,' picnics being a characteristically Australian form of entertainment, but the summer was so wet that she kept putting it off.

There was some tension about these parties, as she tried to arrange them so that Christopher and Ursula would not be thrown too much together, and she tried to exclude the Rounsefells who were down most week-ends, and whose style of conversation she could not endure. But Christopher was bad-tempered if he did not have some of the week-end alone with Ursula, and Wilfred disappointed if he did not meet the Rounsefells.

Wilfred had formed a friendship with Sylvia which was like a love-affair of the intellect. It was full of misunderstandings, spiritual seductions, suspicions, passionate agreements, and exhausted partings.

She was amused by his gawky grace, his naïveté, his enthusiasm for the best, and she was touched by the flame of pure youthful wonder which showed in his eyes when she said something, and for all her pose of exaggerated sensibility she did often say such things, which struck for him a note of absolute unfettered truth.

He was thrilled, too, to learn from her all the latest aesthetic *snobismes*, though he could not always reconcile them with the Church of England, county family respectability which filled his marrow-bones.

She lent him books too, to bring his culture up to date, and throughout the summer he made intermittent efforts to read *Albertine est Disparue* in French.

Christopher lived through the week sustained by the inward vision of Ursula. He wrote her initials U. W. all over the inside cover of one of his note-books. Then fearing that someone might see it he added a C. so that it might be mistaken for his own initials. A youth named Blair did see it, and made some facetious reference. Christopher knocked him down. Blair never met any other Australians, and went through life saying that they were an extremely touchy people.

Ursula caused Christopher so much mental suffering that he began to feel vindictive towards her, little realizing that her own mental suffering was more than equivalent of his.

Liza had not seen Adam in London. He had gone to live at his club. She did not know what this signified. She wrote to him and had no reply. She did not want to see her lawyers about it as she thought that might be a first step towards divorce and she was determined not to divorce him. She discussed the situation daily *ad nauseam* with Ursula, who began to consider desperate plans of running away and living by herself. But she had ludicrous ideas of finance, and did not know whether she could keep herself on her allowance, which was more than most men have on which to bring up a family. Also, she was afraid that if she left Liza, her mother might take to drink or drown herself. And more than that she could not bear to leave the neighbourhood of Christopher, who was her one consolation, her one refuge, her one gleam of happiness.

She lived in equal dread with him that the weather or some other circumstance would prevent their meeting at the week-end.

As often as possible she would escape to Rosie's and play singles with her, to keep her tennis up to Christopher's form. Actually she was a better player than he, but he gave her so much curt advice that she did not realize it.

Sometimes she tentatively expressed her anxiety about the week-end's arrangements to Rosie, who would smile and chaff her and promise to see that it was all right. She acted as pander to the two young people, partly from real kindness and partly to earn the goodwill of Christopher, who, she foresaw, with Beatrice's money, Matty's antecedents, and the possession of Plumbridge Hall, would some day be a man of position. She never missed the opportunity of making useful friends.

One Saturday it rained and there was no tennis. Rosie rang up and asked Christopher and Wilfred to come over and play roulette with herself and Ursula. The stakes were not high. They bought twelve chips for threepence.

After tea Rosie suddenly discovered that she had run out of her special sort of cigarette. Would Wilfred be an angel and drive her into Southwick?

The effects of this manœuvre were unfortunate, though it was self-sacrificing of Rosie, as it was no fun for her to drive with Wilfred, fourteen miles through the rain, there and back. Its obviousness at once made Christopher self-conscious. He stood at the window watching them disappear through the splashing, steaming, summer rain. Ursula sat with the stillness of a girl in love, watching him.

When the car was out of sight he went over to the disarranged tea-table and began to pick the pieces of broken icing from a cake-dish. He ignored Ursula who sat waiting on his mood, as he well knew. All the week he had looked forward to this moment when they would be alone together. He never expected quite to achieve what he anticipated, and he did not know what to do. He had enjoyed the roulette. The fun of the game and Rosie's chaff had enhanced the delicate play of love, of glance and touch between himself and Ursula. Their love so far had been a faint intoxication, an added stimulus to other pleasures, to the swift movement of the tennis court, to the light and shade and the flower entwined grass of the orchard. But the seclusion of this sophisticated room where they were imprisoned by the rain, extracted their love from the mixed ingredients of life and pleasure, and left it confronting them, a stark fact about which something should be done. Christopher was not yet prepared for this. He was annoyed at suddenly having the demand of experienced manhood placed upon him. He nibbled sulkily at the bits of pink sugar.

Then he came and stood over Ursula.

'What 'll we do?' he asked, putting the onus of initiative on to her.

'I don't know,' she said with an appearance of indifference. She wanted him to sit on the chair beside her, and to show some tenderness.

'What did they want to go off like that for?'

'I don't know,' she repeated.

'Don't you know anything?' he demanded. His eyes were glinting. He was half smiling, but she was not sure that he was in fun.

'I suppose Rosie wanted some cigarettes,' said Ursula uncertainly.

'Of course she did.'

'Well, then, you know as well as I do.'

'I know she said she wanted some cigarettes.'

He saw that Ursula was afraid of him. She was really afraid that he would create some discord which would destroy the week-end for her, and leave an aftermath of wretchedness through the ensuing week.

Christopher remembered his own sufferings of the past week, caused by her existence. At the moment her uncertain manner and her fear made him feel that he had her in his power. He wanted to make certain of that, to avoid further sufferings.

'What are you talking about, then?' he asked with an air of derision.

'You said why did she go off like that. I was trying to tell you.'

'You don't understand.'

She did not reply. This was the first time that he had set out to mystify her to make her appear a fool, and she really thought that she must be dull of comprehension. She was on the verge of tears.

Christopher walked over to a table and picked up an illustrated paper which he read with ostentatious nonchalance. He was freeing himself admirably from the thing that had power to hurt him. Three yards away was the face he had agonized to remember, the girl who had made a fool of him by causing him to scribble her initials over his note-book.

When he thought that by his indifference he had obtained complete mastery of the situation he came back to her.

'What shall we do?' he asked.

'Anything you like,' said Ursula with an affectation of carelessness.

'Look at me.'

'Why?' She looked up at him.

'You're barmy.' The implication was that she was foolish to doubt his love.

'I'm not.' Her voice nearly broke.

'Yes, you are.' The glinting derision had gone from his eyes. They were starry with innocent love. He took her hand and drew her up to him. Their eyes drew their faces close together, until their mouths united, a perfect rose of flame.

Ursula was in a kind of swoon, but she was puzzled, and not completely happy.

CHAPTER VI

THE OBVIOUS FLAVOURS

Mr. Hodsall, having said mass to celebrate, he felt somewhat anachronistically, the Translation of St. Martin of Tours, walked in a state of unusual contentment across to the vicarage to breakfast. It was strange, but he far preferred to hold services without a congregation. In the cool, still church where the candle flames twinkled palely below the eastern window, as he murmured venerable and historic words, he was able to lose himself in the virtue and wisdom of the past, and to achieve a state of lofty tranquillity. The presence of Babs Oakes or of his wife, his usual weekday congregation, bringing strained earnestness or complacent righteousness, impaired his sensitiveness to these holy vibrations, or else jangled the vibrations themselves. He realized that there must be war in heaven, and that the vibration of good must absorb and transmute the vibration of evil, particularly in the mass, the dynamic focus of good, but when they worked through such a frail, sensitive, and doubting instrument as himself, it was difficult always to make them effectual.

However, this morning there had been no disturbing influence and he had a sense of well-being as he walked between the cool dewy grass and the grey tombstones.

Coming from the shadow of the church into the sunlight he found the warmth of the breathless morning almost oppressive. Over in a field an oak tree seemed to be dreaming above its pool of shade. By the stile into his garden even the nettles and the troublesome bindweed were tangled in a quiet eternal beauty. They were like the flowers in the background of some picture of a saint in contemplation.

He picked a carnation and coming into the dining-room he laid it beside Carola's plate. He then kissed his wife and read Carola's note with the absent air with which one performs a conventional act.

One morning five years ago Carola had written him a little note, and put it among his morning letters. This had pleased him, and the next morning when he came in from church he had said idly: 'No letter from Miss Hodsall this morning?' So Carola wrote another. Since then every Sunday and Saints Day she had written a note for her father's breakfast table. It had become a weariness to both of them, but when Carola suggested giving it up Mrs. Hodsall had said: 'Oh, father would be so hurt.' To Carola it was an intolerable burden three or four times every week to have to think of something amusing or affectionate as soon as she woke up.

Her father's reward was to place a flower by her plate, generally an easier task, though in midwinter, in an icy wind or pouring rain, to have to halt on his way to breakfast to search for a belated weedy marigold, an aconite, or an optimistic daisy, made him wish equally heartily that the custom could end.

He gave his careless glance at the note, and then read it again:

DEAR DADDY. This is the last note I shall write you, except when I go away. I'm too old now and there's nothing much more to say. I'm sure you'll understand.

Love,

CAROLA.

He laughed, and handed the note to Mrs. Hodsall, who said:

'Oh, how dreadful of her!'

'I think it's very sensible of her.'

'Aren't you hurt, Harry?'

Mr. Hodsall thought a moment and smiled.

'A little,' he said, 'but not excessively.'

He was more relieved and amused. This letter agreed with his mood of tranquil pleasure. He had a superstitious belief in $\ʋ\beta\rho\iota\varsigma$ and Nemesis. So often when he had brought the different elements of his nature into harmony, they would immediately be jangled by some domestic indignation of his wife's.

Mr. Hodsall was afraid of his wife, not of her more forceful personality but of her discovering how little he thought of her character. Her rather brutal righteousness was a continual irritant to his sensitive *tout comprendre c'est tout pardonner* nature. When first he was fully aware of it he was filled with disgust, but then thought logically that she too being a human creature was a subject for understanding and pardon. He set out conscientiously to understand her and succeeded only too well.

She was unaware of his conception of the Christian Religion as the dissolution of self-will in the blinding light of Eternal Values. She thought it meant keeping two maids, and not knowing people who had been divorced. In spite of her downright manner she was not above a little mild trickery. She had not exactly tricked Mr. Hodsall into marrying her. That would be too strong a word, but she had affected to share ideals which she did not understand, and she had confused in her own mind Harry Hodsall's personal attractions with the fact that his father was Dean of Southwick and his mother the daughter of a law lord. When they were married, of course, she would cure Harry of his 'slight unwholesomeness,' as she described his spiritual aspirations. She had much the same standpoint as the local garage proprietor who had told the vicar that it was up to the other fellow to see that he was not cheated. When Mr. Hodsall repeated this as illustrating the corruption of modern business, she said: 'I think he 's quite right, Harry. One shouldn't encourage people to be soft, but, of course, he should be reasonably honest.' Mr. Hodsall was amused by this and other revealing phrases of his wife's, which he used occasionally to chaff her, when he thought there was no fear of her understanding what he meant.

He took his coffee, a poached egg, and *The Times* and sat down to breakfast. Carola came in and smiling a little self-consciously kissed him.

He smiled back at her, and the incident of the note was closed. For some reason neither of them could refer to it openly. Mrs. Hodsall watched them rather crossly, with a sense of exclusion. She liked explicit statements.

Mr. Hodsall as he sipped his coffee, gave his usual perfunctory glance down the deaths column of *The Times*. He did not keep up with many old friends or relatives, but he liked to know if they were still alive. He gave a faint start and looked out of the window. Mrs. Hodsall noticed on his face that expression of mingled peace and regret with which he so often came out of church. It irritated her, as it was a perpetual reminder that she did not satisfy his emotional needs.

'Do eat your egg before it's cold,' she said.

'Roly is dead,' he replied quietly.

If the late and Honourable Mrs. Hodsall, wife of the Very Reverend the Dean of Southwick, had not lived in an era and environment in which infidelity was so inconvenient and unfashionable as to be out of the question, it would be hard to believe that Roly and the Vicar of Plumbridge were both sired by the late dean.

In the most distinguished families, Mr. Hodsall was wont to say, there must remain an element of vulgarity, of greed, and gross contact, however slight, to enable them to survive. The most fastidious scholar, the most courtly diplomat must have this wholesome inoculation. Unfortunately, while Harry Hodsall had been practically denied it, his brother was given a double dose, so that it was not an inoculation but the actual disease. Before he was two years old his inordinate affection and natural dirtiness disgusted his mother and delighted his simple-hearted nurse. He was a human being after her own heart, not like the pernickety Master Harry, whose earliest lispings showed a frightening discrimination.

Roly had eyes of a hot reddish brown, which turned a liquid intimacy on to the merest stranger. His neck was thick, his hair coarse and auburn. He was from the beginning satisfied with the more obvious flavours.

With Harry he went to Eton, but apart from his voice he remained as miraculously uninfluenced by that distinguished school as by the lofty austerity of the deanery. There was a kind of wall between himself and those of his own class which denied him their perceptions. He needs must love the shoddy when he saw it. This applied not only to material things, but to the things of the mind. As much as any boy in Europe he had access to the wisdom and beauty of the ages, but he acquired his political and moral views from the groom, his religious attitude from the man in the street, and his philosophy from the pot-house.

'So many gods, so many creeds, when just a little kindness is all this sad world needs,' he said, and put this into practice, but with so little discernment that his benevolence nearly always brought misfortune to its recipient.

His first effort was to give a ten-shilling piece to a ragged boy who was imprisoned for theft when he tried to change it. He took five shillings out of Harry's money-box to give to the groom to put on a certain winner which lost. He and the groom were to have shared the profits, except for a shilling which was to be returned as interest with the original five to Harry's box.

He did not hesitate to thrust himself forward. When the bishop dined and was discussing a subtle theological point with his father, Roly truculently brought out his maxim about so many gods. When told to be quiet he argued the point with a shallowness which was embarrassing to hear even from a boy of sixteen.

When the duke came to luncheon it was worse. The duke was vice-chancellor of the diocese, and also had the quaint historic title of lay-dean of the cathedral. He was also noted for his connection with the turf. Roly, with hot and earnest eyes, asked him how he reconciled his ecclesiastical appointments with the practice of betting.

The duke replied with an urbane cynicism, at which everybody present smiled appreciatively. This was the sort of polite accommodation which exasperated Roly.

'Yes; but would Christ do it if He were alive to-day?' he demanded.

'If Christ were alive to-day' was another of his favourite expressions, when he was in the mood for religious argument. There was hardly one which could be less acceptable in an aristocratic deanery. Even the duke did not smile.

Roly was, of course, expelled from Eton. This was not for some idealistic misunderstood romance, but for a mere unimaginative grossness. Again a year later he was satisfied with the obvious flavours when he seduced a housemaid. The only things in which he was conventional were his misdemeanours. She was a slovenly and squat-nosed girl, whom Mrs. Hodsall was just about to dismiss as she had come to the conclusion that she was half-witted. Roly, not content with having ruined the girl, though as it turned out this 'ruin' was only moral, further angered his father by announcing that he would marry her. To his feigned astonishment this provoked the dean to the point of fury.

'But that's the right thing to do,' he said sulkily.

It was true that when the dean had been a country vicar he had always ordered seducers to marry their victims. Roly pointed this out.

'The girl's of an entirely different class,' said the dean.

'We're equal in the sight of God,' said Roly in solemn rebuke.

'Heaven help me, I believe you are,' exclaimed his father.

He only prevented the marriage by refusing to give Roly another farthing if he went through with it. On the other hand, if Roly's probably nauseating offspring were allowed to enter the world nameless he would continue Roly's allowance and settle £1,000 on the mother. He despised his son more for giving in.

'A high price for the virginity of such a peculiarly plain girl,' he added, his own wholesome inoculation of vulgarity at last taking effect.

After her confinement Roly's victim bought a small sweet-shop just outside the cathedral close. Her child was a throw-back to more refined ancestors. In fact, he bore a strong resemblance to the dean, who used often to see him playing, golden-haired and grubby-nosed, in the doorway of the squalid little shop. Some day, he thought, he would take him away from his mother, and have him educated in a middle-class school from which he might win scholarships, or if he had not much brain, send him abroad.

But it was Roly whom he sent abroad.

Roly, forgetting his experience with the groom, did another kindness and went to prison. He committed a temporary embezzlement on behalf of another clerk, as they had calculated that there would be less chance of discovery if Roly did it, a false optimism.

When Roly came out the dean sent him, the last of the transportations, to Australia, again using a monetary bribe. When the dean died he left all his money to Harry, with a recommendation to him, but with no obligation, to keep up the allowance, which Harry had done. For the last twenty years he had sent Roly half his private income, for which of recent years he had only a bank's acknowledgment.

Fifteen years ago this drain on his resources had nearly been removed. Roly was in a bad accident near Bacchus Marsh, Victoria. He was unconscious for days, but he recovered and married his nurse. He could be relied on to take the course least convenient for his relatives. All that the Hodsalls knew of her was that her name was Theodora Dobbin. Of her tastes, nature, appearance, education they knew nothing. They were not optimistic.

And now Roly was dead. Here was the notice in *The Times*:

On 11 March at 'Southwick,' Wangaratta, Australia, Rowland de Hervey Hodsall, beloved husband of Theodora Hodsall and son of the late The Very Reverend Dean of Southwick and the late Honble. Mrs. Hodsall, aged 54 years.

Mr. Hodsall wondered if this was Nemesis or an added stimulus to his state of ὕβρις. The death of his only brother should have been a shock which would immediately destroy that sense of all being well with the world, that joyful inner harmony with which he had come out of church. And yet he could not help realizing that a serious drain on his resources had been stopped, and, to change the metaphor, that a volcano on which they had been living for the last twenty years had become quietly, and with gratifying unobtrusiveness, extinct.

Because Roly's quaint activity had not ceased immediately he left England, though they no longer had any cause to fear such devastating eruptions as that which marred the elegant happiness of their wedding day, when Roly had become maudlin, boisterous, sodden, and truculent by turns, had made warm-hearted jokes about concupiscence and fecundity, had exercised his privilege as best man almost to ravish the bridesmaids, and had in his final befuddled condition argued himself justified by reference to the miracle at Cana of Galilee.

He had, in fact, cried havoc. He had on that occasion given complete expression to the urge which directed all his outbursts, the hidden desire to destroy the distinction of his family, to ridicule the graceful deportment, to vulgarize the spiritual aspiration, to make a farce of the fastidious pride which informed the life of the deanery, and which had first rebuked his grubbiness and had repelled his too slobbering affection.

For Roly was not as stupid as he appeared. He had a sort of blindness which made it hard for him to share the perceptions of his associates, and which made him impervious to the dean's reasoning, but the barrier between his own conscious and subconscious minds was much slighter and more transparent. As a poet writes most skilfully in a trance, so Roly in a kind of trance could pick on the exact phrase, the essential vulgarity which could be relied on to make his family squirm. He had no personal standard of conduct, and he would not have been so insistent to the dean on marrying the housemaid if he had thought that the dean would really allow it, though deep down, deeper even than the wish to destroy the austerity of form, was the desire to wallow in a muddled, dirty world of indiscriminate love.

At first, even in the Antipodes, his disintegrating force was at work. In Melbourne he wrote his name at Government House and gave his address as the Deanery, Southwick. He was asked to dine. What atrocious buffoonery he indulged in there, his relatives never knew, but his father had a note from the Governor's secretary saying that an impossible young man, obviously not a gentleman by birth, was passing himself off in Melbourne as the son of the Dean of Southwick. Every now and then faint echoes of his activity reached England. When

Carola was born, the year after the dean's death, Roly wrote to Harry and said he must have £200 at once to keep him out of prison, so that Harry was obliged to send him the money he had set aside for his wife's confinement. Roly always managed to choose the most awkward moments for his eruptions.

And now the volcano was extinct.

Mr. Hodsall undoubtedly had a sense of relief, and yet from the past came welling up a score of memories of Roly, of those hot, reddish brown eyes demanding love, or burning with a cheap indignation. It was impossible not to feel a tinge of regret, of pity, and of personal unworthiness, that one had not been able to extract the true core of love which must have lain somewhere beneath the welter of Roly's vulgarities and misdeeds.

Even so, he could hardly regard this announcement as Nemesis.

He handed *The Times* to his wife, who said: 'Should I wear black?'

'Is the family skeleton dead?' asked Carola brightly.

'Uncle Roly was Father's brother,' said Mrs. Hodsall in solemn rebuke.

CHAPTER VII

A SOPHISTICATED LADY

Tom met Ursula out walking with Pip. He pulled up to pass the time of day.

'Why are you palely loitering?' he asked.

'What can a poor girl do?' said Ursula.

'Why don't you go and play with your Anzacs?'

'It is only Wednesday. My boy friend doesn't arrive till Sat. p.m.'

'He is your boy friend, is he?'

'I don't know,' said Ursula.

'You ought to know.'

'I'm all listless and wayward.'

'You want a tonic.'

'My life is hell,' said Ursula placidly. 'Here's rosemary. Place it on my grave. I'm all fraught with self-pity, like Mummy. We aren't half a household, I can tell you. The servants walk like Agag.'

'How is Liza?'

'Just so-so.'

'I'll go and see her ladyship.'

'You won't do yourself much good.'

They smiled at each other with somewhat derisive affection. Ursula called her dog and walked on.

Tom went to see Liza after dinner on the following

Saturday evening. He found her writing an article on the critical period in marriage. She read him bits of it with evident satisfaction.

'What are you going to do with it?' he asked.

'I might send it to one of the daily rags.'

'Will they take it?'

'They'll take anything by a titled person.'

'You might make more by advertising face cream.'

'I don't need money, and I'm too old-fashioned to turn my face into an advertisement. I'd rather be an honest prostitute.'

'Ursula isn't looking too well.'

'Ursula has no discrimination. She's Adam's daughter.'

'And my niece.'

'That's why she goes so much to see that Mrs. Malaby, I suppose,' said Liza maliciously.

'Rosie's all right. You take her the wrong way,' said Tom with a schoolboy chuckle.

'I hope her character has more integrity than her building,' said Liza. 'Look at those joints, gaping already. I hate this damned house.'

'I think it very attractive.'

'Adam doesn't apparently,' said Liza shortly. 'What the hell am I going to do?' she demanded, turning on him tense, unhappy eyes. 'This is the end for me. I staked everything on this house. I planned it as a final test. I went away for a month as you told me to. Then I wrote to Adam from Monte Carlo and told him at what time I was arriving at Victoria. I had two tests— if he met me at the train *and* came down to Clovermead

I knew everything would be all right. If he couldn't meet me, but came down I would still be hopeful. But he did neither. He didn't even send the car and I had to take a taxi. It was the first time I have taken a taxi from the boat-train since I 've been married. The first time in twenty years. He was in the north, but he could have telegraphed for them to meet me. It was deliberate, I know. It means that he doesn't want anything more to do with my affairs. That is the result of my test, and of your advice, Tom.'

Tom winced. Liza gripped the edge of the mantel-piece in both hands. He knew that she was in one of those distracted moods in which she would destroy the nearest thing at hand to relieve her feelings.

'I only suggested that it might help the situation,' he said diffidently. 'I don't really think it would have been any better if you had stayed in London.'

'At least I could have kept an eye on that bitch.'

'But, Liza, it is no good holding Adam by force, even if you can manage to do it.'

'Then am I just to say: "Yes, do go off with Ella Hindley, I don't mind." Don't be ridiculous.'

'Would it be any satisfaction to you to keep him against his will?'

'Yes, it would. At least I 'd know that she hadn't got him.'

'Well, that 's one way of looking at it.'

'It 's all very well to be amused.'

'I 'm not amused. I think it tragic. But you often laugh about it yourself, Liza.'

'Oh, there's a funny side to everything. There was something funny, I suppose, in that man's having his head chopped off in Munich the other day by a man in a top-hat. I might as well have my head chopped off as lose Adam. When he goes my life falls to pieces. I have nothing, no one else. Ursula isn't interested in me. Her back is turned to me and to all the things of her childhood. It's natural and I can't complain. But I must have some human interest and contact. I can't live like a tree stuck out in the middle of a bare field. My roots are entwined with Adam's. How can he *not* feel that when I feel it so strongly?'

Tom looked at Liza standing tense by the fireplace, her natural grace momentarily lost in a mere hungry leanness. He knew only too well how Adam might feel that the roots entwined with his were only those of some withered plant, one that took and exhausted life, but gave no enrichment in return. There was that quality in Liza, for all her kindness and wit and carelessness. There was a predatory, destructive quality. And Ella Hindley he had heard was plump and placid.

'Don't you see,' exclaimed Liza, 'that for me it is saying good-bye to life? What is there ahead without Adam? Nothing. My body slowly becoming more decrepit and uglier—everything going away from me— Ursula, everything.'

'You could keep Ursula if you liked, if you would not try and force her exclusive attention, and if you could take some interest in that Australian boy.'

'Pouf!' said Liza. 'That's a ludicrous business. They're children. I can't take it seriously.'

'Even Adam can't keep off old age,' said Tom mildly.

'He can make it bearable. As two people grow old together their companionship becomes deeper, and their old age can be as happy as any other time of their life. Look at the Ledburys. They married when they were both twenty-one, and died within two days of each other when they were eighty-one. He was quite well, but he simply couldn't live after his wife died.'

'That is what Ursula and Christopher might do, if they married now.'

'Don't harp on about Ursula and Christopher. I don't want Ursula to marry into the middle classes, too.'

'Young Westlake's origins are a good deal more distinguished than Adam's and mine,' said Tom.

'They're all right—but they know all these deadly people about here.'

'You are a snob, Liza.'

'I'm not a snob but I hate being bored, and I hate being gagged. If I mention my own natural world to these people they think I'm boasting, and if I say what I think, they think I'm indecent, and yet they toady to me. Every association I have with them is false.'

'That's nothing to do with Christopher and Ursula.'

'He's an Australian.'

'As far as I can see the Australians have better manners and more intelligence than the local middle-class people you object to so strongly.'

'I know five peers who 've married Australians and they 've all been divorced.'

'Who? The peers or their wives?'

'The peers, of course. I don't want Ursula to be divorced.'

'But Ursula 's not a peer.'

'That 's beside the point. She might be susceptible. Oh, I know, I 'm being utterly unreasonable and selfish. I can't help it, Tom. I 've got Adam in my blood. My blood has turned against me. You don't know what that feeling is. It is impossible to behave like a rational human being when it happens. I could scream.' She took up a piece of Waterford glass from the mantelpiece. 'I could fling this into the grate. I could take the poker and smash every mirror and window in the room. I not only could do it, but it is an effort not to. I hate this room because I hoped to be happy in it. It makes me feel a fool. I hate every happy memory. That is the worst thing of all, when even the happy memories have become painful—more painful than any other. I can bear to remember when Adam has been faithless and rude. I can't bear to remember the times before. It is as if all the best part of my life is wiped out. Do you know that poem of Maurice Baring's which ends:

> And I had hoped to win for so much loss
> A little gold, and I have purchased dross.

Well, I too am denied the little gold. And even that which I had is taken away. I don't dare to look back,

I not only have to face death ahead, but death behind me—like the Light Brigade or whatever it was.'

'Oh, Liza, that's absurd.'

'Well, it's true, isn't it?'

'Everybody has to face difficulties in love.'

'Who? Ursula and her Australian boy, I suppose? That is not love. That's only excitement. Love is something caught in your blood over years.'

'One can catch a disease in a day,' said Tom professionally.

Liza shrugged her shoulders.

'You ought to try and keep cool when next you see Adam. You are most attractive when you're cold.'

'What is the good of being an attractive refrigerator? Adam may admire me like that, but his admiration will be frozen.'

'That is true,' said Tom.

They looked at each other and laughed.

'What *shall* I do?' exclaimed Liza.

'There is only one counsel of perfection—to be oneself.'

'But I am two people I tell you.'

'Well, be your two selves, but don't be a third person. Don't make up an idea of yourself as a cold, grand person, or a generous, affectionate person, and act that.'

'You are beastly, Tom. That is just what I do.'

'Why not try being yourself?'

'I don't know if I have a real self. I can only follow a pattern. That is what is wrong. Adam wants something more solid. What is the remedy?'

'Lawrence says to sink into the dark night of the senses.'

'How on earth can I sink into the dark night of the senses?' asked Liza petulantly. 'I loathe darkness of any sort.'

'The only other course is to follow that which is good.'

'I can't be earnest. One must live according to one's nature.'

'You say you hate the middle classes, Liza, but you seem to suffer from the prevalent disease of middle-class gentlewomen. You are too fastidious to seek sensual gratifications, and too respectable to be genuinely religious, so you are cut off from life at both its sources, the flesh and the spirit.'

'I knew that ages ago. That is what is wrong with me. I hoped to fulfil my bourgeois nature with Adam, and because I failed I say I hate the middle classes.'

'This is new from you.'

'It isn't. It is as old as I am but nobody knows it. You remember the castle, Tom, everything falling to pieces and that one awful tin bath. The pompous meals and the silver plate and never enough to eat. All our values and our decency were perverted by poverty. They were like the copies of the real pictures, the Van-dyke and the Gainsboroughs which had been sold. They looked all right if you only gave them a quick glance. I don't mean we were shoddy because we were poor. It was the awful atmosphere of *sauve-qui-peut*, which hung over the place. You've no idea of the sordid greed of our schoolroom conversations. The other girls were determined to marry rich, I had a sneaking hankering for a love match. The funny thing is that I am the only one who did marry fairly rich. The other girls in the late twenties grabbed what they could get.

'When I went from school to stay with your sister, in your decent middle-class house—no ancestors, copied or otherwise, no stones falling off the parapet, four bathrooms, masses of food, and not one shabby carpet, it was marvellous. I at once idealized middle-class life. It was secure and honest and there was no strain. Adam going off to the City every morning was a hero to me; I compared him with Hungerford. Do you remember Hungerford at twenty, coming down from Oxford, so insolent, so sly, and already planning what rich girl he could marry? You could see that he had already been in bed with people. You knew that Adam would never be in bed with any one till he married. I thought that if I married Adam my soul would be saved. I would be entering a real life where people were doing things, making their way, not merely living on the past and patching up a cardboard medieval stage scene, which is all our life was.'

'But I thought you loathed our bourgeois characteristics,' said Tom, surprised.

'I only pretend that, I tell you, because I can't acquire them. At least now I do hate some of Adam's, but I didn't at first. I was prepared to swallow them whole. But when he insisted on my difference from himself, and when I did things he didn't like—I couldn't help it. I had been brought up that way—

he insisted on identifying me with my relatives, so to preserve my self-respect I had to fall back on and flaunt the characteristics of the decadent aristocracy. And there is that in me too. I am two people. I like the coldness and levity of my family. It gives me a free feeling. But I only like it as an occasional stimulant.'

'You certainly don't look bourgeois, except when you 're happy.'

'Then my true self is expressed,' said Liza grimacing.

'Then be your true self.'

'Then Adam despises me. Then I become angry and despise him. So the hellish sequence goes on—unless, of course, it has stopped for good.'

Ursula and Christopher came in from the terrace where apparently they had been looking at the stars. Ursula led Christopher by the hand. He felt awkward at having his hand held before other people, and seemed to be smiling and frowning at the same time.

'Well, if Tom hadn't come I should have spent a nice cheerful evening,' said Liza.

'But you were writing your article,' said Ursula. 'You told us to go out because you wanted to think.'

'Oh, I knew you wanted to gape at the moon.'

'There is no moon. There are only stars. Night of stars, oh, night of love,' sang Ursula. 'I do love vulgar music when I 'm happy.'

Liza looked at her with pre-War contempt.

Christopher, as usual, was dumb in Liza's presence. Liza also had a very definite effect on Ursula, which reacted on to Christopher.

M

When Ursula was alone with him she was often silent,
sometimes timid, and inclined to be serious. In her
mother's presence she talked the whole time, rather as
if she were afraid to stop, and everything, even their
love, seemed to be an object of faint ridicule. She was
the twittering bird which Sylvia found so unsympathetic.

'We've been talking about you,' said Tom.

'No good, I suppose,' said Ursula.

'I said you wanted a tonic.'

'Here is my tonic.' She turned to Christopher.
'Aren't you, Sunburst?'

'Oh, my God!' said Liza.

'Am I behaving like the housemaid again, Mummy?'
asked Ursula.

Liza snorted. Christopher was crimson. Tom puffed
out his cheeks.

'I'm going to bed,' said Liza.

'You oughtn't to do that, Mummy,' said Ursula
kindly. 'You'll only lie awake making up conversations with yourself and eating aspirin. If you stay here
we'll play police messages with you.'

'What's that?'

'It's like "consequences." You fill in names and
places and turn down the paper, only you use the form
of a police message on the wireless, instead of the ordinary
sequence. It's fraught with possibilities.'

They sat round the table, biting the ends of their pencils,
scribbling with sudden inspiration, and passing on the
folded paper. Ursula and Christopher sitting close
together contrived to make the results pointed and

personal.   One read: 'Will Dr. Woodforde, who was
last seen in Mrs. Malaby's bathroom, go at once to the
London Library where Ella Hindley has had twins?'

Tom gasped at these naked impertinences, and thought
Liza would really smash the mirrors. Instead, surprisingly, she began to be amused. He felt her watching
him sardonically.

When she went to bed she kissed the three of them.
Christopher was thrilled when she kissed him, not with
pleasure but with pride.

Ursula said: 'Sophisticated ladies kiss every one.'

CHAPTER VIII

CULTURE VERSUS GALLANTRY

WILFRED's attitude towards life was founded on the firm
conviction that the world was an orange or a pomegranate, full of scented colours and juicy pips for his
delight.   But so far he had been foiled in its enjoyment
by the hard shiny skin of the fruit.   He imagined that
soon he would be able to break this and get his teeth
into the juicy contents.

Like Matty he had great faith in culture.   In Australia
he had felt like the Duke Carl of Pater's *Imaginary
Portraits*.   He had made an heroic effort of mind at a
disadvantage in trying to sniff across 12,000 miles or so
of ocean, some faint breath from the countries where,
looking back, tradition was not cut off sharply, the
vista of time obliterated by the portly figure of William
IV, whose period represented for Melbourne the extreme
limit of antiquity.   A mahogany chest-of-drawers of
the 1830's was the Australian equivalent of a piece of
Minoan sculpture.

Through Matty's influence and his own startled,
sensuous perusal of *The Renaissance* he believed that the
skin of the pomegranate was to be broken through some
cultural experience.

'There's some secret behind everything,' he thought, 'that older people won't let you know.' With the idea of discovering this he plodded slowly on through *Albertine est Disparue*, especially as Sylvia had lent it to him, because the Rounsefells seemed to be less reticent about the mystery of life than any one he had met hitherto, and it was, therefore, more likely to be revealed in a book they recommended.

But having an inquisitive and amiable disposition he became friendly with every one except Liza and Rosie. Liza hurt his feelings by being completely uninterested in him and his cultural aspirations. She had said to Tom: 'That boy's the eternal curate.'

Liza had a wide superficial culture which came to her automatically with her quick mind, her wealth, and her social connections. You could not live in London, and occasionally in Paris and Rome and Vienna, and meet a great many people and hear them talk, and go to all the plays and all the operas and all the ballets and all the exhibitions of paintings, and buy the best new books even if you did not read them all, and go to half the weddings and all the memorial services and most of the race-meetings, without acquiring a knowledge of the world and of art and of literature and of music, which was in a way a wide form of culture, even if it did not stop you calling your husband's mistress a 'bloody bitch.' But she could not be bothered making a business of culture, like the Rounsefells. It amused and bored her, knowing so much, but not making a fuss about it, to have to submit to the architectural decisions of Rosie, whose taste still lingered over the worst quaintnesses of the 1900's.

Wilfred could not bear Rosie. When she was present he found that he became stilted in his walk. She had the same effect on him as a group of small boys at the corner of the street. But he was friendly with every one else, including Major Hinde and Mr. Hodsall, particularly the latter, to whom he made semi-confidential self-revelations.

Mr. Hodsall struck him as being very cultivated. When he felt confused or disintegrated from a prolonged session with Sylvia he would go to Mr. Hodsall to be rehabilitated.

'The Rounsefells think everything is silly,' he complained, 'except adultery and a few French drawings.'

Mr. Hodsall smiled.

'They 're only afraid of being old-fashioned,' he said.

'I think there are some awfully good things about them that other people haven't got,' said Wilfred loyally. 'They hate anything stuffy and anything that isn't fresh and real to them, which is why they 're afraid of being old-fashioned. That 's an advantage of being an Australian, whatever Mrs. Malaby says, and of coming to Europe at about my age. The old-fashioned things aren't dead. They 're fresh and vivid with life—all these cathedrals and castles and old houses. They give me a direct impact with the Middle Ages which I couldn't have if I were used to them. It was overwhelming the first time I went into an English cathedral. I was absolutely speechless. I seemed to feel the ghosts

thick in the air—queens and knights and abbots. In
Italy, too, I had an impact with classical times. Those
statues made one's hazy dreams clear and real and lovely.
Some of them shocked Mother, but I don't know, I
was rather pleased with the things that shocked her.
I couldn't say so, but they made my mind feel free,
silent upon a peak in Darien. Do you see what I mean,
sir?'

'Yes, I do,' said Mr. Hodsall thoughtfully.

'Does it shock you—that I wasn't shocked?'

'No cultivated mind is ever shocked—not in that
sense.'

'Yes; but I was not only not shocked—I was pleased
by things which made Christopher go crimson.'.

'You must be very depraved.' Mr. Hodsall smiled
ironically.

Wilfred frowned.

'Nobody takes people of my age seriously,' he complained. 'I want to know why I think things and if
they're right, but no one will tell me.'

'Young people aren't generally anxious for guidance.'

'So many people give one such silly advice. It's
always negative. Why can't some wise older person
advise one how to get the most out of life? That is
what every young person wants. We've been civilized
for thousands of years and I'm still puzzled. It's awful.'

'If I give you advice would you take it?'

'Every one knows what is good,' said Wilfred. 'I
only want them to help me to sort out the good in life,
but on a wide plane, sir.'

'Your demand is tremendous.'

'D'you know, I believe I've discovered a real difference between English people and Australians? English people accept limitations more easily—Australians expect to *arrive* where they want to go. D'you think it is because in the early days they had difficulties to face but got over them?'

'Those were simple difficulties,' said Mr. Hodsall. 'Just the physical difficulties of nature. Our difficulties are like bindweed in our souls, age-old rights and prejudices and oppressions and racial hatreds. The remedy can't help being slow.'

'Alec Woodforde says it must be quick. He's a Communist. I'm not, though. I'm traditional.'

'There is only one remedy.'

'What is that?' asked Wilfred, looking suddenly bright and solemn.

'The love of God,' said Mr. Hodsall, painfully forcing himself to leave his attitude of gentlemanly detachment to utter an eternal truth.

'Oh, yes,' said Wilfred doubtfully. He did not want the perfume of incense released from his pomegranate.

He went to dine with Major Hinde. After all, it was a form of culture to know all about wines, and who was the best bootmaker in Jermyn Street, and what were the details of a correct *ménage*, the arrangements of meticulous comfort.

Major Hinde poured this information over him in a relentless flood, from the moment when, having shown him his new wall-paper, he handed him his sherry, until

Wilfred, dazed and faintly repelled, climbed into his car
to drive home.

Because Major Hinde had not only told him how a
gentleman fed and clothed himself, but also what he
thought. Breathing heavily, his fat knee half an inch
from Wilfred's, his face not much farther away, as he
attempted to escape his barren loneliness by forcing his
views on this young mind, he passed from his contempt
of people who bought ready-made shirts to the subject
of iniquitous taxation, and thence swiftly to the un-
grateful uselessness of the lower orders. As far as
Wilfred could gather the chief end of man was to enable
houses like Major Hinde's to run on oiled wheels.
The number of people he was anxious to put against
the wall and shoot was astonishing.

'These young fellows who wear open shirts and go
hiking,' he growled, 'what use are they? They think
of no one but themselves. I saw that young Alec
Woodforde in a red shirt the other day. A red shirt!
And he went to quite a decent public school, too!
Another war,' he concluded, 'is what they want to put
'em in their places.'

He sat red and stertorous, proud of the martial courage
of this statement. In the War he had lived. In the
midst of death he was in life—the excitement, the gruff,
noble pity for the slaughtered heroes, the salutes, the
magical metamorphosis of himself into an officer and a
gentleman. He paused, his eye watery with nostalgia.

Wilfred sat with troubled brows. It distressed and
puzzled him to find people ill-natured or dull. At home

the least of his mother's callers had come trailing clouds
of glory.   The conventional pleasure which other people
expressed on meeting he really felt.   His imagination
supplied seventy-five per cent of people's charm.   He
imagined them as coming from a background where
the good humour and kindliness of their greeting was
perpetual and undimmed.

Perhaps because of this he became so friendly with the
shamefully shirted Alec Woodforde, who had rather the
attitude of an amiable spaniel, but without cringing,
towards the human race.   Although a prolific writer
of verse it was he who first made to Wilfred the Rim-
baudian suggestion that life was more important than
poetry, and experience than culture.

In illustration of which he led Wilfred to the Lamb Inn.

Wilfred felt socially seduced.   He did not know if it
was usual for the county families to go into village pubs.
Also he would rather have gone into the orchard to
discuss immediate longings and eternal values with any
one so engaging and uninhibited.

'I love pubs,' said Alec.   'I always find a lot of ready-
made mates there.'

'You're a sort of G. K. Chesterton in miniature,' said
Wilfred, quoting, without acknowledgment, Sylvia
Rounsefell.

'Yes.   Only I'm a better poet,' said Alec complacently.   'Chesterton's always sneering at something
—tea or heretics.   I hate Roman Catholics.'

'Why?'

'They're so full of hate.   I hate Protestants, too.'

They're full of hate for the Catholics. The Christian religion's finished now. It's killed itself with hate,' he said airily.

'Oh, I don't think that,' said Wilfred uneasily.

'It's true anyhow. I say, I'm most awfully glad you've come to live here. Honestly I am. There's no one to talk to in this place. No males, I mean. Females are no good for talking to. I say, isn't your brother glorious? If I were a girl——'

Wilfred began to think that Alec must share the inclinations of so many of the Rounsefells' friends, but this suspicion was immediately dispelled by his remarks about Daisy, the girl behind the bar at the Lamb Inn whither they were bent.

'I simply long for her,' said Alec. 'I can't sleep for thinking of her. D'you think I could bring it off?'

Wilfred went pink. He had never been asked such a shameless question.

'What's she like?' he stammered.

'She's marvellous. I wrote a poem about her. Shall I recite it to you?'

'If it isn't very long.'

'No; this is it! He took a crumpled sheet of paper from his pocket and read:

'When winter comes, comes with it revelrie.
Romantic cupid's pixie devilrie
Will seem less hard to fall to, when by night,
From the mossed Tavern stumbling, beery-bright,
You make advances to your dearest dream.
Manœuvres subtle, droll, and gay will seem
To lure her out alone with scattered suns,

Towards violet velvety oblivions
To watch the tall denuded poplars rise—
Or is it good to take her by surprise,
To creep your arms around her while you walk
Without a trivial introductory talk?
Or is it better still to plan your ways,
Beflagged with flattery's sinuous words of praise,
Until because of special favours shown
And compliments and gifts for her alone,
She realizes at last that you desire
That she may take or not her courting sire?
Imaginings have brought such vivid sights
The very thought of which brings plain delights.
And how much more will be that pleasure's hold
If summoning courage great with acts as bold
You put into effect what you have seen
And make confession to your chosen queen.
Oh, I have planned such cunning ways by which
I might withdraw her to some hidden niche
For purposes so gay in realms of thought,
Or take her to some thrifty shingled shore:
Oh, what a chance when whipped by freshening roar
Of off-sea wind, with spirits soaring high
So happy in a mood that's always nigh
To those who seek fine glory of the seas—
Oh, what a chance to hold her close in these
My arms, to take in them her body whole,
Each part of which is sacred as the foal
Is to her mother in the savage field.
The cheering which at Waterloo once pealed
Across a sky of gun-streaked victory,
It filled the hearts of British men like me
With such a surge of feeling undefined
As surely comes to those whose fortunes wind
Through days of friendship, till this fondness pounced
To passion, made to act and not renounced,
A streak of living joy would carve me through,
If only in my arms she'd let me do
A prostrate homage credit to the gods
Of all things great where adolescence nods

In acquiescence to terrific will.
I do not spoil my dream these lines to fill
With thoughts of failure in the Paphian quest.
On visions multiple I sleep, think which is best—
To creep so silently across the sand,
To kiss her feet on grass by salt wind fanned,
And cooled and cleansed in vigorous hurrying tide,
Ah then to softly stroke her hand beside,
To press my face along her bloom-dewed cheek
In craving transportation there to seek
The downy clarity of perfect limbs,
To satisfy at once long pondered whims,
To lastingly veneer her virgin breast
With such symbolic gestures, to give rest
Through the soft-feathered fluttering of this dove
To my imagined overdraught on Love.'

'It's jolly good,' said Wilfred with polite enthusiasm.
'I'd like to read it, then I could understand it better.'

'D' you honestly think so?'

'Yes; did it take you long to write?'

'No; I've written masses. I wrote it in bed one morning before breakfast. I just sublimated my passions and it came pouring out.'

'Can you do that often?'

'What?'

'Sublimate them and pour out poetry.'

'If I'm keen on someone I can. I wrote a marvellous poem about Carola.'

'Were you keen on her?' asked Wilfred curiously.

'Only very spiritually. Anyhow she won't look at me. I tore up the poem when she turned me down. Gosh! I'm ready for some beer. Oh, for a beaker full of the warm south!'

'I love that,' said Wilfred eagerly. 'I went with the Rounsefells one night to hear the nightingale.'

'Whatever did you go with them for? I'd give my nose to go and listen to the nightingale with Carola.'

'Not with Daisy?'

'If I had Daisy down the lane I wouldn't bother about the nightingale,' said Alec.

'But you wrote a poem about Daisy.'

'Yes, but that's just intoxication. Carola's inspiration.'

'I see,' said Wilfred untruthfully.

'Come on! I'll play you bar-billiards, and I'll show you Daisy. She has those lovely breasts that tilt upwards into a point.'

Daisy had the wide, placid face of a peasant, but Wilfred agreed with Alec that her figure quite compensated for this stolidity.

Alec leant on the bar and said: 'Hallo, Daisy, bring me two pints of "old" that have been cooled a long time in the deep, delved earth.'

Daisy, with a rather bovine smile, brought the beer.

'I'm going to be home for three weeks,' said Alec, 'so you must be prepared to see a lot of me.'

Daisy's only reply was a slight broadening of the bovine smile. She went through into the other bar.

Alec pulled the cloth off the table and briskly began to play bar-billiards with Wilfred.

'Don't you think she's seductive?' he demanded. 'Oh, boy!'

He conducted the game with a certain amount of

mildly improper buffoonery, slapping Wilfred on the buttocks and prodding him with his cue. Wilfred's gentlemanly embarrassment disappeared with the pint of old and he began to laugh.

Alec called through to the other bar: 'Hi! Daisy, the beaded bubbles aren't winking at the brim. Two refills please, miss.'

When she brought the beer, he said: 'Will you meet me down the lane to-night, Daisy? Daisy, Daisy, give me your answer do. At ten-fifteen at the corner by the haystack, eh? I'll recite you my poem if you do.'

But Daisy with her bovine smile had returned to the public bar to attend to the wants of the village lads.

Wilfred and Alec having had a third pint of 'old' walked a trifle unsteadily out of the 'Lamb.'

'She doesn't take you seriously,' said Wilfred.

'How can I make her?'

'You're too hearty with her.'

'They don't like you maudlin. I know. I've tried it. Anyhow, what do you think of her?'

'She seems all right.'

'Boy! She's marvellous.'

'You know, I do think your poem's good,' said Wilfred.

Alec halted, his face shining with pleasure.

'D'you really think it is,' he said, 'honestly?'

'Yes. I think it's awfully good.'

'Shall we swear a life friendship?'

'If you like,' said Wilfred diffidently.

'All right, we won't if you don't want to.'

He walked on.

'It's only that I wasn't prepared——' began Wilfred apologetically.

'All right! All right!'

'I thought English people were more reserved.'

'Blow that,' said Alec. 'I'm not reserved. I'm frank. People always know where they are with me.'

'I like people who are frank,' said Wilfred.

Alec began to sing a monotonous but ribald song.

'You're queer,' said Wilfred. 'You like poetry and yet you sing songs like that.'

'That's life,' said Alec. 'Life is everything, fighting, poetry, passion, sacrifice, seduction, struggle, and splendour.'

'I think that, too,' said Wilfred, 'but I don't think I gobble up life like you do.'

Alec laughed, took his arm for a while, and then flung it away again.

'Hell!' he said. 'I'm not going to walk through the village like a pansy.'

They walked on in silence.

'I wish I could have Daisy,' Alec exclaimed dolefully after a while.

'You could wait for her when the pub closes,' suggested Wilfred helpfully.

'By Jove, that's an idea! She has to walk home. Will you come, too?'

'Whatever for?'

'Just to give me confidence. You could buzz off when I get into my stride.'

'I don't think I could get away then.'

'Come if you can, I'll be at your ancestral gates at ten o'clock. My chastity is a simple agony to me,' he added fervently.

At a quarter to ten Wilfred put down *Albertine est Disparue* and crossed to the open window. He sat down on the sill and said ostentatiously: 'It's a lovely night.' Neither Beatrice, who was playing patience, nor Matty, who was pursing her lips at the vagaries of *Elizabeth and Essex*, nor Christopher, who was staring resentfully at the pictures of actresses in the *Sketch*, took any notice of him. If Christopher had done the same thing someone would have been sure to say: 'Where are you going to?' But Beatrice more than once had said a trifle sardonically: 'Wilfred will never get into mischief. I'd trust any girl anywhere with him.'

Wilfred smiled slyly to himself, slipped his legs over the window-ledge, and was gone soundlessly into the night. He had the quality of physical elusiveness. Often one thought he was there when he was not, and vice versa. Hitherto he had only put this talent to tactful and respectable uses. He felt extremely exhilarated at reversing the procedure, and at giving the lie to Aunt Beatrice's tame assessment of his virtue. He had drunk three pints of beer in a pub, and he was about to connive at the deflowering of a village girl. He felt that he was definitely achieving manhood. Certainly it might be a little tame merely to connive at this rakish adventure, but he did not feel as yet that his distinction was sufficiently established to withstand the confusion of such a liaison for himself. He had

the reflected fun without offence to his fastidiousness.
He had no scruples, because the deflowering of village
maidens was, like the slaughter of game, so involved
with the poetry of Shakespeare and the privileges of the
aristocracy as to be part of our cultural tradition.

Alec, lounging nervously under the Gothic gateway,
saw his white shirt-front loom through the dusk.

'What on earth have you come like that for?' he
demanded, glowering at Wilfred's dinner coat. He
himself was in a blue aertex shirt, a blazer, and grey
flannels.

'I had to come as I was.'

'That's useless,' said Alec. 'It'll put her off completely. She's not used to being matey with people
in dinner-jackets. You'd better go back and change.
No, damn, it's too late. Here, turn up your coat
collar and cover your shirt-front. She may not notice.'
His manner was more that of a flustered mother getting
her children off to school than of a young man bent on
gallantry.

Wilfred, muttering, complied. He had thought that
the girl would be flattered by the attentions of young
men in evening dress.

'She'll pass the corner of the lane,' Alec whispered,
though there was no one within half a mile of them,
'in about ten minutes.'

They walked in that direction. When Wilfred
ventured to talk Alec hushed him.

'We'll stand here,' he murmured, choosing the shadow
of a large oak tree.

'Won't that frighten her, if she sees us suddenly?' asked Wilfred. 'It would be better to be strolling down the lane. Then you could say good evening naturally as we pass.'

'P'raps you're right,' whispered Alec crossly. 'But it's Saturday, and she might be late and we might get to the pub before she leaves. She has to wash up the glasses. We'll start to walk when we hear her coming. Keep a sharp look out.'

Wilfred was beginning to cool. He hated being bossed and he thought it rather sordid to seduce someone who washed up the labourers' beer mugs. Still, the aristocracy had always done it in times past. He clung to this consolation.

'Here she is!' exclaimed Alec softly. 'Come on!' He seized Wilfred's arm and they set off down the lane, a little too quickly for confident *flâneurs*.

Unfortunately two figures emerged from the leaf-scented gloom of the night. One certainly was Daisy; the other a wheezy, waddling old man, whose pipe glowed and gave a ghostly illumination to his heavy suspicious face. The reek of tobacco mingled with the incense on the boughs.

Alec halted about fifty yards from the point of this encounter.

'That's only her uncle,' he explained. 'He'll leave her at the corner. His cottage is up the other lane. Come on, we'll have to stalk her. Keep in the shadow, and keep that infernal shirt-front covered.'

They crept silently back on their tracks and heard the

uncle's gruff good night and Daisy's loud, cheerful reply.

Alec and Wilfred scuttled forward. As they came up to her they tried to appear as if they had not been hurrying, though Alec's voice was a little breathless, and his boldness uncertain as he said: 'Hallo, Daisy, where are you off to?'

Daisy hesitated and murmured 'Good evening.'

There was a slight hiatus in the conversation. Alec and Wilfred stared at Daisy who said at last: 'Well, I must be getting along.'

'Come for a stroll,' said Alec.

'I ought to be getting along.'

'There's plenty of time. This is Mr. Westlake.'

'Pleased to meet you,' said Daisy.

Wilfred bowed stiffly. It might be all right to deflower barmaids, but ought one to be introduced to them?

'It's a beautiful night,' he said.

'That's right,' said Daisy.

'There's no twilight in Australia. We never have these marvellous prolonged evenings,' Wilfred continued in his best social manner, anxious to avoid another hiatus. 'My mother doesn't like it. She finds it depressing, but I think it's most romantic, don't you?'

Daisy replied in a puzzled monosyllable.

They began to stroll back along the lane.

Whatever Wilfred's secret longings may have been, his manner, as he later found to his disadvantage on similar occasions, was always that of a gentleman. It was not what he said, but the brittle courtesy with which he said it, that effectually inhibited any amorous laxity or allusive badinage. He was particularly polite to his social inferiors. He had, being inexperienced in these matters, expected the defenceless Daisy to be the half-willing victim of immediate unbridled sensuality. The erotic imagination of the innocent transcends all concrete experience.

However, as this Casanova scene was not forthcoming, Wilfred unwittingly set out to create the atmosphere he most preferred, that of polite social intercourse.

His mind, as well as his body, was in a boiled shirt.

By the time they had strolled back to the corner of the lane, in spite of the warm night and the mysterious trees, he had made any amorous interlude seem as inappropriate as at a conference of archdeacons.

Alec was fuming. At last, desperately, he gave Wilfred a surreptitious kick. Wilfred started, and said: 'Oh, good night.' He bowed and disappeared up the lane to the Hall. Alec said to Daisy: 'Let's sit down for a bit.'

Daisy said: 'I must be getting along.' But she sat down.

'He's a queer one,' she said.

'He's cracked,' said Alec crossly.

'Australian, aren't they?' said Daisy. 'Dad says they're all convicts. Seems funny, doesn't it, convicts living at the Hall?'

'They're not convicts. That's idiotic,' said Alec, cross now with Daisy.

'Dad says they are,' she repeated with filial loyalty.

'Let's talk about something else.'

'I must be getting along,' said Daisy, but she did not move.

They sat in silence for a few minutes. Daisy gave a little giggle.

'You're a funny boy,' she said.

Alec thought rightly that this was by way of invitation, but his imagination was as direct as Wilfred's. He made a too abrupt advance. Daisy was generally complaisant but she expected, at least, a few flattering preliminaries.

She repulsed him and stood up.

'You make me tired,' she said.

'What's wrong?' asked Alec without conviction.

Daisy let forth a surprising stream of vicious ridicule. The general implication of her remarks, made in an affectation of what she imagined to be a public school intonation, was that Alec and Wilfred had spoken to her simply to emphasize their social superiority and then to insult her.

Alec was amazed. He stared at her with his mouth open.

'Listen,' he stammered. 'I didn't mean——'

He put his hand on her arm.

She made an impatient gesture and turned away. He saw that she was crying.

'Look, Daisy,' he said in distressed tones. 'I didn't mean it.' He thought he had offended her innocence.

She began to walk home. He started to follow her and then thought: 'Oh, let her go.' Nothing could happen now, anyhow. It was all rather disgusting.

That outburst was dreadful. When he had joked with
Daisy in the bar, she had not said much but she had
smiled. She had seemed somehow acquiescent. One
could not have imagined her a virago. Really, Alec
was quite horrified at her vulgarity.

He walked gloomily back along the lane. Life was
dreadfully difficult. He was only nineteen and he would
not be able to marry probably till he was twenty-five or
thirty. What did they expect a fellow to do?

.   .   .   .   .

Wilfred, having left Alec, was naturally consumed
with curiosity as to how he was progressing. The night
was warm. He was too restless to go home.

He stood in the lane, sniffing the air, and listening to
the faint sounds of the night. Perhaps he would hear
the nightingale.

He wished that Alec had gone and left him with
Daisy. He forgot that in her presence he was only
capable of conversation about the climate. His imagin-
ative contacts, so different from his actual, again took
possession of his mind.

He simply had to know what Alec was doing. He
climbed a tree in the hedge.

As he expected, in the late gloaming and the light of
the stars, from his vantage point he could just discern
their heads above the grassy bank at the corner of the
lane. If their heads disappeared from view he would
gather that Alec was successful. He did not feel very
comfortable as he could think of no precedent for
spying on a friend's amours.

To his surprise, they stood up, and then Alec came up the lane by himself.

Wilfred slid down the tree. He stood in the lane brushing his clothes as Alec approached.

'What the hell——!' exclaimed Alec.

'What happened?' asked Wilfred.

'What were you doing up that tree?'

'I thought I saw a bird's nest.'

'You 've been spying.'

'I have not.'

'You lousy swine!'

The accusations, excuses, vituperation, accumulated to a speechless climax. The air was hot between them, their eyes glowing black in the dusk. Alec was on the point of striking Wilfred, Wilfred, disliking the idea, of preparing to strike back.

Wilfred's deprecatory air, as in his quarrels with Christopher, won the day.

Alec snorted.

They walked silently towards the park gates. Wilfred's mind was racing through intricate arguments in the attempt to justify himself. Surely there was some precedent for his behaviour. He had an idea that someone in the *Decameron* had done something of the kind.

They stopped outside the gateway.

'What are you going to do now?' asked Wilfred in a troubled voice.

'I don't know. I'm jolly glad it didn't come off really,' said Alec. 'I always feel worst just before dinner. You see I was born at seven in the evening, and my life is always more bursting and urgent at that time of day.'

'I don't know when I was born,' said Wilfred.

'Well, good night. Thanks for coming out.'

'I'll walk back with you some of the way.'

He went as far as the doctor's gate. Alec then came back with Wilfred, and they sat together on the stump of a tree at the end of the lane.

They told each other what they thought about love and aeroplanes, and about being afraid in a war and about prostitutes and death and wireless and God.

'God is only a wireless wave-length,' said Alec. 'I know a chap who explained it to me clearly. He says when that is generally known religion and science will be reconciled.'

At twelve o'clock the moon rose.

At one o'clock the nightingale sang, suddenly, briefly, and then was silent.

'Shall we swear a life friendship?' asked Alec again.

'Yes,' said Wilfred firmly, anxious not to be unresponsive.

Alec seemed to be almost in tears when finally he left Wilfred under the Gothic arch. For him the night was one of indescribable beauty.

Wilfred walked soberly up the drive. The world seemed incredibly large to him, like the inside of an enormous balloon. He felt that he was beginning at last to understand its design. He felt that he understood everything and everybody. He felt lofty and wise and pitying. He was a little depressed about the life friendship with Alec.   He had only sworn it to be polite, because, although he liked Alec very much, he did not love him.   Wilfred had romantic notions about that sort of thing.   To swear a life friendship ought to be a wonderful spiritual experience, a union of minds, the noblest part of love.   Alec, though friendly and full of life, was more earthly than himself.   Their spirits did not mingle.   He could not really mingle his spirits with one whose appetites were so indiscriminate.   This made Wilfred feel lofty and sad.

The front door was locked.   They must have thought he had gone to bed.   Wilfred whistled softly to himself. He did not relish the idea of an interview with Aunt Beatrice if he disturbed the household.   He wandered round the huge house looking for an entry.   At last he found, in the Tudor portion, a larder window protected only by some wire netting which he removed.

In the larder was the remainder of a red currant tart which they had had for dinner.   Nearby was some cream. Wilfred leant against the larder door and ate the tart and cream.   He thought of Alec and Daisy, and pondered the mystery of human appetite.

CHAPTER IX

NEMESIS

THE letters were delivered early at the Hall and brought up with the morning tea. Beatrice read hers when she came out of the bath, and then went into Matty's room to share their contents. In this half-hour before breakfast they discussed the problems of the day, or if there were none, matters of more permanent interest, such as the progress and characteristics of the boys, and the news from Australia.

Matty was naturally a late riser, and the intrusion of Beatrice in her *bois de rose* dressing-gown was not always welcome, this morning less so than usual, because Matty, slightly perturbed by her correspondence, had not yet even fortified herself with her tea. She had a letter from Aunt Albania, asking if she might come to stay.

But this was Beatrice's house, and Matty was afraid that Beatrice might be vexed if one of Matty's relatives applied to the wrong person as its hostess. She so often expected Beatrice to be annoyed that Beatrice could not help sometimes living up to the expectation. If it had been any one else than Aunt Albania Matty would have replied asking her to write to Beatrice, but Matty was even more afraid of her aunt than she was of her sister-in-law.

Aunt Albania was the sister of the late Sir Wilfred Plumbridge. In the eighties she had begun to be reticent about her age. She spent her life travelling about the world. She lived almost exclusively on birds and Burgundy. Every morning at six o'clock whether she was in Iceland in mid-winter or up the Amazon in mid-summer she had seven cold plunges. She visited China in the middle of a war and Portugal in the middle of a revolution. She said that she travelled about to avoid income tax, but she must have spent six times the amount of the tax in avoiding it, especially as she generally had two or three young relatives in her train. In Melbourne she had seen little of Matty as she did not care for intellectual uplift. Her culture was more of Liza's variety. Her favourite poet was Byron and she had an exhaustive knowledge of French novels.

Her indifference to Matty had nothing to do with inhospitality. When she took a house it was crammed to bursting point with guests. In Brompton Square and Bordighera she would give rein to the hospitable traditions of the Australian sheep station. She was known to the officers of most P. and O. liners as Aunt Albania, though comparatively few of them were aware of her surname. She expected other people to be as hospitable as herself, which they generally were to her, as wherever she arrived there seemed immediately to be an influx of enjoyment. Young people crowded round her, not only because she fed them well and

amused them with her astonishing hardihood and her
advanced views, but because she demanded nothing of
them. Nor did she get much, except their society.

She did not think it out of the way to propose herself
and only one great-niece for a week or two at the Hall.
She was a little tired and a lot overdrawn from a motor
tour of Scandinavia. She knew the house was Beatrice's
but she wrote to Matty deliberately, as Matty was a
Plumbridge, and she could not bring herself to ask a
Westlake if she might stay at Plumbridge Hall.

Matty sat up in the wantonly grandiose bed, which
would have been a more appropriate resting-place for
Charles II and one of his duchesses.

'I've heard from Aunt Albania,' she said.

'What, old Miss Plumbridge? Why don't you ask
her down?'

Here was an excellent opportunity for Matty to escape
from her dilemma, but she had that extreme form
of honesty which made her extract the maximum of
discomfort from every situation.

'She has written to ask if she may come,' she said.
'I don't know what to do about it because, of course,
she shouldn't have written to me.'

'Why not? She's your aunt.'

'But it's your house.'

Beatrice shrugged her shoulders.

'As a matter of fact, I regard it as Christopher's house.'

'Wilfred would make better use of it than Christopher,'
said Matty. She felt that Beatrice's generosity to Christopher demanded a gratitude she could not begin to

express, and which she knew too that Beatrice did not want. But the only way she could think of avoiding it was by making this rather ungracious remark.

'Wilfred will be able to look after himself,' said Beatrice. 'He'll always find the softest cushion and sit on it. Besides, Christopher is the elder.'

'From that point of view neither of the boys has any right to it. Walter's son should have it.'

'Well, let him come and take it,' said Beatrice dryly.

Matty handed Beatrice a card.

'Mrs. Malaby has asked us to dine,' she said.

'We shall be grand,' said Beatrice, smiling, 'dining with an English gentlewoman.'

'Don't you want to go?'

'I don't mind. We shall have to, anyhow.'

Matty sipped her tea.

'Do you think that Christopher is attracted by Ursula Woodforde?' she asked.

'Yes, I do. Very much.'

'I don't suppose anything will come of it.'

'It's early yet. They're very young.'

'I don't suppose for one moment the Woodfordes would allow it.'

'Why on earth not?'

'Ursula's an earl's granddaughter.'

Beatrice's eyes snapped.

'If you talk like that,' she said, 'I shall make a gift of this house and half my fortune to Christopher at once.'

'That would be a wickedly irresponsible thing to do.'

'If you talk like a fool you will drive me to wicked irresponsibility.'

Matty's thin cheeks flushed.

'You should not speak to me like that,' she said with a certain dignity. 'I have done what I can for the boys. I can't compete with your wealth and buy them ridiculously unsuitable palaces to live in.'

'There's no need for you to try and *compete*. It's because you won't attempt to enjoy unresentfully what I am able to provide that you anger me. You crab everything. Was this house ridiculously unsuitable for your family when they lived here?'

Matty did not answer.

'Then why is it unsuitable for Christopher? Your white-haired Wilfred seems quite at home here.'

'I want Wilfred to have a taste for scholarship, not for luxury.'

'You said just now that he would make most use of the house.'

'I meant——' stammered Matty and sank into confusion.

'If you could get over your resentment,' said Beatrice more kindly, 'you'd realize that Cambridge and the background of a country house is just what a boy like Wilfred needs at this juncture to bring out the best in him.'

'It's funny that Wilfred doesn't seem to be interested in girls,' said Matty.

'He'll get over that,' said Beatrice laconically.

'Not too soon, I hope. D'you know, I don't believe

he has ever had a sensual thought. When he looked at those dreadful statues in Italy he did not seem to understand what they meant, while Christopher went scarlet at them.'

They began a most delicately allusive discussion of frigidity in young men, which lasted till nearly breakfast time. They both reiterated that it would be safe to trust Wilfred with any girl anywhere.

.   .   .   .   .

There was soon another and far more sinister Australian invasion of Plumbridge than that threatened by Aunt Albania. Mr. Hodsall had less reason than he supposed for congratulating himself that the volcano which was Roly had become quietly and unobtrusively extinct. The morning after the announcement of Roly's death appeared in *The Times* he had a letter from Roly's widow, who had arrived in London and wanted to come and stay at the vicarage. This letter was signed intimidatingly 'your affectionate sister-in-law, Teddy Hodsall.'

Mrs. Roly, on arrival, appeared to fulfil the worst potentialities of an Australian relative. She was fat, sticky, and blowsy, and her voice was a loud, nasal drawl. She wore a bright green artificial silk dress and white shoes and stockings. Round her neck hung a double rope of tiny iridescent shells.

As she was coming out of the station she cried: 'Where's my rain-cape? I must have left it in the train.' She dashed back through the barrier, shouting to the startled guard who was signalling the train on: 'Stop! I've left my rain-cape in the train.'

As she called it 'ryne-kype,' Mr. Hodsall had no idea what she was talking about. He returned with patient courtesy to find her the rollicking centre of a group of porters and small boys, who were grinning at her apologies for delaying the train.

'Wasn't that a scream? I could have split my sides,' she said.

The Hodsalls felt as if the vicarage had suddenly become a centre of *opéra bouffe*, not only because Mrs. Roly, as she ran her bath, or tramped heavy-footed in her bedroom, or bounced down the stairs to breakfast, would burst into a song called 'Love is My Game' but because she loved a jolly atmosphere. 'I like to jolly people up,' she said, with that liquid affectionate gleam in her eye which Mr. Hodsall found painfully reminiscent of Roly.

She made jokes at meal-times in which she tried to implicate Mrs. Hodsall's rather sadistically well-trained servant. She would jump up to put down her plate or to fetch the cauliflower to Carola, who she said frequently was 'a love.'

'I like to lend a hand,' she said.

'It is very good of you, but the maid can do it,' said Mrs. Hodsall with a frozen face.

'Oh, I'll never get used to your grand English ways,' said Teddy.

'This is a very simple household. It is not at all grand.'

'Oh, go on!' Teddy gave a curious leer.

She was as well as jolly, active, and kind, extremely appreciative.

o

'Isn't that bonzer!' she exclaimed on her first arrival
at the vicarage, as she gazed with sentimental rapture
at its mid-Victorian yellow brick façade. 'I do think
an English country house is ever so lovely. There's
nothing like it, to my mind.'

She was full of Anglo-Australian comparisons.

'Your summer's a scream,' she said. 'Why, in Melbourne the butter's just oil—and the flies! You'd never
believe it. I never try to do anything on a real hot day.
I just lie on the floor in a kimono, and sometimes not
even that.' She gave a shrill giggle.

She told Mr. Hodsall that although he was an 'Amen-
snorter,' he was 'not a bit of a wowser.' She had an
amazing fund of 'diggers'' slang.

She wanted to know about all the historic houses in
the district.

'You must take me to see them,' she said.

'Plumbridge Hall is the oldest house in the neighbourhood,' said Mr. Hodsall. 'It has a ghost. That
should interest you.'

'No, really?' said Teddy. 'Does it wear chains and
clank. You can't kid me, though. I don't believe
in ghosts.'

'It is of a white lady.' For some reason Mr. Hodsall
felt it would be uncomfortably intimate to tell Teddy
the story of Lady Jemima, though he had often told it
to complete strangers. 'I hear that the servants quite
believe in it. By the way, there are some countrymen
of your own at the Hall.'

'What d'you mean?' She looked at him suspiciously.

'Australians. Their name is Westlake. Mrs. Westlake's grandfather was a judge in Melbourne.'

'Never heard of 'em,' said Teddy. 'We didn't know
the swells.'

But she seemed depressed at this information. She
did not sing 'Love is My Game' for the rest of that
day.

The Hodsalls were disintegrated by this intrusion.
Mr. Hodsall when he met his wife would give faint,
uneasy smiles, but Mrs. Hodsall did not think the fact
of Teddy funny. At intervals throughout the day she
would go into her husband's study to discuss the
situation.

'How long is she going to stay?' she asked.

'I haven't any idea.'

'What are we going to do? We can't let any one
see her.'

'That will be difficult,' said Mr. Hodsall, 'seeing how
conspicuous she is.'

'She is exactly what I imagined Australians to be like
until the Westlakes came.'

'I suppose there are degrees of education and manners
in Australia as elsewhere.'

'Evidently. But that doesn't help us. If the Westlakes hadn't come people might have thought she was
a typical Australian, and have thought it was just bad
luck that your brother had married one.'

'She is just what I should have expected Roly to marry,
Australian or English.'

'I wish we hadn't asked her down.'

'I'm her brother-in-law.'

'There is no need to insist on the fact.'

'Am I my sister-in-law's keeper?' Mr. Hodsall was verging on one of those mocking, whimsical, vaguely blasphemous moods which most perplexed his wife. He nearly always did this when something dreadful occurred.

'We might have known better than to hope to escape Roly,' Mr. Hodsall went on. 'Every time I have had some release from him it has been followed by a fresh infliction. I have always had to make sacrifices to God or Mammon to keep him off. He is the most significant thing in my life. He is my cross, my limitation. God gave me everything one of my nature could desire—affectionate, distinguished parents, a beautiful home, good health, the best of intellectual and spiritual contacts. Then God said "This is too much," and added Roly. Roly in the schoolroom alternated gross torments with slobbering caresses. He went to school, but my relief was compensated by the humiliation of finding when my turn came to follow him, at my prep school and at Eton, that he had made the name Hodsall stink in every nostril. He went to prepare a place for me, a Gehenna, a purgatory, from which I could only escape by effort, discipline, and suffering. It is to Roly that I owe my apprehension of the underlying truths of the Catholic religion and of life. He left school and my relief was compensated by the disgrace of his expulsion. Later he went to Australia and my relief was compensated by a sacrifice of £300 a year to Mammon. He died, and

I dared to thank God that my cross was removed. But God said "My son, there is no life without the concomitant burden, the cross, the limitation," and He sent —what is her real name, by the way?'

'Theodora.'

'Yes; Theodora. The gift of God!'

'I wish you wouldn't joke about it, Harry. What can we do?'

'We must either bear the spiritual affliction of her presence and offer it as a sweet savour to Heaven, or else make another sacrifice to Mammon.'

'You mean pay her to go?'

'If you must put it so crudely—yes.'

'How much, d'you think?' Mrs. Hodsall frowned.

'As we grow older our cross should become lighter. I should think £200 a year.'

'It seems ludicrous.'

'If we don't Roly will pursue us down the arches of the years.'

'Do talk seriously, Harry.'

'I am serious, my dear.'

'I suppose she wants money.'

'I imagine that's her object in coming here. She does not look affluent.'

'I'll speak to her after dinner to-night. Leave us together in the drawing-room.'

'I'm very grateful to you,' said Mr. Hodsall. 'I dislike that sort of interview.'

Mrs. Hodsall, on the other hand, rather enjoyed dealing with any situation, especially when it meant explaining to people what was right and wrong, and putting them kindly but firmly in their place.

The interview with Teddy, however, was less satisfactory than any which Mrs. Hodsall had ever conducted.

'My husband and I,' said Mrs. Hodsall kindly, 'were wondering if Roly had left you in financial security.'

'How d'you mean, dear?' asked Teddy with a certain alacrity.

'Well, we know that Roly was dependent on his allowance from the estate.' From delicacy she referred to Mr. Hodsall's private purse as 'the estate.'

'Yes?' said Teddy, but with a note of interrogation.

'This ceased with his death.'

'That's right, dear.'

'Well, my husband and I thought you might be in need of money.'

Teddy laughed.

'I could do with a bit. Who couldn't?' she said.

'Perhaps, Theodora,' said Mrs. Hodsall firmly, 'if you were to tell us your plans and your circumstances, we might be able to decide what we could do for you. Do you intend to stay long in England?'

'I haven't made up my mind yet. What was it you were going to say about helping me?'

'We would do what we can if you need help. But we are not well off, you know.'

'Go on,' said Teddy amiably; 'not well off with a big house like this and two maids and a gardener? You can't kid me.'

'We are poor compared with the people about. Your

own countrymen at the Hall have a much bigger house and many more servants.'

At the mention of the Australians at the Hall again an unaccountable gloom took possession of Teddy.

'The point is,' continued Mrs. Hodsall, 'that we could continue Roly's allowance or part of it, if necessary.'

'What, to me?'

'Naturally.'

Teddy sat up with a jerk. Her liquid eyes gleamed, and then became puzzled and angry.

'Do people often die of pneumonia?' she asked suddenly.

'What has that to do with it?' asked Mrs. Hodsall, impatient with this reception of their very generous offer.

'I was thinking of poor Roly. I say, you couldn't let me have a bit now, could you?'

'Are you in immediate need?'

'I could do with a bit.'

'How much would you require?'

Teddy's eye appraised the room.

'A hundred pounds,' she suggested with a slight leer.

'I'm afraid that would be impossible. If you were to return to Australia, or to settle down in some part of the country of which we approve, we might continue the allowance, but the first instalment could not be paid till next quarter day.'

'When's that?'

'In about six weeks.'

A look of baleful exasperation flashed over Teddy's expressive face.

'It's like this,' she said. 'I'm going to stay with mother's people in Wales when I leave here, and they're real toffs. They live in a castle, so I thought a bit of money might be useful to smarten myself up before I go there. See?'

'You have relatives of your own in Wales?' said Mrs. Hodsall, surprised.

'Oh, yes. I used to tell Roly he wasn't the only one related to the dukes.'

'And how long are you going to stay there?'

'I haven't made up my mind yet.'

'Perhaps they will be able to help you.'

'I don't know, I'm sure.'

'When will you be going to Wales?'

'I haven't made up my mind yet.'

'I don't want to hurry you, of course, but I would like to have some idea of the length of your stay.'

'About a week, perhaps.'

'Oh!' Mrs. Hodsall nearly laughed with relief.

'Or perhaps two weeks,' amended Teddy. 'You see, I've really got a mission, like.'

'A mission? Are you a Nonconformist?'

'No fear. I'm no wowser. It's to find poor Roly's boy.'

'Roly's boy!' Mrs. Hodsall, bewildered, was losing command of the conversation.

'Yes, that's why I've come over really. Though I wanted to see Roly's relations too, of course,' she said, smiling archly at Mrs. Hodsall. 'But Roly, when he was dying, was ever so upset he hadn't done anything for his boy. You know the one I mean. Poor kid, it isn't his fault. Roly said I'd been so good, forgiving him about it, and would I go one better and come over here and see the poor kid was all right. So that's what I've got to do really, to obey his dying wishes.'

She smiled with a watery sentimentalism which drove Mrs. Hodsall with a murmured apology from the room.

    ·   ·   ·   ·   ·

Teddy, to the Hodsalls' relief, was not anxious to meet the neighbours. Beatrice, when she heard that the Hodsalls had an Australian sister-in-law as a guest, asked them all to dine, but at the last minute Teddy developed a violent headache and stayed at home.

People who came to the vicarage met her, and for a week or more she was the chief topic of local gossip.

Rosie became almost inarticulate with fastidious revulsion. Teddy was exactly like what Rosie pretended to think the Westlakes were like, so she became rather confused in her social discriminations. She compromised by sympathizing with Wilfred over his frightful compatriot.

'I do feel for you all at the Hall,' she said. 'It must be so dweadful for you to see that fwight walkin' about the village, and to know she's an Austwalian.'

'I don't know,' said Wilfred. 'Do you feel dreadful at seeing old Cripps walking about the village and knowing he's an Englishman?'

Old Cripps was the village semi-idiot, who was perennially arrested for indecent exposure.

In fact, Teddy caused less embarrassment at the Hall than anywhere. Mrs. Hodsall suffered most. She had developed a friendship with Matty in which she took a very dominant part, kindly but firmly instructing Matty in the traditions of the English countryside. Having Teddy in her own home made it difficult for her to maintain her authoritative pose.

But soon the village was electrified by a far more engrossing subject of gossip than the oddities of Teddy.

CHAPTER X

LIZA'S LITTLE GOLD

ADAM arrived!

Liza was so excited that she put it in *The Times*:

'Mr. Adam Woodforde has returned from Scotland where he has been staying with Mr. Wick of Wilkie for the grouse shooting, and has joined Lady Elizabeth Woodforde at Clovermead, Plumbridge, Sussex.'

But this urbane and reticent statement in the Court Circular gave little suggestion of what really happened at Clovermead during the week-end.

Christopher and Wilfred were there when he arrived, as well as Alec who had come to look for Wilfred. The Westlake boys had come home on Friday this week-end, partly because there was a house party at the Hall, and partly because Mr. Tyrrel, their coach, had such bad neuritis that he was glad to be rid of them.

They had come over to ask Ursula to play tennis. But Ursula could not come as her father was due to arrive at any moment. She was sitting on the terrace.

'Mummy's upstairs painting her face in different patterns in honour of the event,' she said. 'She can't decide whether to be wan or florid.'

Alec came hurrying round the corner of the house.

'Hallo, Wilf!' he said. 'Hallo, you glorious bull,'

he said to Christopher. 'I say, Ursula, is it true that
Uncle Adam is about to descend on the dovecot?'

'It is true.   He rang up last night.'

'Hell!'

'Exactly.'

'I don't mean hell, of course—but what's going to
happen?'

'Hell,' said Ursula.   'Mummy's radiant with forgive-
ness and rouge.'

'You are a cold-blooded little wretch.   She'll freeze
your blood,' he said to Christopher.

'That'll take some doing,' said Wilfred.

Christopher blushed.   The others grinned with youthful impropriety.

'Seriously, what's going to happen?' asked Alec.

'I don't know anything about chemistry,' said Ursula,
'but if you put one sort of powder with another sort of
powder into a crucible or a retort or whatever you use for
that purpose, you will blow your crucible or your retort
to pieces.   Daddy is one sort of powder, Mummy is
the other, and Clovermead is the crucible.'

'You are old-fashioned,' said Alec thoughtfully.

'Well, I do think that's an odd remark, don't you,
Wilf?   However, before the crucible explodes I hope
to have a good business talk with Daddy.'

'What about Aunt Liza?'

'I adore Mummy, but I can't protect her from herself
—as Miss Macaulay used to say to me at school: "I can't
protect you against yourself, Ursula."   Dear me, no!'

'Poor Aunt Liza,' said Alec.

'Now, Alec, don't come over here all fraught with pity for my Mamma. She doesn't really suffer half as much as you think. She just acts her life. She has no principles, only taste, and when her desires become stronger than her taste she is at sea. That is the last stage of civilization, when principles are lost in taste. Then corruption sets in. Mummy has reached the last stage. Her heart is gone. She's a frozen actor. Life is a play, let's act it together,' she sang.

'You're like that yourself.'

'Oh, you wound me!' exclaimed Ursula.

'You're like a cold bright little bird,' said Alec.

'Yes, I have Mummy's icy agility and Daddy's concern with the material aspects of life. You see, I know myself. "Know thyself," Miss Macaulay used to say, or was it God? Miss Macaulay is so confused with God in my mind that I can never remember which said what.'

The two Westlakes listened to this conversation, smiling with the awkwardness with which people listen to the intimacies of another family. Christopher was faintly shocked, but proud of Ursula's incisive diagnosis, a thing of which he was incapable.

'Come on, loves. Come and have some tea,' said Ursula. She walked into the house, pulling all the bells as she passed.

'Wedding bells,' she said, as a clangour came from the kitchen regions.

Liza sailed into the room. She was wearing a lovely dress of primrose georgette, a summery hat, and jade ornaments.

'I can't kiss anybody,' she said. 'It will spoil my face.'

'Oh, Mummy,' cried Ursula, 'you 're wearing pillar-box and I told you to wear geranium.'

'Geranium made me look anaemic, darling.'

'I can't help you if you won't help yourself,' said Ursula.

Liza looked puzzled and a little hurt.

A footman came in answer to the bell.

'Oh, Percy, let's have some tea,' said Ursula.

Liza's face immediately became tense.

'Certainly not,' she snapped. 'I won't dream of having tea till Adam comes. I don't know how you could think of such a thing.'

Liza had a dreadful sinking feeling, a premonition, like the first chill that heralds pneumonia. It was slight but experience made it difficult for her to dismiss it easily. If things were going well with her, she had found, they did so from the beginning, without one note of disharmony. She felt a violent anger with Ursula, as if she had deliberately put a blight on this reunion with Adam. She could almost have wept with exasperation, and then realized that above all things it was necessary to maintain a sunny, tranquil mood.

'You look marvellous, Aunt Liza,' said Alec.

Liza's tension was relaxed. She felt a wave of gratitude towards Alec and kissed him. Her pillar-box lipstick left a mark on his cheek. They were all laughing about this when suddenly Ursula saw Adam's car coming up the drive.

'There he is,' she cried.

Liza was at the front door before the others had risen from their chairs.

'Er—hadn't we better let 'em get over the first part first?' said Alec.

'Yes, but we mustn't give them too long or Daddy will be devastated,' said Ursula.

When they came out they found Liza seated beside Adam in the car. She was holding his hand. His air of patient kindness hardly justified her bearing of a radiant, joyful bride.

When the young people appeared Adam slowly slid out of the driver's seat and planted his feet firmly on the drive. He was six foot four, heavily built with a round, red, unlined face. His glance was slow and direct.

'Hallo, Ursula,' he said and kissed her affectionately. He turned a slow amused gaze on to the three young men.

'You seem to have a regiment of followers,' he said. He was like a blood-hound arriving in a kennel of small but more meticulous house dogs.

'I'm full of sex-appeal,' said Ursula. 'These are the two Aussies. Mr. Alec Woodforde, I believe, you know.'

'Hallo, Alec,' said Adam. 'Where's your father?'

'He's healing the sick,' said Alec. 'But I think he's dining here to-night.'

'Good!' said Adam.

Liza, still seated in the car, watched this scene with a happy wistfulness, then seeming to realize that Adam had already left her side, she got out and took his arm.

'Come and see the house,' she said. 'Or will you have tea first?'

'Tea first,' said Adam. 'Then we can see the house at leisure.'

'All right,' said Liza, slightly disappointed that he was not more eager and at once automatically voicing the fact in a mild reproach. 'You might have sent us some grouse,' she said.

'There are some in the back of the car,' said Adam. 'They ought to be cooked to-night.'

'Er—good-bye, Lady Elizabeth,' said Wilfred awkwardly as the Woodfordes began to go indoors.

Liza turned.

'Oh, good-bye,' she said. 'Aren't you coming in to tea?'

'I'm afraid we can't, thank you very much. We have our great-aunt Plumbridge staying with us, and a whole crowd of people.'

'Plumbridge of Plumbridge?' Adam asked.

'Yes,' said Wilfred, smirking modestly.

'I went genealogical in Scotland,' said Adam. 'Couldn't help myself.'

'Well, come in some time,' said Liza with careless kindness.

'Thank you very much. You're coming to our picnic to-morrow, aren't you?'

'Oh, yes. Is it to-morrow? That'll be amusing. Who's going to it?'

'Everybody,' said Wilfred.

'Everybody!' Liza laughed and drew Adam indoors. She was rather pleased. At the picnic she could advertise to the neighbourhood that she had Adam back again.

Alec looked at Wilfred.

'Shall I come with you?' he asked diffidently.

'Of course,' said Christopher.

Ursula made faces at Alec.

'You mustn't go,' she whispered as Adam and Liza were still in the hall. 'You must stay here and diffuse the intensity. Good-bye, my sunburst, my golden bull,' she said to Christopher, and kissed him shamelessly. 'Duty, alas, comes before pleasure. We may sneak over after tea.'

After tea Liza and Adam, followed by Ursula and Alec, went in a procession round the house and garden for Adam to inspect it. His whole attitude was that of an inspector, though Liza pretended it was that of a prodigal husband returned to the bosom of his family. His money had paid for this place, and as a business man he had come down to see how it had been spent.

Adam's only comment was an appreciation of one of the bedrooms. He smiled at the rather excessive quaintness of the rock-garden.

'How do you like it?' he asked Ursula.

'I think it's all very sweet,' said Ursula.

'And what do you think?' he said to Alec.

'I think it's an absolutely lovely house,' said Alec. 'I think Aunt Liza's awfully clever to have arranged it, especially when she had Rosie to cope with.'

'You see, Adam, I'm not such a fool as you think,' said Liza.

Adam said: 'I never thought you a fool, Liza. I

P

always said you were too damn clever for me. I'm the mug.' He smiled ironically. Liza winced.

After the inspection she took him for a walk. They disappeared arm-in-arm round the bend of the drive.

'I know Mummy will overdo it,' sighed Ursula. 'My mother has eaten sour grapes and my father's teeth are set on edge. Let us go over to the Hall in search of our respective loves.'

'What d' you mean?' said Alec, trying to appear mystified.

'Won't Carola be there?'

His face cleared.

'I don't know,' he said, smiling indifferently.

. . . . .

At dinner the sense of Adam's being an inspector, the lord of the vineyard, was more perceptible. The propriety of the household was increased. Adam was like a weighty motif introduced into a flimsy pattern, giving it coherence and order but spoiling its delicacy. The *ménage* at Clovermead when Liza was alone was graceful but erratic. There could be nothing erratic about an establishment over which Adam even temporarily presided. The servants in the shadows beyond the table seemed more self-consciously deft and attentive than usual.

There were only the five Woodfordes at dinner, Tom and Alec in addition to the household. Adam talked non-committal politics to Tom most of the time. Ursula's quips were infrequent. Alec, receiving distracted replies, gave up trying to talk to Liza, who sat in a state of obvious tension, sending away most of her food untouched. Her loss of appetite began with the grouse. This inoffensive and succulent bird appeared to her the symbol of Adam's infidelity.

'But you said you wanted grouse, Mummy,' said Ursula.

'They're too high,' said Liza.

'They were only shot on Wednesday,' said Adam mildly.

Tom looked thoughtfully from his brother to Liza. The conditions of the room were jangled and askew. Liza he knew was wondering where Adam would sleep that night, and by her anxiety making it impossible that he should sleep elsewhere than in his own room. Adam was bored and trying to conceal the fact with this conventional political talk.

When Liza and Ursula had left the dining-room, Adam said:

'I hate this damned house.'

'Liza doesn't like it much either,' said Tom.

'Then why did she build it? It cost enough.'

Tom could think of no answer but the true one, so he remained silent.

'Alec,' said Adam, 'do you mind joining the ladies? The request has no equivocal intention.' He smiled dryly.

Alec laughed politely and went to the drawing-room.

Adam sipped his port moodily.

'How much duty d'you think a man owes to his family?' he asked.

'My family makes so little demand on me that I'm hardly an authority,' said Tom.

'But you go in for moral speculation. I don't. It bores me as a rule, but sometimes there's a use for it.'

'I suppose one is only obliged to fulfil the obligations to which one has committed oneself.'

'The devil is to know what one is committed to when one marries. A young man commits himself to cherish a young girl. But twenty years later she is not that young girl. He has committed himself to cherish a middle-aged vixen possibly, or a blowsy barmaid, or at best a stranger. He is not the same young man, either. Two strangers are tied to each other.'

'They may grow together,' said Tom.

'They may, and they may grow apart. A woman expects too much of a man. He gives her the best years of his life. He slaves all day to keep her in luxury while she goes off and amuses herself. He has to clothe and educate her children, which she insists are her children as she had the bearing of them. A wife and family are simply a drain on one's patience and energy. A man's life is work and meeting his wife's bills.'

'That is only so in a certain class.'

'It is so in my class. The class of the rich man who works. If I were of Liza's class—the idle, sponging, poor-rich, we might hit it off better—but I despise that class. Well, what d'you think a man owes his wife?'

'It's impossible to say. It depends on those thousand

subtle ties of relationship which have been built up over a period of years.'

'I'm afraid I'm not much good at subtleties,' said Adam. 'All I know is this. I have given twenty years to the support and consideration of my family. I'm fond of Ursula, and of Liza, too, in a way; I'm prepared to continue to meet their bills and to give them a little of my society, for what it's worth. But I'm not prepared to give them my body and soul, I've grown apart into a different being, you see. I thought you understood this sort of thing.'

'I do understand that.'

'Well, what d'you advise?'

'D'you want me to give advice about yourself and Liza?'

'That's what I'm asking.'

'It's too great a responsibility.'

'You needn't worry. I don't say that I'll follow it.'

'You see, I know Liza's point of view, too.'

'I wish to God I did.'

'You could ask her.'

'She always turns it into an emotional scene,' Adam said gloomily. 'She accuses me of being cold. I prefer to discuss an important matter coldly. She wants to be heated so that reason can be lost in recriminations, dramatic speeches, and reconciliations.'

'Then you know Liza's point of view.'

'I don't care for that sort of life,' said Adam.

'It is really best in the long run to be frank,' said Tom. 'That is the only advice I can give.'

'If I were frank I should say this to Liza. I quite like you when you 're sensible and I am prepared to spend a certain amount of time with you if you don't make emotional scenes. But I won't spend my whole life with you. I have other interests which I can't neglect or I shall be stifled and bored. I am willing to let you spend most of my money, but, to be frank, you can't satisfy me completely. Why can't we make the best of a bad job and continue on those lines? I leave you free to follow your own life and we may be quite good friends. Don't you think that 's fair?'

'It may be fair but you know what Liza would say.'

'She 'd throw the plates about, eh?'

'I 'm afraid she would,' said Tom. 'You see, she has no life of her own to follow.'

'Why can't she make one?'

'She has no centre of her own on which to build one. It 's much easier for a man of fifty to build his own life, than for a woman of forty-five.'

'It 's the devil,' growled Adam, and glared like a morose, mammoth baby at the electric candles.

'It seems odd to me,' said Tom thoughtfully after a silence, 'that when a man feels imprisoned by association with one woman, he nearly always tries to release himself by making a fresh tie.'

'A man's judgment is more sound at fifty than at twenty-five,' said Adam curtly, and pushed back his chair. He led the way into the drawing-room.

Liza was walking up and down the room, smoking feverishly. Ursula, with Alec beside her, was tinkling

at the piano.   Adam made an effort to give an air of
conventional normality to the evening, and said:

'Why don't you sing something, Ursula?'

Liza burst out:

'I can't stand songs at the piano.   It's too Victorian.'

'Oh, Mummy, you know I have a sweet little voice,'
said Ursula.   'I'm a great entertainer.'

'I sometimes think you'd make a good barmaid,' said
Liza viciously.

'Well, Mummy, you'd empty any bar in five minutes.'

Liza looked at Ursula in amazement, then she put her
handkerchief to her nose and walked out of the room.

Adam looked after her, frowning.

'You shouldn't have said that, Ursula,' he grumbled.
'Your mother's not in a state to stand it.'

'Well, why should Mummy be the only one allowed to
scatter piercing shafts?   She exploits her own temperament.'

Adam stood hesitating.   'I'm sorry, Tom,' he said,
and went out after Liza.   They heard him go upstairs,
and soon voices came from the bedroom above.

'This evening is fraught with frigidity,' said Ursula.
'Would I might be hanged,' she sang.

A message came for Tom to go to a patient.

'You are in luck, Uncle Tom,' said Ursula.   'I wish
I had a patient to go to.'

'You seem to be the most frigid,' said Alec, when his
father had gone.

'Oh, no.   I am merely cool.   Sang-froid and frigidity
are not the same thing.'

Christopher and Wilfred came in.

'Hallo, Aussies,' said Ursula. 'What have you done with your great-aunt?'

'They're all playing bridge,' said Wilfred, 'except Pearl Smyth-Collins, who is sitting by herself looking sour and smart, so we left her.'

'Pearl Smyth-Collins! What a name! I'm so glad you left her. Oh, Sunburst'—she clung to Christopher—'I'm having such a shattering time.'

'What's up?' asked Christopher.

'The crisis in the crucible,' said Ursula. 'Hark!'

From upstairs came Liza's voice raised in a long stream of indistinguishable abuse and pleading. At intervals there was a muffled reply from Adam.

'Mummy is being the aristocratic fish-wife, or a great French comedienne.'

Ursula stood in the middle of the floor and acted a lover's quarrel in fluent French. Her bird-like eyes snapped, and she stamped her tiny feet.

Alec laughed uneasily. Christopher and Wilfred smiled in a puzzled fashion.

'Oh, well!' said Ursula wearily. 'If the aged will destroy themselves, they may as well get on with it. All I ask is that me and my boy-friend may be saved from the wreckage.'

'Are we to be destroyed with the aged?' asked Alec, indicating himself and Wilfred.

'Well, you're a nice pair of nice boys,' said Ursula, 'and I shouldn't like to see you destroyed, even if you are two of the two million superfluous pansies.'

'You've got me all wrong,' said Alec indignantly. 'People don't understand ordinary friendliness nowadays. They expect you to be either cold or vicious.'

From upstairs came the sound of breaking glass. Ursula turned her head upwards.

'That will be Mummy's tooth-glass, or it may be the Copenhagen faun from the mantelpiece. When Mummy breaks the china it means that Daddy's logic has been too much for her. Come, Love, let us leave this House of Sin, and go and look at the moon. For men are admitted to heaven, not because they have curbed their passions or have no passions, but because they have cultivated their understanding. Mummy will not cultivate her understanding and she remains in hell. I am sorry, Wilfie, that you have come to such a disorderly house, but you have your little playmate.'

Ursula and Christopher disappeared through the french window into the garden.

Alec looked at Wilfred with a troubled smile.

'Isn't this awful?' he said. 'This house is a sort of comic hell.'

Upstairs the voices had ceased. They heard Adam come down and go into the library across the hall, closing the door behind him.

'What shall we do?' said Wilfred. 'Shall we go and look for Daisy?'

'No; I'm tired of sex. I want love.'

'What d'you mean?'

'You want to cultivate your understanding,' said Alec.

CHAPTER XI

THE SHEPHERD OF ADMETUS

BEATRICE had taken the opportunity of Aunt Albania's
visit to have a small house-party. Aunt Albania had
brought a great-niece called Myrtle Swan, whom every-
body called, for some occult reason, 'Luxurious Mrs.
Leo,' generally shortened to 'Mrs. Leo' or 'Leo.'
Asked to meet them were Mr. and Mrs. Stock, and
Lady Smyth-Collins with her daughter Pearl, all from
Melbourne, and Miss Wallace, an old friend of the
Plumbridges who had lived in England for thirty years,
but who was originally Australian.

Wilfred was very pleased about the party, even
though Pearl Smyth-Collins was so sour. He thought
that the Hall for the week-end was just what a country
house should be like, full of polite chatter and well-
dressed women. He was anxious that local society
should meet Aunt Albania and the other visitors, who
were the cream of Melbourne society, so he was delighted at the prospect of the picnic. He felt that it
would be a witness both of Westlake distinction and
Australian civilization. It would be hard for Rosie
to patronize Aunt Albania.

Actually it was hard to control Aunt Albania in any
way. Aunt Albania felt that having reached eighty-

two in full possession of her faculties she was justified in being a 'character,' and in giving people something to remember her by. Experience had taught her the source of every human motive, whether a kind action came from the heart or from the brain. She did not take into account that those under eighty who are still in the process of forming their characters are often obliged to direct their good actions from the brain, otherwise they would not be performed at all. The result was that she was often agreeable to those who were selfish and impatient with her, as she was sure that they were sincere, but might deliver some unexpected blow at the considerate. Wilfred, so pleased to have her and so courteous, she was sure must be a humbug, as he was in a way, as his appreciation of her in its first stages, was more social than affectionate.

She required very little sleep. Also she was a little deaf. She awoke at half-past five in the morning. When she had had her cold bath and made her own tea on the small spirit lamp with which she travelled, she was obliged to fill in some hours till breakfast at nine o'clock. At Plumbridge she walked in the garden, wrote a few letters, and then she discovered the wireless. It was in the drawing-room directly under Pearl Smyth-Collins's bedroom. Pearl and the rest of the household spent the hour before their tea arrived with their heads beneath the bedclothes trying to shut out negroid music from Radio Normandie. Miss Plumbridge, having been born in this house, saw no reason not to behave as she chose. Besides, she could not help appreciating that this sort of thing sustained the general interest in her personality.

After two musical mornings, Pearl at bedtime detached the wireless controls, and hid them under the boule clock on the mantelpiece. Miss Plumbridge, failing to find them, went to every bedroom, including the Stocks' and Lady Smyth-Collins's, to demand who had taken them. Incidents of this kind were frequent in her entourage and added considerably to its gaiety.

The other guests were also in a lesser degree 'characters.'

'Snobbery and Lust,' Mr. Hodsall confided to Wilfred in a moment of depression, 'are the two mainsprings of human activity. Man wishes either to improve or to enjoy himself. In the converted they become aspiration and love, but my parishioners are not yet converted.'

The guests at the Hall, on the other hand, were in various degrees of conversion, and being, therefore, unfamiliar to the people of Plumbridge they irritated rather than impressed them. Rosie, Major Hinde, Babs Oakes, and Mrs. Hodsall all knew exactly their position in the world, and had no hopes of bettering it to any appreciable extent. Their snobbery was more critical and exclusive. But the cream of Melbourne society had no idea of its position in the European world. It was still bent on improvement and had an optimistic assurance which maddened those who had accepted the inevitable limitations of their walk of life.

Miss Plumbridge's assurance they accepted because she was old, formidable, and indistinguishable from any gentlewoman of position.

Mr. and Mrs. Stock were the main source of trouble. They both represented appetite, and Mrs. Stock was only faintly concerned with improvement. They were enormously rich. They had uncles and brothers and cousins who were all enormously rich. In Melbourne their name produced the same impression as Rothschild in Europe. They were accustomed to the kind of respect which dukes receive, and had not bothered to improve their naturally rather nasal accents nor to polish their manners. They were good-natured but had never given away a penny except for a certain return in publicity.

Mr. Stock, though he had been rich all his life, was like a nice, but cautious, butcher's boy, who has just had a rise in wages. He was very appreciative of the Hall, and naïvely confidential with Rosie.

'I thought I might buy one of these old places,' he said, 'but I expect the climate's a bit dirty in the winter, though there'd be hunting, of course. And I suppose the gentry about are a bit stiff, eh? Mrs. Westlake's one of your local nobs, isn't she? I didn't know her in Melbourne, but I met her sister-in-law on the ship.'

And yet, in spite of this surface vulgarity, his manners were excellent, and he did as a matter of course all the 'right things.' He played polo, he hunted, he stayed at Claridge's, he called two peers, ex-governors, by their Christian names. Rosie was confused beyond endurance.

Mrs. Stock was equally strange. She was like a plump fairy or some exotic fruit. Her eyelids were blue, her lips vermilion, her fat powdered neck festooned with pearls. On every possible occasion she dressed as for a garden party or a ball, in white lace. Her head was a halo of golden curls. She talked exclusively of horses and her stud groom.

Lady Smyth-Collins, on the other hand, was more concerned with improvement. She was the widow of a Melbourne doctor who had been knighted on a royal visit. Lady Smyth-Collins, surprised but gratified to find herself with a title, determined to live up to it. Mr. Stock did the 'right things' and lived expensively because he enjoyed that sort of life, Lady Smyth-Collins did the 'right things' as a religious duty. She felt that she had been called to the rank and vocation of a knight's widow. She bought her tweeds and went to Scotland in August as a devout Roman Catholic might buy a scapula and go on a pilgrimage. She had taken a small flat in Pont Street, until she had presented Pearl, a pretty but dreary little vixen, rendered unattractive by her perpetual fear of boredom, and by the suspicion that she might be led to associate with someone who was not 'smart.'

On the last occasion when Lady Smyth-Collins had returned to Melbourne from her biennial trip to England, she had been interviewed and asked her opinion of the trend of affairs in Europe. At the time there had been a string of assassinations and a first-class war seemed imminent. Lady Smyth-Collins said: 'I noticed at the Royal Garden Party that hats were inclined to be smaller and worn higher than last year. People are dining later, too, I think. The ballet is still fashionable. In furniture, there is the tendency to use pale colours, off-white and oatmeal. I am having my drawing-room at Willa-Wonga redecorated in oatmeal and coral.'

Myrtle Swan, the niece whom they called 'Mrs. Leo,' was in the thirties. She had an air of indolent charm. If not actually beautiful, her looks were in the tradition of beauty, as distinct from ordinary prettiness. She had the Leonardo type of face and suggested the Bacchus in the Louvre, only more frank and kind. She looked after Aunt Albania with a careless but efficient amiability, and enjoyed what came her way without seeking enjoyment. She was universally popular except with her brother-in-law and his family. He was the socially ambitious son of a wholesale pork butcher in Leeds, who could not bear the disgrace of having Australian connections. She was the exception to Mr. Hodsall's generalization, being untouched either by snobbery or aspiration.

Miss Wallace, unlike these people, was completely converted. From infancy she had loved the highest immediately it was visible to her. From Melbourne University she went to Girton, and finally won a European reputation as a classical scholar. But she was even more venerated by the intelligent for her passion for international justice. From 1914 onwards hers had been one of the voices crying in the wilderness. She spent herself like a flame. During the War she went through Switzerland into Germany to try to cherish a spark of good feeling amid the volumes of hate, and to use her influential friendships to improve the conditions of prisoners. In England stalking with hot contempt past the sentries she brought comfort to the German prisoners. Furious questions about her activities were asked in the House of Commons, and she only miraculously escaped imprisonment. Through the post-War years she raised her passionate voice against every piece of diplomatic folly, and now when all the results she had prophesied had come to pass, she still clung to her faith that, to quote the conclusion of her most celebrated book, 'all things come to beauty in the end.' She was, perhaps, the most distinguished citizen that Australia had produced. Mrs. Stock had never heard of her.

These people, with the Westlakes, the Woodfordes, Rosie, the Hodsalls, Babs Oakes, and Major Hinde, assemble with a small fleet of cars outside the Hall to set out for the picnic.

It was Aunt Albania who had brought Beatrice up to scratch about the picnic. When she was a girl they used to have lovely picnics to Heidelberg (Victoria) and to Fern Tree Gully. They drove out in wagonettes and some of the party rode. They sat about under eucalyptus trees and searched for a sweetish white stuff which fell in fragments from the trees, and which they called manna. They grilled chops held on forked sticks over a wood fire. They adventured into the delicious coolness of the fern gullies, where clear brown streams gurgled, and the air was aromatic with sassafras leaves, and where snakes were dangerous under the mossy logs and among the delicate maidenhair. What occasions of gossip and gallantry were these picnics! Driving home along the dusty white roads, with the sun a lurid

orange in the west, they sang. In these days the society
of Melbourne was composed of simple gentlefolk who
were not afraid to be happy. Aunt Albania for the last
sixty years on every possible occasion had arranged or
demanded a picnic. She demanded one now. She
wanted it to be a big picnic, a real Australian picnic
with grilled chops. The house-party was pleased, and
the local people interested and amused at the idea of
the picnic.

To the Hodsalls' relief Teddy refused to go. They
thought that under this Australian stimulus she might
indulge in appalling jollities. She might try and 'jolly
up' Miss Plumbridge or Lady Elizabeth. From a sense
of hospitality they pressed her half-heartedly, but she
became sulkily obstinate at the very suggestion.

'There will be so many of your countrymen there.
I should have thought you would like to meet them,'
said Mrs. Hodsall.

'I've got a bit of a headache. That's what it is,'
said Teddy confidingly. 'Don't you worry about me,
dear. I'll go to bed early.'

She had been behaving rather strangely for the last
few days. She seemed to be waiting anxiously for some
tidings. She read the obituary notices in *The Times*
first thing every morning, but took no interest in any
other news. She was always first down to breakfast.
Once Mrs. Hodsall came in and found her examining
the vicar's letters. On another occasion she opened a
letter addressed to her sister-in-law, and explained it as
absent-mindedness, owing to her being accustomed to

Q

open all letters addressed to 'Mrs. Hodsall.' She said she was waiting to hear from her relatives in Wales.

'I think there's something queer about that woman,' said Mrs. Hodsall to her husband. 'Why won't she come to the picnic?'

'She probably doesn't want to meet those other Australians. They're of a different class.'

'I thought all Australians were the same.'

'Evidently they're not. Why should they be, any more than all English or all Scots?'

'D'you think she's really Roly's widow?'

'She has his signet ring and knows a good deal about us. Besides, whoever, not being Roly's widow, would want to impersonate her?'

'That woman might. I shall nail her down in the morning.'

'I imagine it will be like trying to nail down a peculiarly slippery eel.'

However, by the morning Mrs. Hodsall's opportunity of nailing down had fled.

The picnic was held on the downs above Southwick, near a place where there was a long glade of yews, which were unique in their gnarled antiquity. They were supposed to mark the burial ground of British kings, and to have been the scene of Druidic rites and sacrifices.

The boys arranged that the drive to the picnic should be in the form of a treasure hunt. Aunt Albania was thrilled at the idea of this. Pearl Smyth-Collins was equivalently bored. She thought any amusement that was not paid for in hard cash childish and unworthy of her attention. She had slightly affected Mrs. Leo with her distaste for the expedition. They were to drive Aunt Albania in her car, but at the last minute they said they did not want to go.

There was a little scene on the drive outside the Hall, while Aunt Albania nodded her head for a moment, rather like an obstinate pony, and then peremptorily ordered them into the car.

'What a marvellous old lady!' Rosie said to Wilfred. 'Is she Austwalian, too?'

'Yes, she is,' said Wilfred with satisfaction.

'But somethin' else by owigin, I suppose?' said Rosie.

'Don't you think she's as common as we are?' asked Wilfred engagingly.

Every one standing about heard this remark. There was a startled moment of silence. Then Mr. Stock gave a huge guffaw. The others smiled, except Aelred Rounsefell, Matty, and Lady Smyth-Collins, who looked horrified. Rosie went to pieces.

The treasure hunt was inclined to be a frost. Rosie did not recover her aplomb in time to enter into the spirit of the thing. Aelred in a mood of lofty contempt for the Philistines drove straight to the picnic ground, Liza and Adam did the same, being in no mood for light-hearted puerilities. Mrs. Leo would not drive fast enough to satisfy Aunt Albania, who liked to take her corners at sixty, while Pearl only got out of the car to look for clues under protest. Christopher, with Ursula beside him, and with Alec and Wilfred in the back seat of the 'gin-palace,' drove wildly about the countryside encouraging the indifferent competitors. Beatrice arrived first, and the prize was given to Lady Smyth-Collins who thought this was done out of respect for her position.

Aunt Albania arrived second. Mrs. Leo stayed to do something to the car. Pearl went on, leaving Aunt Albania to make her own way up the rough hillside. When Pearl arrived at the picnic ground she stood apart, looking hostile with distaste both at the landscape and the figures, at Christopher and Wilfred because they were so young and had lived in Kew (Victoria) instead of in Toorak, and at Alec and the Hodsalls because they were not rich.

Actually the landscape was lovely. Westward the long harbour stretched in a silver haze from Millnore to Southwick. To the north the wooded hills slept peacefully in the afternoon sun. Immediately below them were the twisted, ancient yews.

There was a sense of excitement between the three boys. They were exhilarated by their rather reckless driving and by their sense of being on top of the world, by the high, clean air. They shouted and chased each other. Alec seemed the most full of animal spirits. He seized Christopher's legs and brought him down, saying: 'You magnificent creature, I must engage you in battle.'

Christopher, to Wilfred's surprise, instead of being livid at this assault responded in the same spirit. Alec at last, purple and panting, stood up and combed his ruffled hair.

'I'm absolutely gloriously happy,' he cried. 'I could drink four gallons of old and mild.'

He caught sight of Aunt Albania, toiling alone up the steep hill from her car, and tore down to help her.

Pearl Smyth-Collins stood apart feeling entirely contaminated by this lack of sophistication.

'That girl would blight any entertainment,' Beatrice muttered to Matty.

Beatrice had spread herself on the picnic. She was becoming accustomed to being rich. She did not want to be vulgar but she found it difficult to spend her income. She was also rather irritated by Aunt Albania because she was inclined to ignore the fact that Plumbridge was Beatrice's house. Aunt Albania wanted the picnic to be a simple meal of grilled chops and sandwiches and tea made in a 'billy.' Beatrice sent on the cook and two men in the luggage van with trestle-tables, canvas stools, glass, silver, and champagne in ice-buckets.

'How marvellous!' cried Rosie. 'I think it's so wonderful the way Austwalians are never afwaid of bein' lavish. We English would never dweam of makin' a show like this.'

'I suppose you have meaner forms of vulgarity,' Wilfred muttered, but fortunately this time no one heard him.

The table was a small glittering patch under the vast sky. 'How perfectly lovely to dine up here,' exclaimed Miss Wallace. 'It is like dining on Olympus.'

Mrs. Stock was used to a great deal of attention.

If she were not receiving enough she would blandly cut across the general conversation with some reference to her own affairs. She heard Miss Wallace mention Abyssinia to Mr. Hodsall. The pleasant chatter was suddenly silenced by her loud clear voice announcing: 'I have a horse called Ethiopian. I don't want to change his name because it's unlucky. But I don't think he'll have any luck with a name like that.'

'I'd call him Mussolini,' suggested Aelred ironically.

Mrs. Stock laughed comfortably.

'That's an idea,' she said.

'I wouldn't give even an animal that name,' said Miss Wallace.

'Well, it's a better name than Haile Selassie,' said Mrs. Stock. 'He had no luck.'

'He's saved his soul which is more than we have done,' Miss Wallace said warmly.

Aunt Albania nodded her head. 'In Australia——' she began. She was worried because the chops had not been grilled over a wood fire on the spot.

'You wouldn't have us go to war for Abyssinia,' said Mr. Stock tolerantly.

'I would have the strong protect the weak when their cause is just.'

'It's the business of the Government to look after the interests of British people, not after a crowd of niggers.'

'It's their function to look to the honour of the British people as well. Our honour is of even greater value than our material interests.'

'Oh, that's idealism!' He waved his hand as if someone had offered him a cheap cigar.

'If there were no idealism we'd still be in the dark ages. The idealists may run a hundred years ahead of the bulk of the people, but they drag them along somehow.'

'If we'd gone to war with Italy in the autumn, Germany would have taken the opportunity to seize Austria.'

'That is not really so. I have just come from Germany.'

'That's a country I shall never visit,' said Lady Smyth-Collins firmly.

'You mean because of their treatment of the Jews. I know a great many people let that blind them to the justice of Germany's claims. In fact, I know some people who refuse to visit Germany for fear of being influenced in her favour.'

'I wouldn't let a few massacred Jews worry me,' said Mrs. Stock. 'A Jew once sold me a horse with a faked pedigree.'

'I'm not thinking of the Jews. I was thinking of the War,' said Lady Smyth-Collins.

'Oh, you want to forget that,' said Mrs. Stock. 'The French are no better than the Germans. They're half Communists.'

'I think that politically the French are a mean-natured people,' said Miss Wallace.

'Yes; that is true,' conceded Lady Smyth-Collins. 'D'you know that sixty thousand Australians were killed, fighting for France in the War, but when I stayed at Grasse with Madame du Quesnoy, not one of her neighbours, some of whom had delightful houses, asked me to afternoon tea.'

Even Mrs. Stock was rendered speechless by this curious assessment of comparative value.

'You don't always get good value for your money,' complained Aunt Albania. She was still thinking about the chops and had not fully taken in Lady Smyth-Collins's remark.

Alec said: 'I think you ought to get a jolly good dinner for sixty thousand lives.'

Tom frowned at him down the table.

Mr. Hodsall said diffidently to Miss Wallace:

'Do you agree that any good can come out of a war?'

'You can't separate the means from the end, can you?' Sylvia appealed to Miss Wallace.

'I think not,' said Miss Wallace. 'In fact, I'm certain you can't. One's indignation at a brutal policy at times inclines one to go to war. The trouble is that in any war, however just the cause, every force of evil, of murderous hatred and lies, is released and can't easily be controlled again. And the peace is dictated not by the men who might first have been prompted by the cause of justice, but by the adventurous politicians who have superseded them, and who express the revengeful passions of the people, and so the peace terms are the certain seeds of another war.'

Mr. Stock did not much like this argument.

'You want to keep out of war because it's bad for

business. That's sufficient reason,' he said with an air of finality. Adam, with the freemasonry between rich men, nodded agreement with him.

Miss Wallace's fine fingers crumbled her bread. Her eyes flamed.

'That is a view I entirely repudiate,' she said. 'What is business for which every value, human and divine, must be destroyed? One sees small boys standing all day holding placards at the doors of shops. Business keeps them there and throws them out unemployed when they reach the age for insurance. Business keeps some men sweating harder every day in terror of losing their jobs while a million others rot in the streets. Business would have a war if it paid. It would allow any human agony if it paid. Business forces the destruction of vast supplies of foodstuff while half the people in the world are underfed. And now it lifts its filthy head unashamed. Oscar Wilde said that hypocrisy is the tribute that vice pays to virtue. Nowadays virtue does not even have that tribute. If I were a Christian I should say that the devil is openly worshipped. A young man said to me the other day: "The rate of exchange is the thermometer of our credit abroad." That was the only sort of credit he could recognize.'

'I quite agree,' said Liza. 'The only effect of efficient business is to allow the scum to rise to the top.'

Adam looked wretchedly at his plate. So did Lady Smyth-Collins.

She was horrified. She thought she was associating with the upper classes. She had not dreamed that

any one would have the bad taste to express an idea—
worse still to mention Oscar Wilde—and, incredibly
bewildering, to say: 'If I were a Christian.'

'Hooray, I'm a Communist,' cried Alec. 'I have to
mix with the working-man. I know what he feels when
he realizes that five-sixths of his effort is to put money
into someone else's pocket. He has the sense to see it
now, and the present system can't last. There'll be a
terrific smash-up soon, and then there'll be a brave
new world.'

'Then you'd better drink up your champagne while
you've got it,' said Adam.

Every one laughed. Alec looked a little confused.

'If I were free I'd go and fight for the Spanish
Government,' he said.

'And I should certainly fight for the patriots,' said
Mr. Stock.

'Well, you can, can't you?' said Alec. 'You are free,
I mean.'

Mr. Stock grunted.

'That's ridiculous,' he said.

Miss Wallace looked with glowing approval at Alec.
Agreement in battle lighted a kind of love between
them.

'But why have the smash-up?' she asked him. 'With
good will the brave new world could come without
misery and the destruction of our cultural heritage.'

'Yes, that's why I'm not a Communist,' said Wilfred.

'A man must consider his own interest,' said Adam
quietly.

'That's only natural,' said Mr. Stock, aggrieved.

'If one assumes that it is natural to be ruthless and evil one will be so. But it is no longer even self-interest. As this young man says, Big Business will destroy itself through its own short-sighted greed. If the haves will recognize their common humanity with the have-nots you can avoid the hell of civil war. It only needs good will. But whatever happens the future is with the people,' Miss Wallace concluded.

'And what will happen to the aristocracy?' asked Lady Smyth-Collins.

'There's no aristocracy left,' said Liza. 'We've all become Jews at heart.'

Lady Smyth-Collins was confused and upset by this remark, especially coming from Liza. If one of the ancient and established aristocracy said that there was no aristocracy, where did she, Lady Smyth-Collins, come in?

Beatrice did not enjoy this conversation much. She sat silent at the end of the table, occasionally giving instructions to a servant. At any rate, even if people were angry, they weren't bored, so the picnic could hardly be accounted a failure.

'That's right,' said Mrs. Stock. 'They don't cut much ice nowadays. The last two Governors of Victoria were both lords and both quite poor, really. They used to borrow Willy's polo ponies. Still, they've been useful to us over here.'

'I was very pleased to lend Jack my ponies,' said Mr. Stock with gruff good nature.

'You'd give away your last sixpence,' said his wife, stating a wild improbability.

But the homely good nature of the Stocks was powerless to check the Spanish conflagration which was raging between Major Hinde and the Rounsefells at the other end of the table, with Alec and Ursula and Wilfred as chorus.

A young bank clerk from Southwick had brought his girl out to the yews on the back of his motor bicycle. He was surprised and hardly pleased to see the assortment of expensive cars standing about rather drunkenly on the uneven ground. He left his motor bicycle a little apart from them, and with his arm round the girl began to walk up the hill. Up there under the high evening sky he intended to initiate her into the mysteries of love. But instead of solitude he came upon the astonishing sight of Beatrice's picnic, a large number of people dining at a table as if they had been transported there on a magic carpet, a tiny bright blot of sophistication on the natural majesty of the downs. The diners were all talking at the tops of their voices. Heated affirmations and shouts of derisive laughter came to him across the stretch of green. Isolated words rose above the clamour—Gibraltar—Moors—Franco—Blum—and a clear voice saying: 'They exhibited the corpses of six nuns.'

The young bank clerk stared in incredulous disgust.

'Are they bats?' he demanded.

He led his girl down the hill again, and asked Liza's

chauffeur what the show was. He was told that an
Australian lady was having a picnic.

His sense of propriety was outraged. It was against
nature to sit at a dinner-table on the top of the downs.

His moral indignation drove out his gallant intention
so that he had to take his girl chastely home, which made
him very angry. He was most violent against Australia
in the next test matches, and whenever thereafter he heard
Australians mentioned he said stoutly that they were mad.

The discussion had become so heated that immediately
the party rose from the table it divided into small excited
groups in which people could give vent to those expressions of complete contempt for their opponents which
they did not dare to use to their faces.

Mrs. Stock was most indignant.

'How dare that woman talk to Willy like that?' she
demanded of Lady Smyth-Collins. 'Who is she, anyhow?'

'Her mother was one of the Barretts of Tasmania,'
said Lady Smyth-Collins. 'They are quite well known
in Hobart.'

'They have no money,' said Mrs. Stock contemptuously.

Aunt Albania, distressed at so much disagreement and
at the fact that the chops had been brought out in a
thermos box instead of grilled over a wood fire, was
nodding her head violently.

'Old Mrs. Barrett had a private zoo,' she said re-
miniscently. 'It was full of Tasmanian devils. I think
they're extinct now, but I'm not sure.'

Liza had enjoyed the racket, the destructiveness of

heated argument, and seeing Adam uncomfortable. She
felt sufficiently cheered to come over and ask Mrs.
Stock if she had any tips for the next race meeting and
to compare successes at Goodwood.

Matty apologized profusely to Miss Wallace for sub-
jecting her to such unintellectual contacts.

'One has to make them,' said Miss Wallace. 'It is
no use for the people who think clearly to meet only
each other.'

The Rounsefells did not seem to agree with this.
They stood apart, their sensibility wildly affronted.
Although Major Hinde had most offended them they
blamed Australia and the Australians.

'What a ghastly place Melbourne must be,' said Aelred.
'Look at that woman, just like a cow dressed in pearls.'

'I think a cow dressed in pearls would be rather pretty,'
said Sylvia. 'Let's go and talk to Wallace. How on
earth did she get in with this crowd?'

Sylvia had pretended to Wilfred that she had never
heard of Miss Wallace. Actually she was pleased at
meeting her. They commiserated with her at having
to consort with so many Australians.

'But I am an Australian, too,' said Miss Wallace, 'and
I am proud of my country. There are selfish and stupid
people everywhere—in Australia as well as here. But
the bulk of Australians have simplicity and good will,
and those are two qualities of which Europe is desperately in need.'

'I don't know what people mean by simplicity,' said
Sylvia.

'I mean the acceptance of obvious values,' said Miss
Wallace. 'The acceptance of justice and kindness as
the natural standards of conduct.'

'But I am simple. I accept them,' cried Sylvia.
'Everyone accepts them.'

'Yes; but there is the tendency among too intelligent
people to confuse moral standards with psychological
reactions.'

'Can one be *too* intelligent?' asked Aelred.

'Perhaps I should have said too intellectual. But there
is a sort of aggressive intelligence without humility.'

'Oh, but I loathe humility,' said Sylvia, laughing.
'I hate all that Christian grovelling.'

'Still, it has been an ingredient of some very admirable
characters,' said Miss Wallace.

'Who? Who?' demanded Sylvia. 'I don't believe
that I would admire any character who showed humility.'

Matty, to the Rounsefells' annoyance, drew them away
from Miss Wallace to introduce them to Aunt Albania.

Miss Wallace found herself standing near Adam.

'You are the people who could bring the kingdom of
heaven if you wanted to,' she said. 'You have the power.
Don't you *want* to see people properly fed when there is
food, and living happily instead of tortured in wars?'

Adam lifted an ironic eyebrow.

'Men must live according to their nature,' he said.

'They can make their nature what they will, noble
or base.'

'I'm afraid they haven't the inclination to make it
noble,' said Adam.

'I hate more passionately than any one the Laodiceans,' said Miss Wallace.

The small self-justifying groups gradually wandered off in different directions, some up on to the summit of the downs, others back to the rather sinister glade of yew trees.

Adam gave a brief bow to Miss Wallace, and drew Tom away while Liza was talking to Mrs. Stock.

'This is a rum show,' he said. 'The Australians seem very argumentative.'

'The Rounsefells started it.'

'What d' you think about these intellectuals?' he asked. 'You've more in common with them than I have. What I feel about them is that they never get down to life itself. They look on and criticize, but everything they have and do seems to have been digested a couple of times already. No fresh meat. Sometimes I've tried to read some of those high-brow books that Liza buys and leaves about uncut. It seemed a waste for no one to read 'em. I can't see anything in 'em. D' you think you intellectuals get more out of life than we do —business men like myself?'

'I'm not particularly intellectual,' said Tom.

'You're in sympathy with them. Though you don't look like one. I can't stand 'em myself. But I'd like to know who gets the most out of life.'

'Every one,' said Tom, speaking slowly and rather pedantically, 'must live according to his own nature, as I heard you say just now. Whoever does that is getting the most out of life for himself. The intellectual is nearly always largely feminine. The woman experiences life by being penetrated by life, physically and spiritually. She likes to be touched in the depth of her soul, and to know herself in this way and feel herself revealed. The male wants to remain whole and intact and keep his godhead encased. By chewing at life and love, and digesting it over and over again, the feminine-natured intellectual hopes to come to the revelation of himself. The purely masculine man hates anything that is going to reveal his inner soul, the seat of his power, what Lawrence calls the dark god, or something like that. So he occupies himself with practical things, sport and making money, which do not touch that central being at all. He does not care for religion because then he has to open his inner self to God. When he wants release he takes it in a purely physical way with a woman. The trouble is that being bottled up in so much darkness his godhead often dies altogether, while the soul of the half-feminine intellectual is shrivelled with too much light.'

Adam laughed.

'I'm afraid that is already rather over-chewed for me,' he said.

'I was simply trying to explain what seems to me the difference between two sorts of men,' said Tom.

'Yes. And it shows I must stick to my own sort,' said Adam. 'I see Alec calls himself a Communist. Does he know what it means?'

'I don't know. We don't discuss things much. He lives apart from me.'

R

'What the hell is the use of a family?' said Adam.

Tom murmured something unintelligible.

Adam turned back towards the site of the picnic, where the men had taken down the trestles and were removing the last traces of that festivity.

Liza, evidently in a state of tension, was standing beside Lady Smyth-Collins and giving random replies to her questions about the procedure at Court. Adam joined them. He signed to Tom to occupy Lady Smyth-Collins's attention, and led Liza away. As she turned to follow him she gave a questioning glance at Tom and saw in his eyes a sort of sober pity. She knew that talking to his brother, Adam had come to a decision. She looked round helplessly for some aid, but there were only three groups of strangers strolling about the hillside. She could not make a scene here. She must be the victim of reason. She followed her husband with the dejection of a dog about to be chloroformed.

     •   •   •   •   •

Christopher hated arguments. He did not mind a good row with Wilfred or any other youth, when personal abuse was likely to be succeeded by physical violence. That gave him release from himself. But he hated a conflict of ideas. He said nothing during the arguments at dinner, but the veins showed at his temples and his eyes grew small and angry. He had no means to shine in this sort of scrap. About him Wilfred, Ursula, Alec, and the Rounsefells flung their bright invective, and Wilfred and Ursula were most in agreement.

The quick succession of ideas hurt his mind with the strain to follow them. As far as he could understand them he repudiated them instinctively. Every one except Major Hinde, the Stocks, and Mr. Woodforde seemed to think that some kind of humane Communism was both desirable and inevitable. They were all on the side of the Spanish Government, not that it was particularly humane. But Christopher, if anything, was by sympathy a Fascist. The unity, the ban on intellectual exploration, the beliefs in force, were suited to his temperament. This argument was leading Ursula away from him and aligning her with Wilfred. It was giving Wilfred every advantage, displaying those mental qualities in which Christopher knew himself to be painfully lacking.

By the time they rose from the table he was inarticulate with jealousy. The young people drifted into a group. Wilfred said: 'I don't care if the Spanish Government has committed atrocities. It doesn't affect the argument. People may commit atrocities and yet not affect the original justice of their cause.'

Alec saw Christopher's state of mind, and said: 'Oh, we've had enough of politics. Let's go and look for the bones of ancient Britons among the yew trees.'

Lady Smyth-Collins had brought a shooting-stick which she had left lying about and Alec in idle curiosity had picked it up. He prodded Christopher with the sharp end.

'Come on, you blond beast,' he said. 'Come down where we can't see the wood for the trees.'

Christopher grabbed the stick, and each holding an end they walked down towards the yews. Wilfred, Ursula, and Carola followed them.

Wilfred, when a train of ideas started rushing through his mind, found it impossible to stop. He went on talking to Ursula, his voice raised in excitement. 'All these people talk as if you had no choice beween Communism and the Middle Ages. I don't see why Communism is the holy gospel once for all delivered to the saints. There must be some bad in it and there must be some good. It's bad to destroy our culture, but it's good to give equal opportunity to all people. The two things don't necessarily go together. It's only the people who prefer weak-minded violence to patient intelligence who say that they must.'

Christopher walking with Alec was listening to Wilfred and Ursula. He thought that the reference to weak-minded violence was directed at himself. He wanted to turn round and separate Wilfred and Ursula, whose alert minds were drawing them together, but he was somehow hypnotized by Alec and the presence of Carola. There was something about Alec's spontaneous friendliness which made him ashamed to show the savage streak in his nature.

When they came to the trees Alec let go of his end of the shooting-stick and turned round.

'Do stop politics,' he said, 'and let us play a game.'

'What shall we play?' asked Ursula; 'oranges and lemons or Communists and Nazis?'

'We'll play hide-and-seek.'

'That's too childish.'

'I am childish,' said Alec. 'It's part of my charm. You can all hide and I'll count a hundred.'

They argued a little and then agreed to go and hide.

Christopher was now so angry that he deliberately turned away from Ursula and Wilfred and followed Carola into the yew trees. Carola climbed up into a tree to hide and signed to him to go somewhere else, lest he should be seen and draw attention to her.

'Hurry up,' she whispered.

At this trivial dismissal his sense of being slighted became intolerable. He felt that since the beginning of dinner there had been a conspiracy to ignore him. At one stage in the communistic argument, someone had mentioned Russian materialism. Someone else had said the Russians were the most mystical nation in the world. They angered him by talking of things of which they had no experience. He was inarticulate, but he knew unaccountable surges of love and anger and fear which he thought made him as mystical as any Russian. That first day in the orchard at Plumbridge he had been the subject of some strange force. He could not bear to hear any one highly praised, or to have some unusual quality attributed to another. He thought it was intended as a reflection on himself.

He knew that he was a splendid human specimen. Because Alec paid that tribute to him he had influence with him. But the others, Ursula and Wilfred, used their quick clever minds to belittle his manhood. If Ursula loved him she would not speak to Wilfred. His jealous anger was like a force, ready to burst his veins. He could stand the strain no longer. He must have things clear. At that moment he saw them, standing close together among the dark trees.

Wilfred's mind was still racing on. There was so much more that he had to say to Ursula about the respective merits of Communism and traditional culture, that he could not give attention to the game of hide-and-seek. He went with her into the glade of yews, still talking eagerly but in a subdued tone.

'You do see what I mean, don't you?' he said.

She saw exactly what he meant. She agreed with him almost entirely. She was touched and amused at his eagerness. The air was full of roused feelings, and the discovery of identical views was liable to produce a warmth, a faint transient love between the most improbable people. But there was nothing improbable in a sense of love between Ursula and Wilfred. She touched him with a kindly gesture and impulsively he kissed her hand. It was then that Christopher came upon them.

'Get out,' he said to Wilfred.

'Don't be a fool,' said Wilfred.

Christopher's hand clenched the shooting-stick.

'Will you get out?' he said. He was breathing heavily. It was as if he were holding with great effort something that was likely to burst, and urging someone with laboured breath to release him from the strain.

Wilfred had seen Christopher angry before but never like this. He lost his poise. He tried to control,

as usual, the situation with levity, but that was the one
thing which Christopher could not now endure. There
was a note of fear in Wilfred's voice as he said uncertainly:
'I'm blowed if I'll get out.'

Ursula, too, was startled. She stepped back.

It seemed as if the dissensions of the evening, the
clash of philosophies and interests, were focused here
in one point of passion. Christopher's eyes almost disappeared in their sockets. He lifted the shooting-stick
and brought its metal seat down with all his force on
Wilfred's head. Wilfred bent side-ways only to receive
it on the temple. He fell unconscious to the ground.

For an eternal moment Christopher and Ursula stared
at him lying there.

Ursula looked at Christopher.

The blood had drained from his face. It was growing
dark now under the gloomy trees. Christopher's face
was ghastly against the gnarled blackness of the yews.
All his passion was spent. His eyes held an extreme
anguish, as if his own nature were more than he could
bear. The beauty of his head, of his golden hair above
his pale tortured face, made him appear like some symbolic figure of damnation.

Ursula for the moment forgot Wilfred lying at her feet.
Her indignation was lost in a dreadful pity for Christopher's suffering. She could not speak. The vortex
of emotions in this dark hollow of the trees was beyond
her experience, beyond possibility of expression in words.
Something had been dragged up from the dark centuries of human pain, the deep underlying design, the

current of passion and atonement had flashed to the surface.

Christopher turned and fled. As he ran he flung away the shooting-stick. It struck a tree and fell with a tinkle on to a bottle which had been left by some trippers.

Ursula bent over Wilfred. Lying there unconscious he still had the gawky grace, the angularity, even exaggerated, that would excite the derision of small boys. There was something almost grotesquely gentlemanly about his injured body.

There was a huge bruise and a little blood on the side of his forehead. She called his name and dabbed the bruise with her handkerchief, then realizing that this was useless she ran up out of the glade to find her Uncle Tom.

Tom was up on the site of the picnic, where most of the party were saying good-bye and thanking Beatrice for a pleasant evening.

'Quickly,' cried Ursula, arriving breathless among them. 'Wilfred's had an accident. He's unconscious.'

She stood in the middle of the staring group.

'Where is he?' asked Tom curtly.

'Down in the yews. Hurry.'

Tom bounded off down the slope. The others crowded round Ursula with useless questions. Matty had darted off after Tom.

Someone saw Christopher's car bouncing away at a reckless speed along the grassy road, and said: 'Where's Christopher going?'

'I expect he's gone for a doctor,' said Beatrice.

'Didn't he know Dr. Woodforde was here?' asked Rosie.

'How did it happen?' asked Beatrice.

Ursula looked at the ring of excited inquisitive faces.

'He fell from a tree,' she said slowly.

'Ursula! Ursula!' Tom called from down by the yews. 'Where is he?'

'Oh, can't she hurry?' cried Matty.

Alec knew nothing of all this. He came happily out of the yew glade with Carola and saw Ursula tearing down the hill.

'What's up?' he sang.

'Wilfred!' she called. 'Come and help.'

Tom and Alec carried him to the place where the cars were waiting. Every one had come down the hill and stood about where he was lying unconscious on a rug. Fortunately the van with the food and trestles had not yet left, and there was some ice from the champagne buckets which Tom put on Wilfred's head.

Sylvia talked to Beatrice about concussion, using a good many technical terms. She was eager and interested.

After a while Wilfred regained consciousness. He said: 'Crackers!'

Then he opened his eyes and saw the ring of people staring at him with sympathy or curiosity, and Tom holding the ice on his head.

'You're all right, old man,' said Tom. 'You had a fall.'

'Christopher,' said Wilfred, and closed his eyes again.

Matty and Beatrice exchanged a glance. Tom said: 'I think we 'd better get him home, Mrs. Westlake, as soon as possible, and get him to bed with hot bottles at his feet.'

Ursula sat apart, on the steps of a car. Alec came over to her.

'How did it happen?' he asked. 'He fell from a tree, didn't he?'

'No,' said Ursula. 'Christopher felled him with that shooting-stick.'

'But you told them he fell from a tree.'

'I know. I couldn't give away Christopher to those people—to people like the Stocks. They wouldn't understand.'

'I don't understand, either,' said Alec.

'You would if you had seen Christopher after he had done it. His life is agony to him.'

'But knocking Wilfred senseless! Wilfred of all people. He wouldn't hurt a fly.'

'He threw a butter-dish once at Christopher. He told me so himself. He thought it was funny. Brothers are like that it seems.'

'But I can't understand it. He couldn't have meant to do it. Christopher, I mean. He loves Wilfred, really.' Alec wrinkled his forehead in puzzled distress. 'Where is Christopher now?' he asked.

'He drove away. He looked awful. I think he thought he had killed Wilfred.'

She bit her lip in an effort at self-control.

Alec went back to the group round Wilfred which was parting to allow access to the car.

'Help me in with him,' said Tom.

Alec put his arm under Wilfred's shoulders. 'You'll be all right, Wilf,' he said.

'I've a hell of a headache,' said Wilfred. They settled him in the back of the car, with Matty and Beatrice. As the big car moved slowly away over the bumpy ground Alec kissed his hand to Wilfred, who returned a sickly smile. Mr. Stock looked doubtfully at Alec and then every one, with an air of relief, began to talk cheerfully, except Lady Smyth-Collins, who with considerable vexation was demanding if any one had seen her shooting-stick.

Owing to Wilfred's going in the big car the Stocks were driving Lady Smyth-Collins and Miss Wallace back to the Hall. Long after the other cars had gone Lady Smyth-Collins kept them searching over the twilit downs for her stick. When it was quite dark she gave it up in despair, but she mentioned her loss several times on the way home.

.   .   .   .   .

Lady Smyth-Collins soon had more serious cause for complaint. When the Stocks' car turned into the park they saw that the Hall was a blaze of light. Every light in the house seemed to be turned on and most of the curtains left undrawn.

Tom's car was at the door with Rosie waiting in it.

'I didn't like to go in when they are so wowwied,' she said.

As they came blinking into the Hall they found the rest of the party standing about silent and embarrassed. Matty apparently was on the verge of hysteria, Aunt Albania was nodding her head, while Pearl Smyth-Collins stood apart looking not only sulky but vicious.

Mrs. Stock, who did not notice anything unusual, said: 'Those downs would make a good place for a training stable.

Beatrice said: 'A dreadful thing has happened. A——' —she hesitated—'a burglary. Would you mind going to your rooms and seeing what you have lost?'

'Are the police here?' asked Mr. Stock.

'No,' said Beatrice. 'I haven't rung them up yet.'

'You should let them know at once,' said Mr. Stock sternly. 'It doesn't give them a chance if you delay.'

'Would you just see what you have lost and come back here? Then I shall do whatever you wish.'

'I don't travel with much jewellery, except what I wear,' said Mrs. Stock complacently. She was wearing sufficient—a double row of pearls, an emerald brooch, and some rich-looking rings.

Lady Smyth-Collins had suffered the worst loss, a pair of diamond ear-rings. Miss Wallace's jewellery was more of the decorative but inexpensive type mentioned in the book of Revelation — chrysoprase, carbuncle, and chalcedony. The burglar had bothered to take nothing of hers beyond a gold chain. Aunt Albania, as she had already discovered, had lost only a few old-fashioned gold ornaments. The girls had both lost

their pearl necklaces and Pearl a new brooch from
Cartier which her mother had given her barely a month
ago.

'You really ought to ring up the police at once,' said
Mr. Stock rather crossly, but not as insistently as if he
had lost something himself. Even his dress studs had
escaped, being put away by the footman in last night's
boiled shirt.

'My nephew is the thief,' said Beatrice.

'Nonsense,' said Mrs. Stock sceptically.

'It's an aberration,' said Tom. 'I think we'd better
explain everything, Miss Westlake. Wilfred did not
fall from a tree. Ursula made up that story to protect
Christopher. I knew it was untrue, both from the nature
of the wound and from the fact that there was no tree
close enough to where he was lying. Christopher
felled him with a shooting-stick. He was overcome by
a fit of jealousy. These things happen to young people.
Their passions are intense and they have no perspective.
It is no use blaming them. My niece tells me that
Christopher thought he had killed his brother, which is
why he cleared out. For the time being his emotions
had completely unbalanced his reason.'

'I don't see why we shouldn't ring up the police,' said
Pearl. 'He's a criminal, isn't he?'

'If I make good your loss, perhaps you will not insist
on that course,' said Beatrice.

'One moment, please,' said Tom. 'Any anti-social
person is a criminal as far as that goes. The person who
gives nothing to society is as anti-social as the person

who takes what isn't his. That's beside the point.'
He frowned, groping for the thread of his argument.
'You can imagine that a boy who thought that he had
just killed his brother would feel himself to be in the
extreme anti-social position. He has repudiated every
social convention. Compared with what he has just
done, robbing his mother's guests is a triviality. The
world is against him. He has to have money to escape
and he takes what is to hand, regardless of its ownership.
At the moment he is mad, but he will soon come out of
the madness and return what he has taken, especially
when he hears that Wilfred is all right.'

'He will. Of course, he will,' sobbed Matty. She
made a gesture of gratitude towards Tom.

'I don't know about all this physiology or whatever
you call it,' said Mrs. Stock cheerfully, 'but, of course, you
can't send the police after any one, you know. I never
heard of such a thing.'

'In my grandfather's time,' said Aunt Albania, 'there
was a burglar here. The butler locked him in the
pantry and woke up my grandfather, who told him to
fetch him a gun. When he had brought the gun he told
him to let the burglar go. My grandfather potted at
him as he was running across the park. He only meant
to frighten him and pepper him up a bit, but he
wasn't used to shooting in the moonlight and he killed
him. He compensated the widow,' she added reminis-
cently.

The anecdote was received in surprised silence except
by Pearl who said again:

'I think we ought to send for the police.'

'That is a terrible suggestion,' said Miss Wallace hotly. 'Are our possessions the only things that count? The combined wealth of every one here is not worth one human life.'

'Oh, I wouldn't go as far as to say that,' said Mrs. Stock, a little hurt.

'I think I should point out,' said Lady Smyth-Collins to Miss Wallace, 'that my daughter's and my own loss is considerably more than yours. All the same I agree that people of our class should hold together. I mean we should not give people the chance to say things against people of our class.'

'I shall, of course,' repeated Beatrice with faint contempt, 'make good any loss. I'm afraid I can't replace things of sentimental value.'

'That's very kind of you,' said Lady Smyth-Collins, 'and I quite understand your wishing to do it, but I could not take advantage of such an offer.'

'Don't be soft,' said Mrs. Stock.

'I don't see why I should lose my brooch,' said Pearl. 'And Myrtle's lost her string, too.'

'I don't mind,' said Mrs. Leo. 'I'll get the insurance. Anyhow, I'd rather have something else that I can buy with the money.'

'There is, of course, the possibility that Christopher didn't take the things,' suggested Tom.

'I'm afraid it is only too certain,' said Beatrice. 'He came back to the house for ten minutes. The servants heard him rummaging about upstairs, and one of the housemaids saw him coming out of Mr. Stock's dressing-room.'

'Well, I'm afraid there's nothing to be done,' said Tom. 'Nothing that any decent person could do. I'm afraid I must go. Mrs. Malaby is waiting in my car. You'll find that Wilfred will be all right in the morning, Mrs. Westlake. It's a good thing that he's been sick.'

He nodded good night to the others and went out to his car. Driving home he told Rosie what had happened.

'I always thought there was somethin' sinister about Chwistopher,' she said. 'I expect it's the Botany Bay comin' out.'

Back in the Hall Aunt Albania said:

'I suppose you'll want to turf us out to-morrow, Matty.' She moved so exclusively in the society of very young people that unconsciously she adopted their slang.

This remark lightened a little the gloom in which the house-party dispersed to bed.

Lady Smyth-Collins before she went upstairs rang up Ursula.

'I want to say how splendid I think it was of you to try to shield Christopher,' she said, 'though perhaps, dear, you had forgotten that it was Wilfred who suffered. Also I'm afraid he was unworthy of your protection. He has stolen all our jewellery and run away.

'I wonder if you would do something for me,' she continued. 'Would you drive over to the yews with me in the morning and help me find my shooting-stick? You would know where it was most likely to be. I should hate to lose it as it was given me by Lady

Bletchingdon, the wife of our governor-general, in recognition of my work for the Victoria League. Hullo! Hullo!'

There was no reply, only a clattering sound.

'These country telephones are most unsatisfactory,' said Lady Smyth-Collins.

CHAPTER XII

THE HONEST BRUTE

No one who had been at the picnic slept well that night. Those who, like Tom and the Stocks, had little cause for mental distress, were tormented by itching. The grass had been full of harvesters.

Adam had decided to leave Liza. He had told her so, just before Ursula came rushing out of the yew trees, saying that Wilfred was injured. Liza had looked like death. He felt rather mean taking advantage of the presence of other people, but one had to take mean advantages when dealing with Liza. The rest of the party was too far off to hear what he was saying and near enough to prevent Liza's making a scene. Her expression of dismay was almost comic when she realized that. Driving back, the presence of Ursula and the chauffeur had prevented further discussion.

He intended to drive on to London at once. He was going to make a decisive cut, to do it with a sword. It was kinder in the long run. When they arrived back at Clovermead Liza, patting her nose with her handkerchief, went straight up to her room. He had an impulse to pat her arm and comfort her, but knew that he must not give way to it. She would at once use it to make an emotional entanglement. And he did not really

know how much Liza's grief was genuine and how much
it was a trap to catch him. She probably did not know
herself. So he just had to appear more of a brute than
actually he was, and let her go uncomforted to bed,
on perhaps the last occasion they would meet. When
she came down in the morning she would find him gone.
He would have liked to end twenty or more years of
married life with more grace, more testimony of mutual
gratitude for the good it had held, but that apparently
was a luxury a woman would not allow a man.

When Liza and Ursula had gone in, he turned to the
chauffeur and told him not to take the car to the garage,
but to leave it at the end of the drive. He thought
that if Liza heard him starting from the house she would
be upset and have a sleepless night. He did not know
that the harvesters had already doomed them to that.
Liza would probably say that he had sneaked away
from her. Should one consider other people and appear
a sneak, or be an honest brute? That again was a problem for people like Tom, not for himself.

He went up and changed. He was about to pack
himself a suit-case, but thought this would look like
more sneaking, so he rang for a servant.

'I have to go to London to-night,' he said. 'Her
ladyship won't be coming up till later in the week.'
He had to save Liza's face, though she would not thank
him. He carried his own suit-case downstairs. In the
hall he saw Ursula, lying on the floor with the telephone
fallen beside her. He made an exclamation and dropped
his suit-case.

Lately he had not felt much relationship to Ursula.
He had an uneasy feeling that she knew a great deal
more than he did about the processes of the human
spirit and even of the human body.   She rather frightened
him.   She seemed so very much to be Liza's child, full
of levity.   She was too assured for him, and yet he had
a degree of contempt for her.   He knew that Ursula
made fun of his rows with Liza.   He did not know
that her bright derision was to conceal the dismay she
felt at the falling to pieces of her background.   Now
seeing her lying there, he was suddenly aware how much
the bright hard manner of these young people was an
affected armour, under which they were far more lost
and defenceless than his own generation in its youth,
which had a dozen faiths to support it.   God, the future,
the security of one's home, and the virtue of one's parents
had been buttresses whose strength one did not question.

He lifted Ursula in his arms—she was surprisingly
light—and carried her into the library where he lay her
on a sofa.   He was worried that she was so light, and
he thought what a hell of a time she must have had with
Liza.   When Liza could not get at himself, he might have
known that she would take it out of somebody, and,
of course, Ursula would be the one to suffer.

As he lay her on the sofa she opened her eyes and
looked at him.   She smiled faintly and said: 'Hullo,
Daddy.'

'Hullo.'

'What's happening?'

'Apparently you fainted.'

'I never faint.'

'You were at the telephone.'

'Oh, yes.' She frowned. 'It was about Christopher.'

'What about him?'

'He's committed a burglary.'

'You'd better have a drink.'

'Yes. I had really.'

Adam went to the dining-room and fetched a brandy and soda.

'Drink that,' he said, 'and then you can tell me.'

Ursula sat up and sipped the brandy.

'This tastes filthy,' she said. 'What is it?'

When she had finished it she handed him the glass.

'He hit Wilfred on the head with a shooting-stick because Wilfred was talking to me.'

'What has that to do with Christopher?'

'Everything. You see, we are secretly engaged.'

'You said Wilfred fell from a tree.'

'I know. I told an honourable lie. I couldn't help feeling what a noble figure I cut, but I spoilt it by letting the cat out of the bag to Uncle Tom.'

'You can't be engaged to Christopher.'

'Why not? He'll be very rich when his aunt dies. That's the only thing that matters nowadays. She was fifty-four last birthday.'

'Apparently he has criminal instincts.'

'It's a mistake. He can be so gentle and kind. No one understands him. If someone really loves him he will be rescued from his torments—like Faust or someone—or have I got it wrong?'

'I don't know. I only read detective novels,' said Adam.

'Daddy, you ought to educate yourself more.'

'If you have to keep a family you have no time for education.'

'Are you going to leave Mummy?'

Adam looked at her thoughtfully.

'Not yet.   Not for a while,' he said.

'Not for how long?'

'Not till I am satisfied that you are quite well and strong again.   You've worried yourself into this state.'

'If Mummy knew that she'd keep me sick and weak for ever.'

Adam smiled grimly.

'I see you have Liza taped.'

'I wasn't only worrying about Mummy. I was worrying about Christopher, too. I didn't expect life to be like this at all really. It's all fraught with discord. Mummy says she loves me, but she doesn't hesitate to shatter me with scenes when she thinks you are slipping her up. I don't want to be like one of these selfish modern girls you read about who say: "I must be true to myself and lead my own life," but honestly, Daddy, I don't think I ought to have the sole responsibility of my parents' conjugal relationships or whatever you call it.   And then I thought that when a girl became engaged to a nice young man he was a tower of strength to her, and would understand her pretty, wilful ways. But it's the other way round. I have to understand the pretty ways of a jungle tiger. The world's mad, or else I wasn't told what every girl of eighteen ought to know. I feel as if I was walking all the time on quicksands or clouds or on the thin brown crust of an enormous soufflé. There are times when I could absolutely scream and scream and scream.'

She smiled, but her strain showed in her eyes.

'Look here.   You must go for a holiday,' said Adam. 'Would you like to go to Kitzbuhel or somewhere with a friend?'

'I can't go away and leave Christopher. Oh, what is happening to him? Do ring up those people and find out.'

'You must forget Christopher.'

'Don't talk `nonsense, Daddy. I can't forget him any more than I can forget my own head. My true love hath my heart. I in him and he in me. There's no division. I can't forget him as if he was an umbrella in a bus. He's so different from every one else—from Alec and Wilfred. They're very nice and all that, but they have no polarity.'

'What d'you mean?' growled Adam.

'You know—the tension of poles or something like that. Christopher is evil and Christopher is good. When I am with him I feel as if I was caught in the primal struggle of nature. I flame into life.'

'You sound to me as if you're becoming hysterical.'

'I may be at the moment, but I tell you I won't give up Christopher.'

'But you tell me yourself that the boy is a criminal.

He has committed a burglary. Any girl I ever heard of would be finished with a man who did that.'

'Oh, Daddy, you don't understand! You give things names — burglary, adultery — my generation is not like that. We are not respectable any more. We want values—not labels.'

'You don't understand that values and their negatives have to be labelled,' said Adam. 'You 'd better go to bed. Wait a minute.'

He went out into the hall and hid his suit-case under a console table. He did not want Ursula to see that he had been on the point of flight. He was angry at having to conceal an appearance of vacillation. When Ursula had gone to bed he rang for the butler, and said that he would not be going to London, after all, at any rate not till the next day as Miss Ursula was unwell. Then he went out and drove the car round to the garage. Liza could think what she liked if she heard it.

As he strolled back to the house he felt trapped and tied. Women had caught him and tied him down with a thousand tiny adhesions. If he snapped one, another was strengthened. Now there was this business of Ursula and that young Australian.

He had thought that as he grew older life would become more simplified. Instead of that it became more tangled and confused. It was impossible to deal with people who played according to a different set of rules. Liza followed no rules at all, and now Ursula was drivelling about values. These young people talked an infernal amount of nonsense. They wanted to shatter the world to bits, but had about as much idea as a sucking-pig of how to rebuild it. Let them try to run a big business. Then they would know what it meant to deal with stupid people, with lazy people, with shifty people. They would realize how unfit the bulk of mankind was to form and live in an ideal brotherly-loving world. They might even realize how unfit they were themselves—when they came to know themselves. At present they allowed their warm-hearted aspirations full play before they were correlated to and quenched by the greedy natural man.

Adam bit the end off a cigar and sat on the edge of Liza's new terrace to light it. He thought gloomily of the morning, of what would happen when he told Liza that he was not going to leave her. She would think he was staying out of love for her and would slobber over him.

Women were the devil. That Miss Wallace, for example. She was worse than Liza. She demanded nothing less than your immortal soul. She was like Christ telling you to sell all you had and give to the poor. It was damned silly.

CHAPTER XIII

'ALBERTINE EST DISPARUE'

MR. HODSALL walked from the church through the cool
garden to the vicarage. He was in a condition of
perfect tranquillity. The sleepless night, caused by the
bites of harvesters, had lowered his vitality, but his
religious exercises had soothed him. In these moods
he would think: 'Death won't be so bad for me as for
most people, as I have so slight a hold on life.' He would
have liked to stay out here in the dewy garden, and to
have a deaf-mute bring him a light breakfast. At times
the idea of meeting his wife was painful to him. He
found her vitality almost brutal. This morning he felt
unusually disinclined to bring his mind down to the
consideration of domestic problems which she generally
forced on him at breakfast.

He turned into the rose garden to strengthen himself
and to control in advance any irritability he might be
inclined to show. But before he had completed these
exercises he saw Mrs. Hodsall, cloudy with anger,
approaching him. She did not call him from the end
of the garden as she would have done if she had been in
an even moderately good temper. She came right up
to him before she spoke, a thing which only happened
on rare occasions, such as when she had found cock-

282

roaches in the larder, when her rubber shares had slumped, and when she had discovered that the house-maid was only a fortnight from motherhood. He wished that she had given him time to harden his spiritual armour before springing some unpleasant surprise on him. Some manuals of devotion gave ejaculatory prayers for use on such occasions, but Mr. Hodsall had a sense of the ridiculous or of proportion which inhibited him from linking up Almighty God with cockroaches.

'She didn't go to bed at all,' said Mrs. Hodsall with suppressed fury. Mrs. Hodsall was inclined to join battle with a cryptic announcement, referring to the cause of the disturbance as 'he' or 'she' and then being more annoyed that her listener did not know of whom she was speaking. However, this morning Mr. Hodsall had a good idea that she meant Teddy, as last night, when they came in from the picnic, they found a note on the hall table: 'Headache so bad that I 've gone to bed. Please do not disturb me.—Teddy.'

'As if we should be likely to disturb her,' Mrs. Hodsall had said contemptuously.

'What did she do?' asked Mr. Hodsall. He had visions of his sister-in-law sleeping drunk in a ditch, or else wildly poetic, walking naked through the woods. He felt that like Roly she was capable both of squalid indulgence and of exhibitionist sentimentality.

'She 's gone. And taken everything she could lay hands on. Elsie went to lay the breakfast-table and found the canteen empty. All my brooches and rings have gone, too.'

Mr. Hodsall looked miserably at a red *Étoile de Hollande*. He knew that his wife was blaming him because his sister-in-law had stolen her rings. And he knew that she wanted him to know that she was being very generous in not mentioning the fact that Teddy was his sister-in-law. And he knew that she wanted to know what he was going to do about it.

She stood there like a sergeant-major waiting for an aphasiastic recruit to describe the trajectory of a bullet.

The trouble was that there was nothing he could do. The silver was gone. It was unfortunate, but that was all there was to be said. Carola had a ridiculous gramophone record which ended with a man, who had been told some disastrous news, saying in American: 'I don't know what to say, I 'm sure.' He had a ribald impulse to quote it, but he refrained and said instead:

'It is unfortunate.'

His wife went, if anything, a trifle redder.

'What is the use of saying that, Harry?' she demanded.

He knew, too, that she knew that he did not care half as much as she did. It was having to affect a concern which he did not feel that made him afraid to speak at all. He knew that she was waiting to assess the amount of concern he showed, and pounce on him if it were inadequate. He thought how difficult it would be for his wife to die, with her tenacity of life and its possessions.

'There is little one can say. I am sorry, my dear, that my sister-in-law should have stolen your jewellery.'

'I am not blaming you, Harry. I want to know what we should do. Should we send for the police?'

'It had not occurred to me.'

'It occurred to me at once.'

'There would be an unpleasant scandal.'

'I know. Otherwise I should have rung up immediately.'

Mrs. Hodsall was in the furious state of a righteous person when some other consideration prevents her from performing a righteous and punitive action. Mr. Hodsall would not have enjoyed a scandal, but more than that he had a sneaking regard for the blowsy, dishonest, affectionate creature who had decamped with his plate. He smiled.

'Well,' he said, 'perhaps at last we've heard the last of Roly.'

'Thirty pounds' worth of silver is nothing to joke about,' said his wife. 'We shall have to buy more—to say nothing of my jewellery.'

'We must regard it as the price of escape from Roly —thirty pieces of silver.'

'I said thirty pounds' worth of silver. There were sixty-two pieces in all—including the gravy spoons. What I can't understand,' she went on, 'is why she chose to take these things instead of accepting an allowance.'

'Yes. That is odd.'

'Perhaps she's a kleptomaniac.'

'She may be,' said Mr. Hodsall indifferently.

'I wish I could make you *feel* that something was

important,' said his wife, flashing on him a glance of righteous indignation.

. . . . .

Two days later Ursula called at the vicarage. She asked to see Mr. Hodsall alone in his study.

'Isn't there something called the seal of the confessional?' she asked.

'Yes; there is.'

'Does it work in the Church of England?'

'I hope so,' he said.

'I don't want to make a confession,' explained Ursula, 'but I want to tell you something in the strictest confidence and to ask your advice.'

'You may rely on me.'

'You won't tell——' She hesitated.

'I shan't tell my wife.'

Ursula blushed.

'You see, Mummy 's useless to go to in any difficulty. She listens for two minutes, then she compares it with her own troubles and you find you 're discussing her affairs instead of the thing you asked her.'

'I see,' said Mr. Hodsall, smiling.

'It 's about Christopher,' said Ursula. 'You know he ran away?'

'When?' asked Mr. Hodsall, surprised.

'After the picnic. He thought he had killed Wilfred. This is all in deadly secrecy, you understand. Well, then he stole everybody's jewellery at the Hall. When they came back from the picnic they found that they had all been robbed. I suppose he had no money to run away on, and they were all rich people. I know it was wrong and dreadful of him but you don't know Christopher. Some people are fairly decent and some are fairly bad, but Christopher is both very good and very bad at the same time. He's all fraught with good and evil. He's frightfully positive.'

Ursula stopped and pulled a letter out of her bag.

'This shows it. I had a letter from him this morning. Here it is. He thought he had killed Wilfred and yet he rang up the Hall and put on a strange voice and asked how he was. If he had killed him he would have run a terrible risk in doing that. Anyhow he heard that he was all right, and now——'

'Yes?' Mr. Hodsall encouraged her.

'You know about me and Christopher, don't you?'

'I had an idea,' he admitted.

'Well, now he wants me to go and join him.'

'And are you going?'

'That's what I've come to ask you. I can't promise that I'll act on your advice, but I simply must discuss it with somebody. My brain's bursting. You see, Mummy's such a *fool*.'

'I shouldn't think that Lady Elizabeth was exactly a fool. At least, not in the light of this world.'

'Oh, don't let us discuss Mummy,' cried Ursula. 'My affairs always get engulfed in hers. You see, Christopher doesn't mention stealing the jewellery. That's what worries me most. I think he intends us to live on it. If it weren't for that I'd go to him. Even

if there were no Christopher I 'd have to escape somewhere. Daddy has decided to stay with Mummy for a
while, but I don't expect it will be for long, and then
the whole thing will begin again. My father is a brute,
she 'll say. Therefore it is my business to suffer vicari-
ously for his brutality. She plays tunes on my emotions
as if I were a violin and sometimes the strings nearly
break. She talks of my duty to my mother. But it
isn't my duty to wallow in her self-pitying orgies. I have
a right to my own life. Haven't I, or am I being modern
and selfish?'

'I think one is only called on to help those who are
prepared to be helped. I 'm afraid Lady Elizabeth
doesn't want to be helped. She wants to be indulged.'

'Of course, there is a lot of good in Mummy,' said
Ursula defensively.

'I 've no doubt.'

'Anyhow, that isn't the point. I think I could help
Christopher. I have some money of my own. We
could live on that and send back the jewellery. We
could go right away and begin a new life, away from all
this mess. And yet will I go to a worse mess? Will
Christopher's good or bad come to the top? I can't
turn anywhere.'

'One can't always go away and leave a mess. It is
better to stay and clean it up.'

'I can't clean up Mummy's mess. It 's a widow's
cruse.'

'But Christopher can face the consequences of his
actions.'

'That would mean prison. It would ruin him for ever.'

'Christopher did not steal the jewellery from the Hall. At least, it would be an astonishing coincidence if he did.'

'Who did, then?' asked Ursula, mistrusting as too good to be true this sudden resolving of her chief cause of distress.

'I'm afraid that my sister-in-law was the thief. She took our plate and my wife's few rings and brooches at the same time. We said nothing to avoid a scandal.'

'That's what they did at the Hall!' said Ursula angrily. 'Oh, why will people be so respectable?'

'It seemed harmless enough to preserve the appearances of respectability,' said Mr. Hodsall. 'It was only our loss—at least, so we believed. But now that I know there are other victims we shall have to do something about it. I must go and see Miss Westlake.'

'And what am I to do?' wailed Ursula. 'Oh, how could I have believed that he took it? I should have known that he didn't. If he knows that I believed that he'll never speak to me again. I can't be noble. I thought I was being noble in telling a lie about Wilfred's knock on the head, but I spoilt that. And this time I didn't even begin to be noble. No decent girl in any book believes that her young man can commit a crime, even if he's caught in a bank with a bag of dynamite. I believed it on absolutely no evidence. But, oh, Mr. Hodsall, I've had to deal with such odd people. You know what Mummy is—and Christopher has behaved in such an extraordinary way himself sometimes, and

T

Mummy's brother's an absolute bad hat, even for a peer. I haven't the instincts of respectability.'

'The instincts of respectability are not very admirable,' said Mr. Hodsall consolingly. 'They are only concerned with appearance.'

'Then you think I should go to Christopher?'

'No. I don't think that would be very wise. You may not have behaved like a heroine of fiction. Neither has he behaved like a hero. Very few people do. But if you were to run away together now you would behave like the heroine of a very bad novel. It would be improbable.'

'But don't you think life is rather improbable? People do such extraordinary things. I know thousands of facts that you'd never believe. Anyhow, this is beside the point. What am I to do? If I don't go to Christopher he must come to me. I know he'll be ruined without me. But I shall never be able to persuade him to come back.'

'Perhaps I might be able to persuade him to come back,' suggested Mr. Hodsall.

Ursula looked at him appraisingly.

'You?' she said.

'Do I appear so very ineffectual?' asked Mr. Hodsall.

'Oh, no! It's awfully good of you. I was only surprised. That's all. It seemed odd to think of a clergyman having any influence with Christopher.'

'You admit that improbable things happen.'

'Oh yes, they do. My family's frightfully improbable.'

.　　　.　　　.　　　.　　　.

Wilfred had slight concussion. Tom said that he should stay in bed for two days. On the afternoon of the second day Matty came in to see how he was, and found him cheerfully playing with a puzzle, which consisted of getting three elusive balls simultaneously into three separate holes. *Albertine est Disparue* lay on his bedside table.

'Why doesn't Christopher come to see me?' he asked. 'He'll have to see me some time and the longer he puts it off the more embarrassing it'll be.'

'Christopher is not here,' said Matty. 'He has gone away.'

'Where to?' asked Wilfred, surprised.

'We don't know. He disappeared from the picnic.'

'Phew! Why wasn't I told?'

'We didn't think you were fit to be told.'

'He's a fool,' said Wilfred. 'He'll get over it and come back.'

'I don't think he will,' said Matty.

'Of course he will, Mum,' said Wilfred kindly, seeing her distress. 'Don't let it worry you. He's trying to make us realize how valuable he is. When he finds we take no notice he'll come sneaking in to breakfast one morning.'

'He won't,' said Matty. 'He has committed a dreadful crime.'

'What?' said Wilfred quietly, wrinkling his forehead. He thought it possible Christopher might have killed someone.

'He stole from our guests. Lady Smyth-Collins's diamonds and the girls' pearls.' She told him how they had come home and found the house ransacked, and how one of the housemaids had seen Christopher coming out of Mr. Stock's room.

'That's the most absolute bunk I've ever heard!' exclaimed Wilfred. 'Christopher may be a potential murderer, he's not a potential thief. That's the last thing he'd do. Good Lord! I know him well enough to know that. Mum, I absolutely can't understand you and Aunt Beatrice believing it. Why didn't you send for the police?'

'We all agreed it was better to save a scandal. They were all very generous to us.'

'D'you mean to say that you let all those people think Christopher did it? Oh, my God!'

'Wilfred!'

'Oh, good heavens, then. If you'd had a policeman he would be sure to have found footprints under the pantry window or something. Of course Christopher came out of Mr. Stock's room, as it was his own room that he'd been shifted from. He probably wanted some clean shirts. Honestly, people are mugs. What on earth will people think of us now?'

'I'm thinking about Christopher,' said Matty grimly.

'So am I, but I can't help seeing every side of the affair,' said Wilfred.

'Wilfred,' said Matty earnestly, 'if we find Christopher, I want to go home.'

'What d'you mean?' asked Wilfred, looking at her suspiciously.

'I never intended to leave Australia for good. It is purely owing to the accident of Beatrice's fortune that we are here.'

'We are here. That's the main thing,' said Wilfred sullenly.

'I feel that our position here is false.'

'Why on earth——' Wilfred made a gesture of exasperation.

'It isn't only that,' said Matty. 'Aunt Albania was talking to me about this house the other night. She said that there was a curse on it, ever since that eighteenth-century Plumbridge who rebuilt it shot his wife here. That was one reason why my grandfather refused to live here. His father had died in extraordinary circum-stances in the cellars. Aunt Albania wouldn't tell me exactly what had happened. She said that this dreadful behaviour of Christopher's did not surprise her in the least. Sometimes, when I go up to bed at night, I feel that there is a sort of arrogant cruelty about this house. The grand staircase and those huge carved mantelpieces make me feel that it despises us as intruders.'

'I love them,' said Wilfred furiously.

Matty flinched, and ran her nail along the hem of her handkerchief.

'You used to love our little home at Kew,' she said.

'So I did,' he said. 'You can love more than one thing.'

'You won't come back there—not for mother's sake?'

'Oh, but, Mum——' he cried.

'Will you?' Matty's voice suddenly became hard. She saw the emotions she had disturbed, and thought it was safe to put the test.

'You're worried now about Christopher,' he said coaxingly. 'But all that business about a curse on the house is nonsense. Christopher has always been liable to bang me on the head. He often bullied me at Kew and you didn't say there was a curse on the house. When he's back here, you'll forget about it, and now he's got it off his chest he'll probably behave decently for a while. Besides, I must go to Cambridge, mustn't I? I mean it's necessary for my career.'

'If Mr. Uniacke had not left Beatrice his money you couldn't go to Cambridge. I could not afford to send you there.'

'Why do you always try to make me feel like a charity child?' cried Wilfred. 'I'll go and live in the gutter if you like. The reason is that you want to keep me down so that I'll always look up to you.'

This sudden blurting out of a deep truth shocked both of them. Matty was too hurt to speak, Wilfred too ashamed to apologize. And he could not apologize without admitting that his resentment was unjustified, which he was not prepared to do.

'How could we go back to Kew after living here?' he went on, in fretful self-justification. 'You wouldn't like it yourself when once you got there. It would be awfully tame, just as things that thrilled me when I was

twelve wouldn't interest me now. I love being here.
I love England. I feel absolutely at home here. I
don't mean that I don't love Australia, too. It makes
me livid when people like Mrs. Malaby talk as if it was
full of squalid shanties and savages. But all the same,
Mum, you must admit that the centre of the civilized
world is over here, and I love being in the middle of
everything. I want to go to Australia again, often,
but not yet. And although Mrs. Malaby doesn't know
what she's talking about, and I wouldn't admit this to
any English person, you know that there are an awful
lot of Australians that make you feel uncomfortable.
The worst of being an Australian is that you have to
be responsible for every Australian, but Mrs. Malaby
doesn't have to be responsible for every English person.
If an Australian behaves foully, people say: "Oh, a typical
Australian," but if an English person does the same
thing they don't say: "Oh, typical English!" They say:
"What a common man!" The funny thing is that Mrs.
Malaby is more like one type of Australian than any
one else about here. She thinks money is everything
and has hardly any sensibility. And you must admit,
Mum, that there are a terrific lot of Mrs. Malabys in
Melbourne. Look at Mrs. Stock, though, at least,
she's friendly and amusing. There may be as many
decent people per cent in Australia as in England, but
the population is so much smaller so it is more of a job
to find them. There are a terrific lot of ghastly people
in every country,' he concluded devastatingly. 'But
one has so much more scope over here.'

'I have made no friends here,' said Matty. 'I had quite a circle in Kew.'

Wilfred put his hand on her arm.

'You will, Mum. The Rounsefells know all kinds of intellectual people. You should cultivate them. Ask them here to dinner fairly often, and ask Lady Elizabeth to meet them. They pretend to be Communists and to live for art and ideas, but they're quite human really and they love good food.'

'Lady Elizabeth doesn't like intellectual people,' said Matty. 'Besides, I am rather afraid of Mrs. Rounsefell. I can't see myself as her friend.'

'Oh, Mum, can't you scrape up any confidence in yourself?' groaned Wilfred. He put his hand to his bandaged head and lay back on the pillows. His face was white and strained. He dreaded that somehow Matty would drag him away from Plumbridge, and he had put all his strength into repudiating her intention.

There was a knock at the door and a footman appeared.

'Mr. Hodsall has called, madam,' he said, 'and Miss Westlake says would you come down?'

Matty, with less concern than she would have shown at another time, told Wilfred that he must sleep, and that she would come and dress his bruise before dinner.

She went slowly downstairs. She did not see how she was going to escape from Plumbridge and this kind of life, even when Christopher had returned. It was strange how little actual sympathy she felt with Christopher. She felt the disgrace and the worry of not knowing what was happening to him, but she was more deeply hurt by Wilfred's attitude. She had expected his sympathy, but she felt now, more than ever before, that he was set on his own interests and ambitions, and that his love for his mother was regulated largely by the amount she was able to help him in them.

Mr. Hodsall and Beatrice were in the little drawing-room. Mr. Hodsall explained briefly about the disappearance of Teddy, plus the silver.

'We had better question the maids,' said Beatrice. 'The men were at the picnic when the robbery took place.'

She rang and sent for the head housemaid.

'Did you see no one,' she asked her, 'except Mr. Christopher between the time we left for the picnic and the time we returned?'

'No, madam. Though if any one had come in we mightn't have noticed them because of Bertha.' Bertha was the second housemaid.

'What was the matter with Bertha?'

'She was screaming with fright. We couldn't stop her.'

'What on earth for?' demanded Beatrice testily.

'She'd seen the ghost, madam.'

Beatrice snorted.

'Where did she see it?'

'It was a lady in white. She walked along the gallery and went into Mrs. Westlake's room. Bertha had gone up to draw the curtains and turn down the beds.'

'I wasn't told.'

'No, madam, because Mr. Lucas said it annoyed you
to have the ghost mentioned.'

'D'you mean to say that you knew there'd been a
burglary, and yet you didn't mention this apparition?
All right. That'll do. It's incredible how stupid
people can be.'

Beatrice could hardly control her vexation.

'My sister-in-law was wearing a white dress when we
left her,' said Mr. Hodsall. 'I'm afraid my apologies
must be utterly inadequate.'

'It is not your fault,' said Beatrice. 'We must find
Christopher.'

'Yes, we must,' said Matty tearfully, dramatizing herself as the distressed mother.

'I know where he is,' said Mr. Hodsall.

'You do!'

'He wrote to Ursula Woodforde. She has just been
to see me.'

'Where is he? I must go to him,' cried Matty.

'I don't want to intrude myself,' said Mr. Hodsall.
'But I told Ursula that I would go.'

'But it is my place to go,' said Matty. 'I am his
mother.'

'If Mr. Hodsall would be so kind,' said Beatrice,
'I think it would be better if he went. You know what
Christopher is with members of his family,' she added
dryly.

'I shall also inform the police about my sister-in-law,'
said Mr. Hodsall.

'I am awfully sorry,' said Beatrice. 'We were spared that. In fact, I don't see why we should ask it of you, as our guests were so lenient with us.'

'Your guests were unwilling to bring disgrace on your nephew. I doubt if they would willingly make sacrifices to spare my sister-in-law. Especially if they had met her,' he said ruefully.

.   .   .   .   .

Upstairs Wilfred lay back on his pillows. He had his first inkling that all was not right with the world. He always expected everything to be delightful, that his life would be one long succession of expanding and increasingly interesting vistas. His chief trials, Matty's tiresome humility and Christopher's temper, he had regarded merely as rough pebbles on the path of a charming garden. He imagined that they could be removed. He thought he would cure Matty, not realizing that she would literally have to be born again to be cured, and he had become fairly inured to Christopher, and was satisfied to say that he hated him, while often taking pleasure in his society.

Now these were no longer surface irritants. He had allowed recognition to the fact that his mother had an ignoble mind, that she deliberately wanted their lives to be petty and sentimental and shrinking. He loved her more than anybody and he felt an urgent need to repudiate the thing he loved.

Then because he loved her so much he began to make excuses for her. She had lived in Australia so long that naturally she could not accommodate herself easily to this different life. And then she must be dreadfully upset about Christopher. But how could they have thought that Christopher had stolen their paltry jewellery? It was so sordid, so mean-spirited of them. Poor Christopher.

His critical shell being broken a flood of family sympathy possessed him. He seemed to understand and feel in himself every passion that had moved Christopher. He knew how he would look as he drove away, that awful hurt look he had in his eyes, after he had done something brutal. He imagined him hiding in some beastly hotel. He knew the wretchedness of isolation, at the best of times an affliction of Christopher's, which he must now be suffering. He felt that he was the only person who really could understand his brother, and his sympathy, his bond of brotherhood, was an agony to him, in which he endured every pang which he imagined must now be Christopher's. He saw the whole pattern of his brother's life as a tragedy which he was bound to share.

He lay back on the pillow. His face was white and the tears squeezed out of his closed eyes.

In the late evening Alec put his head round the door and said:

'May I come in?'

He sat on Wilfred's bed.

'How's your old skull?' he asked.

'All right. I'll be up to-morrow,' said Wilfred. 'I could have got up to-day only they made a fuss.'

'You look like the family ghost.'

'I'm a bit tired. That's all.'

'I've written another poem.'

'About Daisy?'

'No; shut up. I don't feel like that now.'

'About Carola, then?'

'No; it's not sentimental.'

'Read it to me.'

'Soon. What have you been doing with yourself?'
He picked up *Albertine est Disparue*. 'Is this any good?'

'I don't know,' said Wilfred honestly. 'The Rounsefells lent it to me.'

'They get my goat.'

'Why?'

'They don't want food for their minds, they want
chewing-gum. They grab every new idea that comes
along, masticate it, and then spit it out, or else leave it
on the bed-post overnight.'

'They're a bit rude sometimes,' said Wilfred, 'but
I like them. They have freer minds than any one I
know.'

'It's all right to have a free mind, if it means it's
free to follow the direction you want to go. But they
haven't any direction. They just sit in a pretty pool
admiring their own reflections.'

'Mrs. Rounsefell looks jolly nice, anyhow. She
dresses beautifully.'

'So do a lot of people who are of no use.'

'Everybody can't be of use. You must have some
leisured people or you won't have any culture.'

'That sort of culture has to go. You'll have a long, sterile mechanistic period and then a new sort of culture will develop in which every one will have a share.'

'Then I might as well shoot myself,' said Wilfred hotly. 'Because the present sort of culture is the only thing I care about.'

'You like things more than people.'

'Perhaps I do. So do Communists. They like their beastly machinery better than individual lives.'

'Oh, don't let us talk politics!' exclaimed Alec.

'You started them.'

'I don't care. Let's talk of something else. It's bad to excite you.'

'You can't suddenly talk of something else,' said Wilfred. 'You can't think of anything to talk about if you try and do that. You can read me your poem if you like.'

'I'm not in the mood now. I will later.'

'We'll have to talk about the Rounsefells, then,' said Wilfred. 'Everybody in Plumbridge talks about the Rounsefells or else about Lady Elizabeth and Mr. Woodforde.'

'Shut up,' said Alec. 'Don't let us wrangle. I couldn't bear it if you quarrelled with me.'

'Why not?' asked Wilfred, sitting up interested.

'I don't know. I just couldn't bear it. It would be the last straw.'

Alec picked up the puzzle and fiddled with it for some minutes. Wilfred watched him in silence. At last with a grunt of disgust, he put it down unsolved.

He put his hand in his pocket and pulled out a folded sheet of paper torn out of an exercise book.

'Is that the poem?' asked Wilfred.

Alec nodded and began to read:

> 'The grey bird
> And the blue one,
> Their song's heard
> When the day's done.
> Filled they
> The parkland,
> Made day
> The dark land,
> Made bright
> As darkened
> The cold night.
> Now harkened
> All folk
> In wonder.
> None spoke,
> Nor thunder.
> Just quiet
> Repose;
> No riot
> Arose.
> In Heaven
> Their song's heard;
> The blue and
> The grey bird.'

The still, subdued light from his bedside lamp, the quiet half-comprehended beauty of the poem, the face of his friend, brought to Wilfred a strange sense of peace. He opened his lips to speak, but emotion caught his throat, and he lay back silent upon his pillows.

'What does it mean?' he asked when he had his voice under control.

'I don't know exactly what it means,' said Alec.
'I wrote it when I came home from the picnic. I
couldn't go to sleep for thinking of you and Christopher,
so I went out into the garden in my pyjamas. Everything was very quiet and I had a feeling that whatever
rotten things happen, the good things will blot them out
in the end. I mean that people will do far worse things
than Christopher did, but in the end the love they have
in them will be heard.'

'Yes,' said Wilfred thoughtfully.

He had changed his mind about the life friendship.
It seemed now the most illuminating thing that had ever
happened to him.

He closed his eyes.

Alec stretched his legs out before him and stared at
his shoes.

'Is your head bad?' he asked after a while.

'It isn't too good.'

'I'd better go.'

'No, don't go—that is, unless you have something
to do.'

'No; I've nothing to do.'

Outside the rooks cawed and the shadows lengthened
in the stately park. The last thin ray of sunlight faded
from the wall, so that the room was in darkness beyond
the yellow pool from the bedside lamp. Wilfred slept.
Alec sat there idly turning the pages of *Albertine est
Disparue* until Mrs. Westlake came to do Wilfred's
bandages.

CHAPTER XIV

GIVE ROSIE THE RICHES

CHRISTOPHER had not bothered to hide himself very thoroughly. He had gone to the hotel in Knightsbridge where the Westlakes had stayed on their first arrival in England. He had no idea that there was any question of the law being put on his heels. It was true that he did in the first emotional storm of his flight imagine it possible that he had killed Wilfred, but when he had rung up the Hall and, pretending to be one of the guests at the picnic making polite inquiries, had discovered that Wilfred was comfortably in bed with hot bottles, he had only been concerned to avoid the people of Plumbridge, who, he imagined, were spending their days talking of nothing but himself in tones of angry condemnation.

He had not heard from Ursula, who was afraid that if she wrote refusing to come to him before Mr. Hodsall arrived, he might leave the hotel and do something desperate, such as returning to Australia as a stowaway.

This was unlikely as he had saved what seemed to him an enormous sum of money, and which at times he felt completely justified his proposal to Ursula. At other times, when his schoolboy's habit of mind was in

the ascendant, his plans appeared to him so preposterous
that they could only make him an object of ridicule.

He spent his days in London in walking wretchedly
round the park in the mornings, and in going to suc-
cessive cinemas in the afternoons and evenings until his
eyes were sore and his brain as cluttered with images
as the screen. He went back to the hotel for meals.

On the third evening as he came out from dinner he
saw Mr. Hodsall sitting in the lounge.

Christopher, looking shy and furious, tried to slip
past to his room, but Mr. Hodsall stood up and came
towards him. Unless he ran and made himself foolishly
conspicuous he could not avoid him.

'Christopher,' said Mr. Hodsall.

'What d'you want?' mumbled Christopher.

'I want to speak to you.'

'I'm just going out.'

'I have a message from Ursula,' said Mr. Hodsall.

The blood surged to Christopher's face. He looked
anxious and childish, miserable and angry.

'Where can I speak to you?' said Mr. Hodsall.

'Upstairs,' said Christopher.

They went up in the lift and he led the way to his
room, where he switched on the hard, bright light,
shaded only by a white globe.

He offered Mr. Hodsall the only chair and sat on the
bed. Mr. Hodsall ignored the chair and leant against
the window-ledge.

'Why did she send a clergyman?' asked Christopher
with unintentional rudeness.

Mr. Hodsall smiled but he was a little rattled.

'It was perhaps an old-fashioned thing to do,' he said. But if people are in difficulty or trouble they still sometimes come to the clergy.'

Christopher sat examining his finger-nails. Mr. Hodsall looked at him thoughtfully.

'Ursula wants you to go back,' he said at last.

Christopher mumbled a refusal.

'Why not?'

'What 'll they think of me?'

'They won't think a great deal about you. They talk so much in small communities not from any real critical perception, but because they are unhappy in themselves.'

'Why can't Ursula come to me?' demanded Christopher.

'Would that be to her advantage?'

'I don't see why she shouldn't.'

'When people say, I don't see why she shouldn't, or I don't see why I should, nearly always they see perfectly clearly why they *should* act against their immediate desires.'

Christopher did not answer.

'You said just now,' Mr. Hodsall went on after a pause, 'why did Ursula send a clergyman. It is true that the clergy are largely discredited. It is not to be wondered at. We are supposed to be intellectually dishonest and to put material considerations first. We often are and we nearly always do. But with all its faults the Church is the only institution nowadays that is definitely committed to uphold the principles of good. It

is the only body pledged to try and lead mankind to
where all good things are safely gathered in, to where
all things comely are reconciled. Perhaps Ursula came
to me because she knew that if I had no personal axe
to grind I was bound to apply the principles of good.'

'How d'you mean?' said Christopher.

Mr. Hodsall looked out of the window, down at the
traffic of Knightsbridge, at the long low cars and the
fat red buses steadily roaring past. He contemplated
these for a while then turned back to the room.

'There is no problem in life but one,' he said, 'to
admit love into your heart, and to act at his direction.
I can see what is right intellectually but I have little love.
But you are young and warm-hearted and can give
yourself to the direction of love. Someone told me
that you had great potentialities for either good or evil.'

'Who said that?' flared Christopher.

'It does not matter. Don't be angry. Every one
whose life has had any significance has had this dual
potentiality. You have the core of love in you. You
can make it into a possessive, self-indulgent, evil growth,
or you can cultivate it until your love becomes one with
Universal Love. Perhaps you don't understand?'

Christopher shook his head.

'You love your brother whom you have seen.' Mr.
Hodsall smiled. 'I don't mean Wilfred, I mean—well—
Ursula. That lights a pure flame in your heart. That
is the same flame as the sanctuary light, as the love of
God. But it can easily be made to burn smokily, by
possessiveness or unqualified lust. You have to com-

pare the flame of your human love with the flame of
divine love. You must continually make this reference
back to divine love, or your love will degenerate and
die. That must be the discipline, or if you like, the
cross of your life. When you find your love is not
burning in a pure flame, and you bring it into contact
with the divine flame, then the evil in one is burnt out.
It is spiritual pain, this admission of the evil in one's
desire, but it is a pain we must suffer if we are not to lose
our love and with it our life.

'I know what I am saying is true,' said Mr. Hodsall.
'I see its truth illustrated every day. Take, for example,
those people at the picnic. Each one of them could have
resolved the difficulty of his life by this reference to love.
Lady Elizabeth's wretchedness is not because she loves
but because she wants to possess. If she made the
reference of her love to divine love and let that resolve
her anxiety and her avidity, I know that a pure love
would burn in her, to which her husband would gladly
return. Nothing can resist the power of purified love.

'Or take the Rounsefells. They have intelligence and
a diffuse goodwill, but they will not make contact with
that divine flame. Their hungry minds flit from one
theory to another, until their souls are dissipated with
intellectual curiosity. There is no light and darkness
for them, but only stimulus and boredom. They cannot sit in stillness and feel the strength of love which
could stabilize their lives and bring them that illumination which they so urgently desire.

'Or take your fellow-countrymen, the Stocks and Lady

Smyth-Collins. They are at a simple stage of evolution and are fairly happy, because of their good nature. But if they were directed by love, its fire would burn out their false values, and they would have a real significance instead of the faintly ludicrous façade of importance which they have built up.

'Take even young Alec Woodforde. He has a natural love in his heart which cannot fail to affect those who see it, but it is unredeemed by reference to the supernatural force of love, so that he wastes much of it in misdirection and in sporadic desires. I don't deny that his life would be harder if he made this reference, but it would have an eternal beauty, instead of the transient animal beauty of youth.

> Low lie the bounding heart, the teeming brain
> Till sent from God they rise to God again.

'I have really come here to ask you to make this reference. I don't think it is dangerous to tell you that your life to me seems to have more significance than that of any of those whom I have mentioned. In you the forces of good and evil are strong. Your passions are violent. Because of this if your love is made one with divine love its strength will be beyond that of others. In you part of the war in heaven must be fought. You, in some degree, must suffer in yourself the death of evil. And it will be harder for you than for the others, but nothing is asked of us more than we can bear.'

Christopher, while Mr. Hodsall was speaking, sat

forward with his face in his hands. There was that in his attitude which suggested that the pain which was demanded of him had already begun.

Mr. Hodsall went quietly from the room.

.   .   .   .   .   .

Christopher and Mr. Hodsall returned together to Plumbridge in the morning. Christopher was inclined to be silent, but seemed anxious to show a friendly gratitude to Mr. Hodsall. He helped him rather unnecessarily with his suit-case, and offered him solicitously the choice of corner seats in the train. He then went to the bookstall and bought him *The Times* and the *Tatler*. This latter unsuitable gift touched Mr. Hodsall's feelings almost more than anything that had happened in the last twenty-four hours.

Apart from the deliberately casual reunion with his family, which Beatrice with an effort prevented Matty from making theatrical, Christopher had no embarrassing meetings at Plumbridge. To avoid them Beatrice and Matty took the boys to London until after their examinations, and from there on to Salzburg, as they wanted to hear some music. They only returned to Plumbridge a week before Christopher and Wilfred were due to go up to Cambridge.

While they were away the subject-matter of village gossip was reduced by half. However, there were two or three items of interest.

The first was the arrival at the vicarage of another Mrs. Roly Hodsall. Teddy, who had been caught by

the police, was not Roly's widow. She was a London
prostitute who had married an Australian soldier. In
Sydney, disgusted to find that he was not rich, she had
left him and taken to theft for a livelihood. Finding
herself naturally proficient she had returned to England
to widen her field. On the ship she made friends with
Mrs. Roly, a delicate woman to whom she had been
extremely kind, and in return had learnt the confidential
details of her life. Immediately on landing in England
Mrs. Roly had been carried off with pneumonia to a
nursing home. Teddy, having stolen her signet ring,
had taken the opportunity of descending on the vicarage.

Mrs. Roly was a quiet, well-mannered woman whom
Mrs. Hodsall was quite pleased to take about. She was
incredulous of Teddy's activities.

'But she was so kind. I can't understand it. I
don't think that I should have survived the voyage
without her. You 've no idea of the trouble she took
for me. Why, she spent a whole morning looking
for my ring.'

'She was wearing it,' said Mrs. Hodsall grimly.

'It destroys one's faith in human nature,' declared
Mrs. Roly.

'It need not. Her essential nature was kind,' said
Mr. Hodsall. 'I always felt that.'

His wife snorted.

Mrs. Roly's most surprising information was about
Roly himself. Apparently his accident had affected his
brain or his glands in some fashion that completely
changed his character. As far as the Hodsalls could

gather without making too brutally direct inquiries, his latter years had been spent in an excessive, pernickety gentility. Mr. Hodsall thought he must have been pleasanter unregenerate.

The other item of Plumbridge gossip was about Adam and Liza. Adam miraculously, so people thought, had returned to her for good. This was not because of Ursula, but because of Ella Hindley, who, when he had told her that he was going to remain awhile longer with his wife, showed that her placidity was entirely bogus. Adam decided that if one must endure fish-wife scenes, an aristocratic fish-wife was, after all, preferable, and that there was something less smothering in Liza's levity than in the hot, earnest adhesions of a serious-minded woman.

Having both suffered a shock, he and Liza settled down fairly happily together.

When the Westlakes returned, the gossip naturally was once more focused on the Hall. People talked a good deal about Ursula and Christopher, but not even Rosie knew that their respective parents had agreed to a secret engagement, though there was to be no talk of marriage for two years.

But the Westlakes gradually floated away from local society into that of the very rich. In the autumn the duke returned to Plumbridge and called at the Hall. The boys were invited to shoot.

One morning Alec strolled rather dejectedly through the village, having just seen Wilfred and Christopher off to Cambridge. He was afraid that their experiences there, and the fact of Beatrice's wealth, might slowly cause an estrangement.

By the post office he met Mr. Hodsall, and after some desultory conversation he disclosed his fear.

'I don't think you need worry,' said Mr. Hodsall. 'A great many people go through Cambridge without forming any particular friendship. I mean if your friendship with the Westlakes is established, the fact that they will make many associates there will not necessarily weaken it. And there will be the connection through Ursula.'

'Yes. That's true,' said Alec brightening.

At that moment Rosie joined them. She had just heard about the duke's calling at the Hall and was all agog.

This made Alec depressed again, as he was sure that ducal associations would seduce Wilfred away from him.

Mr. Hodsall, aware of this change in his mood, said: 'How hardly shall they that have riches enter the kingdom of heaven.'

Rosie laughed, then, emboldened by something ironical in Mr. Hodsall's manner, she retorted:

'Oh, no! For once I agwee with the Austwalians. Give me the wiches and I'll wisk the kingdom of heaven.'